Outside In

By
SL VanderPyle

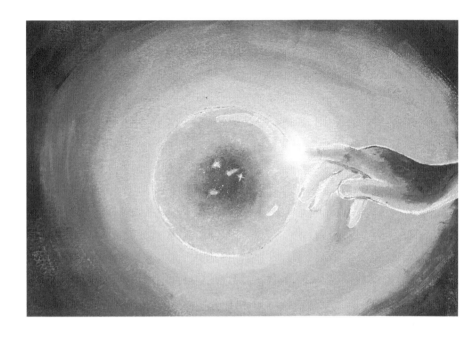

Chapter 1 The Visit 6

Chapter 2 La La Land 13

Chapter 3 The Manor 18

Chapter 4 Discovery 31

Chapter 5 Mr. Kort.....................................34

Chapter 6 Where'd He Go? 40

Chapter 7 The Museum 46

Chapter 8 Preparations 66

Chapter 9 Aden 80

Chapter 10 Perfectly Charming 86

Chapter 11 Magic 92

Chapter 12 Unreal 103

Chapter 13 Sadness 126

Chapter 14 Mom......................................135

Chapter 15 Haunted................................154

Chapter 16 Freak Out 171

Chapter 17 Fade Out...............................175

Chapter 18 Alone 182

Chapter 19 The Master 192

Chapter 20 Back......................................197

Chapter 21 Explanations 198

Chapter 22 Home 200

Chapter 23 Dad 205

Chapter 24 Tests of Another Kind 210

Chapter 25 While You Were Sleeping 217

Chapter 26 Moving Forward 222

Chapter 1 The Visit

Grams and Pops are warm-hearted, wonderful people. From the day I arrived, Grams went out of her way to make me as comfortable as possible. She knew I had come there to recover, and she would love me back to health her way, through food and comfort.

She cooked me the hearty cheese-covered dishes I'd loved in my childhood and put the electric blanket on my bed in the guest bedroom; the rose room as she called it. It had pink carpet, pink walls, pictures of pink roses on the walls, and a frilly floral patterned bedspread. It was enough to make a healthy person have a panic attack, but I didn't tell her that.

Freshly baked pies and pastries, my favorites, kept appearing on the counter, although I ate little of them. (I had to keep up with my strict nutrition regimen.) She even made sure there was vanilla flavored creamer for my morning coffee; my one indulgence (sugarless of course).

I wasn't sure if she was trying to make me comfortable, or fatten me up; but such is our family's way. We show love through food, and I had become fairly thin from all of my grief, stress, and anxiety. Honestly, that was one thing I was happy about. My life was a mess, but I was thin.

***

The first few weeks after Aden died were a blur. I went through the motions and acted the part of a woman who had everything together, just like I always had. Zoey Jacobson, always the reliable one.

I had always been so alive. I loved art, and picnics, and animals. I loved music, all kinds, from all genres and eras. I laughed during tense situations and made jokes at the wrong times. I loved deeply and was a kid at heart. An amusement park could make me positively giddy and I was entertained by the simplest things. My mother used to tell me that I was going to enjoy life more than most, that I had the ability to find fun in just about anything.

Well, that was before. Before she passed away, before Aden, before I was broken.

I played the unshakable, young widow to all of Aden's law firm partners and political friends. I greeted all the guests and played perfect hostess to his parents when they stayed at the house while in town for the funeral. They were cordial but distant.

None of those people mattered though. After the funeral, they were gone. I was nobody to them, just Aden's widow.

I was drowning in emotions. I felt guilty for Aden's death. I *was* the reason for his unhappiness, after all, or at least that's what I believed, and I felt it was my fault he'd gotten himself killed.

I was terribly lonely, but I had been lonely for years. There was a huge part of me that just felt relieved, and that just brought on more guilt.

I prayed a lot during that time, but never really believed my prayers were heard. I believed in God, but he was most likely angry and disappointed with me. I was.

The night Aden was killed, I had accused him of infidelity. In a moment of rage, he hit me hard across my face. Something he had never done before. He had tried to apologize, but I flinched at his approach. The rage resurfaced and he stormed out. An officer came to my door early the next morning to tell me Aden had died in a drunk driving accident. The woman that was in the car with him was killed as well. His mistress.

More guilt.

My dad helped me through every step of the way, happy to be back in my life on a regular basis. After several months I began to realize how codependent I had become with Aden, and how far I had to go to be a healthy person again. Honestly, I always knew it, I just couldn't do anything about it while Aden was alive. I had been submerged in the grip of another's control, and now I found it difficult to make a decision and I almost never voiced my opinion.

Eventually, I decided to wean myself off the antidepressants, valium, and whatever else was helping me cope, and began trying to be social again. My friends were very patient and happy to have me back in their lives. My best friend, Susanna, was always willing, although sometimes reluctantly, to take me home when the stress of social situations became too much for me. I usually just found a way out anyway, avoiding social situations all together. I would have anxiety attacks and my home was my only sanctuary. I wasn't used to freedom, and it took a while for me to adjust.

I wanted to feel safe, so I began going to church again. I also enrolled in a self-defense class. Gabriel Kort's Martial Arts and Fitness Dojo. According to the women there, he was the best looking instructor in town, but that was the furthest thing from my mind. I needed to know how to defend myself. I needed to feel in control. Little did I realize that martial arts doesn't teach you how to defend your heart.

Aden had left me some money, enough to allow me some time before I had to go back to work. He left me the house, which was now paid for via his insurance policy, and he left me the cars, a fairly new Volvo and his Mercedes.

The house felt unusually empty and the bed was bigger without him there. Even though I hadn't wanted to share a bed with him for a while, I still felt terribly alone and exposed that I began sleeping on the couch. I still had trouble falling asleep and wished, at times, that I hadn't stopped taking my sleeping pills. I found it was a little easier to go to sleep with the TV on, even if it was just playing infomercials. I was coping, but not living.

***

My Grandparent's house is in a lovely valley, nestled deep in the woods, about five miles from the little town I had grown up in. Burney, California. A perfect place to get away from the hustle of life and recover.

Outside was a garden, a swing set, (still there from when I was a child) and a shed. Everything else was forest and beyond that, majestic mountains on all sides. It's a truly serene place to be.

I could have gone into town, but I wasn't really interested in seeing my old friends, or rather in them seeing me. My cell phone wasn't working well out that far, and I didn't really feel like calling anyone anyway.

For the first few days, I sat at the house and talked with Grams and Pops. Their TV received one channel and they had no idea how a computer worked, let alone having the internet. Life was indeed quiet. It was perfect. But by the end of the first week, I was growing bored. As we watched the Friday evening news in comfortable silence, I realized I was ready to leave the house.

The next morning I got out of bed and decided to go for a walk. The forest was calling me to come and explore all of the childhood places that I had loved so much. The lava rock formations that had settled there several eons ago had been my playground as a child, and I doubted there was a tree I hadn't climbed.

There were trees with small hiding places along their trunks that may still have held the tiny treasures that I stored there as a child, and of course, the animals of the forest who's curiosity for me was as great as mine was for them. As I thought about venturing out I felt a fire begin to kindle within me. A spark of childlike wonder that I had not felt in a long time; it fueled me.

Grams insisted I eat breakfast before I went out, just as she had always done. The sentiment made me smile and I was surprised how easy it was to feel safe there. I found myself smiling more, even laughing; it felt good. I even allowed myself to eat things that were on my forbidden list, well, bacon at least.

After breakfast, while I was putting on my tennis shoes and getting ready to head out, Pops came out from his bedroom. He handed me a compass.

"Thank you." I put the compass in my backpack and zipped it up.

I hadn't brought much with me. A bottle of water, a first aid kit, and a thin jacket, just in case it got chilly.

"Zoey, it's easy to get lost in these woods, be careful," Pops instructed with a look of concern on his face. I was getting a lot of those lately and frankly, I was getting tired of it.

"Pops, how could I get lost? I practically lived in these woods."

Pops nodded his head thoughtfully and smiled. "There's a clearing not far from the lava rocks to the east, on the other side of the little bridge. It is a place where animals gather. The stream flows through there and the deer like to come and drink under a huge Oak. I suppose it makes the animals feel safe. You should check it out, it's real pretty." He winked at me and walked into the kitchen where Grams was singing and putting dishes away.

I smiled and wondered why that felt so suspicious, but that was Pops, I guessed, and I let it go.

I quickly helped Grams put away the remaining dishes and kissed her cheek before heading out.

It felt good to be back out in nature again. I meandered east of my grandparent's house and deep into the woods. Birds sang loudly and the wind blew softly through the trees. The air was brisk and dry, very unlike my home in Florida. I breathed in the cool air and smiled.

Tall pines swayed and creaked with squirrels chattering in their branches and I could hear cicadas singing somewhere in the distance.

The forest floor was covered in packed dirt and leaves that crunched as I walked. The first of the dogwoods were blooming. There were oak trees scattered sparsely among the pines and mulberry bushes flourished where the sunlight stole through the pine branches and traveled to the forest floor. These beams of light shone through like spotlights on a myriad of undetermined spots on a stage where the actors didn't matter; only the scenery.

I had been walking in the forest for quite some time when I finally arrived at the lava rock formations. It wasn't that they were difficult to find or even that far away, I was just enjoying myself so much that I took my time. I found two of my old climbing trees and I discovered that I could reach one of my old hiding spots without having to climb up the tree. Inside I found an old beaded necklace with a scratched up, plastic, blue crystal wrapped in a piece of faded cloth. I imagined the crystal still held the power to heal and laughed to myself.

I felt my imagination coming back to life; something that had died was breathing again. I slipped the necklace on over my head and pressed on; I had a quest to follow. I must find the clearing and set free the kidnapped princess beyond the Elven village. I took out my compass and found East.

The lava rock formations themselves weren't huge; actually much smaller than I had remembered them. They rose up at the highest point at about ten feet. Jagged, rough, and full of small spaces for snakes and lizards to live. They curved around in a half-moon, highest in the middle; right about where I began to climb. They were not overly difficult to traverse, however; especially now that I was an adult. I was mindful of my footing and careful to watch for snakes. The cool spring air filled my lungs and I was a child again.

The rocks became a huge mountain and I imagined them high and majestic among the clouds. Only I, the great warrior, could make it past the huge troll that guarded the bridge on the east side. I pulled myself over the last of the boulders and I could see the giant bridge that was guarded by the infamous, vicious, man-eating troll.

It wasn't long before I set foot on the first stone of the monstrous bridge, ancient and long, that stretched hundreds of feet above a raging river.

I crept as quietly as a ghost, until my foot snapped a twig and caught the attention of the mighty troll. He lumbered up from under the bridge where he lived in a nasty hole, full of bones and decay. I could see his massive back muscled and furry. His scraggly hair was long and hung in tangles to his belt, and his stench wafted through the afternoon air, smelling of rotten meat and sweat.

I ran to the middle of the bridge and turned, drawing my sword; the blade of my father and his father before him, and took a defensive stance. The jewel-encrusted hilt caught the light and reflected brilliantly the colors of the gems on my skin. The troll turned and our eyes met; his face filled me with terror and my breath was caught in my throat, for it was the face of Aden. I stifled a scream, holding my hand to my mouth. My sword clattered to the ground as I backed away.

"Zoey!" he yelled. "Freakin' grow up! Stop acting like a child."

The illusion faded, and I was back in the forest standing on a small stone bridge over a shallow rivulet. No magic in the old beads around my neck, no princess to save, no giant bridge or Elven village, just me; alone.

Panic and anxiety caused my insides to shake and I knew the panic attack was coming. I began to sweat. The fire of my imagination died down to embers, and I sat on the edge of the bridge and cried. Anxiety seemed to follow me wherever I went and at that moment I just wanted to be home where no one could see or touch me; where I was in control. Where I was too busy for Aden to haunt me.

I sat there for a long time with my face in my hands, counting to ten over and over. "I am in control, I am safe, everything is okay," I whispered to myself.

I closed my eyes and straightened my spine, taking cleansing breaths before I opened my eyes. There, in front of me, stood a young boy in a bow tie, smiling at me. I gasped, surprised, but before I could say anything he spouted, "Sorry about this," and pushed me backward over the edge of the bridge and into a void that should have only been a few feet.

Chapter 2 La La Land

Some of the best things in life require a fall to get there. You fall asleep, you fall into a wonderful dream, you fall in love. Did you know that falling into yourself is like that? To stumble upon something beautiful is often a once in a lifetime appointment.

I didn't lose consciousness the first time, or at least I didn't think I had. I simply fell, and found myself in an unfamiliar place. It was a lot more violent and messy than falling in love. I say simply fell, it was more like flailing and screaming till I hit the grassy bottom in a totally different place. The bridge was no longer there by the time I hit the ground. The air was knocked from my lungs, and I coughed and writhed, gasping small gulps of breath.

My side, below my left rib, was sliced open. I moaned in pain. Feeling around beneath me, I realized I had landed on a small, sharp rock, that I would have chucked as far as possible had I had any air in my lungs or I wasn't hissing breaths of pain at the moment. When I pulled my hand back it had blood on it.

I can't tell you at what point the bridge had disappeared during my fall, but it felt as though I had fallen a lot farther than what I should have. The bridge hadn't been that big.

I looked around for the mysterious child that had pushed me, but saw no one. It was as if I had fallen into a different place entirely and for a moment I was sure I must be dreaming. The colors around me were brighter than usual; more alive. I could hear a waterfall in the distance and a sharp breeze blew through the trees, suddenly colder than it had been a moment earlier.

I lay shivering, trying to determine how I had ended up in an unfamiliar place when I had just been on the small, rock bridge over the stream. I should be in the stream, but I lay deep in a forest on the grass.

I remembered leaving my grandparents' house for the forest and walking for hours. The forest had always given me peace and solitude. I knew those woods, I grew up there, but somehow I'd gotten myself lost.

A kid, there was a kid, he pushed me...

I gingerly sat up, moving a brunette curl out of my face, I looked around myself and found my backpack. I dug around and pulled out my first aid kit, then did my best to clean and bandage my wound. It was a long gash that probably needed stitches. Blood ran down my side and soaked into my white shirt leaving a red stain growing along my ribs and down the side of my jeans. I pulled my shirt back over it and irritatingly threw the bloody gauze and trash back into my pack, irked about the torn and stained blouse.

"Ugh, I liked that shirt!"

All around me was a forest of color and texture; beautiful flowers of all colors and genera. I breathed in the strong, many fragrances and my mind swam with memories. Every scent evoked an elusive feeling that would come and go before I could grasp what it was. Something from my past, a person whose face I couldn't quite see, a place I recognized without actually knowing where it was.

Jasmine, the strong aroma of soil after a good rain, pine, mixed with the cool spring air. A forest of emotions; good and bad, fleeting and deep. I can only describe it as pure elation, a place that evoked more emotion than any place I'd ever set foot in. The air brought memories, the scenery brought tears to my eyes.

Standing slowly, I winced at the pain at my side. I cautiously slipped on the thin jacked that I'd taken from my pack. Then I pulled the pack over my shoulder on the other side.

The forest was quiet, save for the leaves that blew in the breeze, and a tall slender boy that sat atop a branch and hooted at me. He wore a bow tie and knickers. He chuckled and said, "You aren't out of the woods yet, are ya?"

"Hey! It's you. You pushed me!" I accused. "Get down here you little twerp!"

He tisked at me. "The name's Carl," he said with a little wave. "And you're Zoey Jacobson," he continued, smiling slyly.

"How do you know me?" I snapped.

"I have the inside scoop," he answered. "You're shorter than I imagined though," he looked me up and down and smirked. "You look like your mom, you have her green eyes and high cheekbones." he studied me, rubbing his chin.

"How would you know?" I snapped. "You're too young to have known my mom!"

My chest did that tightening thing as it always did at the mention of her, and I took a deep breath to steady myself. I could have sworn for an instant that I smelled her perfume.

He smiled keenly. "It's strange, isn't it? The way your memories float around here like lightning bugs."

I opened my mouth to answer, but somewhere in the distance, I was interrupted by the frenzied baying of a beast. It was like no animal I'd ever heard before, but somehow I knew it was hunting. I also knew I was no longer in my forest, I was sure of it. There was nothing like *that* in my forest. It was a haunting howl like that out of a horror story and I wanted no part of whatever manner of beast it had come from. My heart kicked into high gear and the adrenaline that suddenly hit my bloodstream made me feel queasy. I surveyed the area for someplace to run.

"How I do love a good chase," he said, shaking his head and tsking at me. "But you really should run along inside!"

I glared at him, poised to defend, just as I'd been taught in my self-defense classes.

The insidious boy laughed. "I was not implying that I would give chase, that would be ridiculous," Carl explained, his voice flaunting and pompous. He looked at his fingernails and rubbed them on his shirt, as to remove a speck of dust. "I was speaking of the Jester and his Wild Card."

I pictured my grandmother saying my grandfather was "such a card." I wondered how that could be a bad thing. Braced to jump at anything, I couldn't help but ask: "Aren't cards and jesters meant to be entertaining?"

The boy rolled over and hung by his legs over the branch, looking at me upside down. His eyes narrowed as he spoke. "How dark is your sense of humor?" he laughed loudly.

"What do they want with me?" I demanded. I didn't know whether to hide or run or just wait and see what would happen next. I didn't even know where I was or how I had gotten there. On top of everything, I was talking to a child; an irritating, haughty, creepy, riddle boy! My side was hurting and most likely needed medical attention. The sick feeling grew as my heart raced in my chest. I didn't know whether to be scared or pissed off.

"They smell the blood," he remarked, pointing to my side.

"No thanks to you!" I snapped. "Why did you push me? And where am I?"

Carl pulled himself back up on the limb and began to pick at the bark with a manicured fingernail. The tree shook violently and groaned until he vanished and reappeared, sitting on a stone a few feet away from me.

I screamed, startled, and frankly, I was pretty freaked out.

"The Master told me to help you get inside," he explained.

"Who is the Master? And how did you possibly think that meant to push me off a bridge? I could've broken my neck!" I looked around. "And I'm outside, not inside. What are you talking about?"

"You really should get going, Miss Inquisitive. The Jester will be here soon."

I glared at Carl as I imagined choking the little Snot.

Carl rolled his eyes. "Fine…" he stretched out the word in annoyance. "The Wild Card is just a mindless demon dog that would just as soon rip you to shreds and gnaw on your bones, but the Jester wants to play before he kills you. He is a trickster, that one, the great deceiver. He takes many shapes. He hates the Master and wants to destroy anyone whom the Master loves."

"The Master?" I whispered, mostly to myself. Then, what he had actually said, hit me.

"This Jester guy, what is he, like some sort of serial killer?" I asked, my voice becoming increasingly more shrill.

Carl laughed. "He wrote the book."

"Well, what do you propose I do, *Carl*? Where should I go?"

"Go home, of course."

"I just told you, I don't know where I am. How do I get home?" I asked, jolting at the slightest noise.

"The only way to go back is to go forward, the only way out is to go in, you gotta fall before you can get back up," he replied. And then with each finger wiggling, he waved at me, his eyes narrowed as if to say "toodle loo." And he disappeared.

I frantically looked around, but found no trace of him. "Kid, er, Carl! Please, come back. I don't know where to go, where am I?"

The disembodied voice of Carl, laced with annoyance, echoed through the clearing. "Choose a path and follow it," he said. "You can't move forward if you don't move at all."

Stupid kid.

I looked around for a place to run and noticed three paths worn in the dirt. One to my right, one to my left and one straight in front of me. I wouldn't have been surprised if my shoes suddenly turned into ruby slippers.

Then I heard howling again. *It doesn't seem close,* I thought, trying to decipher which direction it was coming from. It was a sound like none other, it was ravenous, wanting, and psychotic; wild. Fear gripped me again. The boy had said go forward. I stepped onto the path straight in front of me and I began to run.

Chapter 3 The Manor

I ran for my life, stopping only a couple of times to see if I could still hear any sign of pursuit. My breath was coming in ragged gasps as I stood to listen. I heard the rapacious cry once more; it still seemed far off, somewhat closer... maybe? Nonetheless, I was taking no chances. I had a stitch in my side, never having run that fast at the gym. I was tiring quickly and that only fueled my fear.

Most of the trail was a blur of colors, mostly green, as I sprinted. Bushes and grass-lined the trail. The trees were tall and I could feel them rooting me on. *"Go, run, you can make it!"* I faltered and almost fell, but caught myself and pushed on.

Finally, I reached a place where I had to stop, I could run no further. I slowed to a quick walk and looked around. The path had taken me from the forest to a small rise and a clearing beyond, green and lush.

The overall feeling of this place was peculiar, my emotions were off the charts; vivid and palpable. I was frightened and cautious, yet I imagined I'd find someplace safe. I felt as if I had a quest, a purpose. I had to get home, or at least to the place the boy had said to go. I imagined myself like Dorothy. *There's no place like home...* chanted through my mind and I mentally rolled my eyes and took off at a jog.

Ahead, as I crested the small hill, I could see a huge manor towering in the distance beyond the field. The front section was two, maybe three levels, with a glass dome at the top. Behind that, another portion jutted up five stories and went out to form wings on either side.

My lungs burned, and again I stopped to catch my breath, taking a moment to check the bandage at my side. The cut stung and ached, but the bandage showed no sign of blood seeping through. I pulled my shirt back over it and mumbled an irritated complaint while pressing it with my palm. The pressure didn't seem to help much and I grimaced at the pain.

I took a moment to take the compass out and see which way I was going. The needle spun in circles and never stopped on a direction. Flustered, I shoved the compass back in my pocket and looked around me, then took off running again. I was almost there.

I crossed the field and my path became a cobblestone lane leading to the beautifully, mournful manor. Two large pillars stood abreast double wooden doors at the top of a wide staircase. The pillars were missing large chunks of stone that had broken off and fallen to the steps in heaps of rubble. I stopped at the doors and scanned my surroundings, gasping for breath.

The manor looked as though it had been neglected for many years. Its beauty still exhibited through the decay. Intricate millwork covered the enormous doors. They arched at the top with large knockers on each door. They were made of bronze and had been oxidized by the elements.

There was no going around this monument. The mansion was huge and stretched out half a city block in both directions. If I had had time to wonder about its regal inhabitants, from ages past, I could have stayed there all day and fantasized, but I felt the need to get somewhere hidden and relatively safe.

I knocked on the door and waited, impatiently. I didn't hear anything, so I tried the handle. It was unlocked and, as I pushed it open, of course it creaked loudly, just as I would have imagined it would. What would an old abandoned mansion be without a creepy, creaky door?

I stepped inside and the door closed behind me. My entrance stirred up dust causing me to cough. It echoed in the large expanse and I froze. My heart still hammered in my chest. I quickly turned to lock the door behind me and then leaned against it, as I took in the room and waited for my heart to slow.

"Hello?"

"Hellooo," my voice echoed in reply.

Rays of evening light cut through the room from way up high. Dust particles floated through the air and all was silent. The foyer was large and the ceiling went up to the third floor. There, at the top, was a glass dome with intricate designs etched in the glass; well, what glass was left anyway.

Straight in front of me, on the other side of the room, was a hall that went under an archway beneath the stairs and a huge ballroom in the center of the house surrounded by opaque windows.

The stairs started on both sides and came to a balcony on the second floor. From there, hallways stretched out in both directions, and stairs went to other floors off to both sides. The second-floor balcony wrapped around either side of the entrance of this room.

The walls were covered in drooping wallpaper and chipped paint. The furniture was layered in dust and cobwebs.

High backed chairs were pushed back against one wall. Across the room, a large mirror with coat hooks lining its edges hung between two windows. A dusty, white, lady's coat hung on the top hook; nearby, a matching pair of gloves sat on a small round table. I recognized that dress coat from one of my mom's old clothing catalogs. When I was a child, I had folded down the corner of that page, returning to it often to admire the lovely coat. I thought it strange, there it hung, dusty and unused.

In the center of the room, under the dome, lay the remains of what once was a beautiful chandelier in a shallow puddle of filthy water. Large, teardrop crystals littered the floor, bouncing tiny specks of light all around them. The Chandelier was enormous, with candles that lined the middle in a diamond pattern. Way up in the dome I could see the broken chain that had dropped the once beautiful fixture.

I walked around the chandelier, getting my tennis shoes wet in the effort, trying to reach one of the candles that were tangled in the remnants of crystals and iron. I didn't know what lay ahead of me, but I surmised a candle would come in handy at some point. Every movie I had ever watched about an old house, haunted or not, would at some point be dark and scary. I managed to pull a candle free and stuffed it into my backpack. I didn't know how long I would be there or where I'd end up. I felt like a character in an old Nancy Drew novel my mother had read to me when I was younger.

Strangely, I felt safe in the large house, not to say that I was feeling comfortable. I just didn't think I was in danger at that moment. The house intrigued me. I felt like I had been there before; though I was sure I had never seen it in my life. It called to me in a way I can't describe. More of a feeling than words, a longing that sadly whispered: "welcome home."

"Hello? Anyone here?" I shouted again, but only received my echo and managed to frighten a pigeon out of the dome.

I walked through the hallway under the stairs. It was a tunnel with a curved ceiling that went under the balcony and through the mansion to the other side. Portraits lined the walls. The light, however, couldn't reach here, at least not at this time of day, making it too dark to see the faces in the large frames. A way to light my candle might have come in handy, but I had no such luck.

I held myself with my arms in an effort of self-preservation. The house held such a feeling of loneliness, it made my chest feel heavy. Sadness filled the corners like shadows and beckoned for life, comfort, love, like a living thing. I realized I had tears streaming down my face and quickly wiped them away. *What is wrong with me?* My mental state was so heightened, it was as if I flitted from emotion to emotion without warning and was feeling hard-pressed to keep it together.

I started to feel a tremor. Slowly, then building, the mansion began to quake. Everything shook, portraits fell from the walls and I could hear something break in the room behind me. I huddled down against the wall in the recess of a set of double doors, and put my hands over my head as bits of plaster rained down from cracks in the ceiling and dust filled the air.

After a few seconds, it stopped and all was quiet once more. I didn't really feel I was in danger of the house falling on me. It had obviously stood the test of time and earthquakes are common in California (if I was, in fact, still in California that is). I rose, brushing the plaster off my clothes and out of my hair, and then proceeded towards the light of the next room.

The hall had been surprisingly long. When finally I emerged into a large living room, there was a huge iron gate at the end of the arched hallway. It was ornate and corroded and it closed in the center where the two gates met. I decided to close it behind me. It had an old lock with a skeleton key already inserted into it. I closed the lock and took the key and then turned to examine the room I had just entered.

Candles were lit and a fire was burning in a large fireplace on the opposite wall. The room was clean and bright. The furniture was colorful and even whimsical in design. A stark contrast to the entrance room on the other side of the tunnel.

A large ornate mirror leaned against one wall. Oddly curved bookshelves packed with books covered another. High backed chairs that looped at the top and an overstuffed couch sat in front of the fireplace. There were small tables that held little trinkets and curiosities, and the walls were striped in wide gray and white and had large frames devoid of pictures hanging at odd angles all over the room.

There were no windows in this room. There were doors, but they were all closed. Behind me, on both sides, was another set of staircases the same as the staircase in the entrance room. The staircase went up to a balcony and a row of doors. The doors on either side of a central ballroom closed off an inner hallway that wrapped around the ballroom.

Another large chandelier hung from the middle of the room, beautiful and perfect, and the dome at the top, just like the entrance room, had a large metal cover. It resembled the shutter on a camera and closed in the middle. This one was shut tight.

I moved further into the room, looking around. "Hello?" I said loudly, this time to be answered by a man standing by the fireplace.

"Hello, Zoey," he said, softly.

I screamed.

He chuckled. His smile reached his eyes and he held out his hand.

"Don't be afraid," he responded.

"Where am I?"

"You have gone within yourself. I brought you here."

"You..? How, why?" I asked, but didn't wait for the answer. "I got here all on my own after I fell off a... bridge." I trailed off, realizing how dumb that sounded.

"You asked for my help," he explained.

"I've never seen you before," I argued, but felt that maybe I *had* known him from somewhere.

He smiled, "Most people don't."

"Who are you?" I inquired.

"I am the Master and your caretaker."

"Oh. You're the Master," I muttered. "Do you mean the caretaker of this house?"

"Yes."

"My caretaker? This place is mine?"

He nodded, "This place is *you*."

"Like, metaphorically?"

"And literally," his expression was serious.

I laughed, "What am I, inside out?"

"You are outside in."

I stared at him incredulously. His expression didn't change. "Do I know you?"

"Yes, I have known you all of your life. You met me when you were very young."

"What are you doing here?"

"I have always been here."

"So, are you my subconscious?" I chuckled, playing along. "Are you my Jiminy Cricket?"

"I am the still, small voice inside of you."

I thought for a moment. "If you're the caretaker, then what's with that room?" I asked, thumbing over my shoulder towards the gate and the dilapidated entrance. I didn't mean for it to sound as snarky as it did, but I didn't apologize.

He didn't get irritated, he didn't seem upset in the slightest. He simply answered my questions.

"I will only do what you allow me to do."

I wrinkled my brow. "*I* didn't let you fix it?" I asked, indignantly, pointing a finger at myself.

He nodded. "You like to stay where it is safe and you don't like to let others in. Therefore that room is left to decay. It wasn't always that way, but you have been wounded." He looked sad, or maybe compassionate. The look made me angry, I didn't need pity.

He continued. "You think you are protecting your heart, but abandoned places only fall, eventually."

Okay, he's weird. I thought.

I sat down in one of the chairs and gingerly took off my backpack, trying to remember if I had ever met this man before, while trying not to bump the wound at my side. He seemed familiar to me, although odd and a little evasive. He knew a lot about me, apparently. It made me uncomfortable, and although I felt safe with him for some reason, I had questions.

He was middle-aged I guess, yet to look into his eyes he seemed timeless; ancient. It was as if I could see eternity in his eyes. I had never seen eyes like that before. I found myself staring at him. He smiled warmly at me and I quickly turned away. He didn't seem perturbed however, he didn't even seem embarrassed that I was staring. He was just calmly standing there waiting, perhaps, for me to drill him with more questions. I blushed in spite of myself.

I must have bumped my head, or maybe I touched some kind of psychedelic plant in the forest. Oh, crap, maybe I'm having a mental breakdown.

A million questions went through my mind. *Where am I? Am I dreaming? What am I doing here? This feels too real to be a dream.*

Weariness washed over me and I realized I was tired and hungry. I hadn't eaten since breakfast and it must be getting late. I looked at my watch, but it had stopped at a quarter past five. I looked up to inquire about the time and realized I didn't know his name.

"I'm sorry, what do I call you?"

He smiled, "I go by many names, but as a child you called me Jace."

"Okay, Jace. Do you know what time it is?"

"Time moves differently here. You have all the time you need."

By now I had a perpetual look of confusion on my face, and didn't seem to be able to get a straight answer.

"Is any of this real?" I gestured to the room. "I mean... are you real?"

Jace smiled again. His demeanor was kind and peaceful, making it difficult to see him as a stranger. Maybe that was why I couldn't seem to treat him as someone I didn't know.

"Nothing is real here except the things that are real. And yes, I am more real than anything," he explained.

Yeah, he's definitely strange, I thought. So, I changed the subject. "Do you know the Jester?"

"Yes, I know him well. He's a nasty character. Don't worry, you are safe with me."

"So, he's real. Do you know what he wants with me?"

"He wants to kill you," he said matter-of-factly.

"Why?" I raised my voice without realizing it. Again Jace was un-bothered and spoke gently to answer my question.

"Because he hates. He is hate. There is no love in him. He was once a beautiful creature who brought joy and music to the King, but he desired power, he desired to take the King's throne. He was thrown from his position to a lowly existence, exiled, but still sub-ject to the King. He now hates the King and seeks to destroy all whom the King loves. He is deceived by his own mind and seeks only his own pleasures."

Kings and Masters, mansions, and monsters? I thought. *I'm in a fantasy! There must be some psychological meaning to all of this.* I put my hand to my throat and realized I was still wearing the plas-tic jewel. *I must have hit my head and I'm dreaming; passed out in the forest.* I began to feel anxious again.

"Okay, well I need to get home! How do I get home without run-ning into that guy?" I asked, looking over to the gate.

"You will have to open the doors."

"What doors? The front doors?!"

"The ones you won't let me into, the doors you're afraid to open."

"I'm afraid to open the front doors!" I spurted. "He's out there, and I can't get out that way anyway. I came from that way. Carl... do you know Carl?"

He nodded.

"Carl said I had to come here, or well, he said to go forward, not back!"

I was frustrated and impatient. I didn't mean to yell at him, it all just spilled out. "Would you please tell me what is going on?! I am not keeping you from going anywhere! I just want to go home and you haven't really answered anything."

"You will understand soon," he said calmly. His calm was just irritating me at this point.

"Look, I don't have time for this. My Grandparents are going to be worried, then they'll call my dad and... I gotta get back."

"They will not miss you, like I said, time is different here."

I was about to protest when my stomach made a loud growl. Jace politely excused himself, turned, and left the room through one of the doors behind him. I was alone once again.

I stared at the door where he had gone. He intrigued me, and irritated me. *I don't have the patience for this.* I sighed deeply.

Somehow I knew I wasn't in the forests of Northern California though. I was somewhere else entirely. I was having a nervous breakdown, dreaming, or I was dead; I didn't know.

I didn't remember a time that I had ever seen this man, yet I knew I had known him from somewhere. He said I knew him when I was young, yet I had no memory of him. He said he was the voice inside my head, or something like that, but that's crazy. How do you meet your conscience? And since when is my conscience a middle-aged man?

Although I was confused and irritated, I still found myself drawn to him. He felt safe, he felt like my Pops, only those eyes, there was something in those eyes. He had something about him that made me feel exposed, like he could see to my soul. I was conflicted. I wanted to trust him and that scared me more than anything.

Trust no one, and no one can hurt you. Everyone leaves eventually.

I got up from the chair and paced around the room admiring the decor. It was an enchanting room. The stair railings were beautiful mahogany polished to shine. The steps were covered in light velvety carpet. The whole room was elegant and yet had a playful feel. I liked how the frames were hung at odd angles and the bookcases were quirky in design. I liked that there were pops of color among the white and gray marble floors and walls. Little trinkets and doodads sat on tables like a sparse museum.

The candles burned but never got smaller; it was the same with the fire in the fireplace. It burned but the wood was not consumed, it wasn't even warm.

There were pictures of landscapes sporadically placed among the empty frames. Above the fireplace there was a painting of a waterfall, the next was of Lake Britton, where I learned how to swim, the sun sparkling across the water. A feeling of recognition flickered through me and I turned back to the waterfall. The wide weeping rocks and twin chutes were unmistakable, it was Burney Falls. We had hiked down to the basin of those falls on too many occasions to count when we lived in California. The next framed image was an oil painting of the house I grew up in, ugly green paint and all. As I looked around I realized I knew where all the places were. Just then, Jace walked back into the room and beckoned me to follow him through the door he had left through a few minutes ago.

Through this door was a massive dining room, capable of holding hundreds of guests comfortably. It was brilliantly lit and immaculate. In the center of the room was a huge table. There were candelabras all along the table's top and large vases full of colorful, fresh flowers. The room was filled with the fragrance of fresh bread and florals. Everything else was brilliant white.

How can this place be mine if I have never been here before? I don't own a mansion!! How do I have an enormous palace in the middle of the forest, filled with pictures of people I know and love? Where am I?

On the far wall was an elaborate fireplace with a roaring fire in it. There were windows on either side. Stone lions lay beside the fire as if to warm themselves. The fireplace was so large one could have walked into it without the need to duck, but the room was a perfect temperature.

Why are there some clean rooms and some abandoned rooms? Why does it seem everything here is something I have seen before?

Outside, the light was waning. *If there isn't time here then why is the sun going down?*

"It moves differently here, and it is going down because you believe it is time it should," answered Jace, as if he could read my thoughts.

"Oh," was all I could think to say.

Jace led me to the table where dinner had been laid out in a beautiful spread. Everything seemed to be made just for me. The dishes were something I would have chosen, the dinner was one of my favorite meals, cheesy lasagna and garlic bread, salad, the works. And the décor reflected different areas of my personality. If the living room was my whimsical side, this was my elegant side.

"Thank you, Jace," I whispered.

Jace nodded and smiled at me. "It was my pleasure."

He pulled my chair out for me as I sat at the corner seat, and then took a seat next to me at the head of the table. I was overwhelmed that all of this was for me. It was odd and wonderfully kind and yet unnerving.

Time was moving along strangely, or not moving, that part confused me. First I was running for my life, frightened, and now I was being waited upon by someone whom I should know, but didn't remember. He obviously knew me.

I sat eating in silence for a little while. I realized, sitting this close to Jace, I could smell him. I couldn't help but breathe in his scent, it was like a spring day. He smelled like cool air and rain. He looked at me and I realized that I was staring, again. He only smiled. Embarrassed, I tried to 'save face' by asking a question.

"Jace, you said this is my house, but I have never been here. Where am I?"

"You are always here, you've just never seen it. This is the place where I meet with you.."

"Jace, you don't make sense."

Jace laughed.

I gasped; my breath caught in my throat. It was just like anyone else's laugh, except it wasn't. It had depth, like tones you can't hear, you feel. Like music. It felt like a babbling brook and fireworks, like sweet icing on your tongue and a symphony. It made the air celebrate, if that makes any sense. It doesn't, I know.

"All will become clear to you soon, Zoey."

For some reason, which I didn't understand at the time, my heart jumped at him saying my name. There was something very different about Jace. He was like Elrond or Gandolf, he was a character of power from a fantasy book, but better. I was so full of conflicting emotions it made me feel tired. I didn't even argue, though I was still confused.

I looked around the room at the ornate light fixtures and noticed the large portraits along the far wall. Graced with simple, elegant frames, the people took center stage, smiling at me from their staunch and poised positions. So lifelike were my relatives that I wouldn't have been surprised if one had winked.

Who had put up all these pictures? Who would know me this well? Nobody knows me, not the real me. Nobody! I don't let anyone in. Not after Aden. Never again.

"You let me in, Zoey, and that is what matters."

I stared at him, once again answering my question without me voicing them. I was afraid to even think it, but I did. *How does he do that?*

"You put up all these pictures?" I asked.

"No, Zoey, you did. They are all part of what's inside your heart."

"Well, I know that, but how did they get here?"

"*We* are inside of you."

"We're in California." I articulated, with a look of confusion on my face; incredulous.

We're inside of me? That's what he had said before and it still didn't make sense, and I knuckled my temple at the oncoming headache.

Jace nodded and set down his fork, then wiped his face with his napkin. He crossed his hands in front of himself and spoke.

"Zoey, after tonight, you will not be seeing me like you are now. I will always be with you, just call my name."

"But Jace, I have questions! I..."

"I will send another to help you."

"No. I don't want anyone else!" I protested, setting down my drink and sloshing it on the table. "I can find my way out alone!"

I was floundering; panicking. If this place was in me as he said, then I didn't want anyone coming in, I knew that much at least. "I don't need anyone else! I just need you to tell me what to do." I dabbed at the spill with my napkin.

"All will be answered, but you were never meant to be alone, you must let others in. You are tired now and you need rest. There is much to be done."

I was very tired and not just a little flustered. I had finished my meal and sleepiness washed over me. I looked out the window to see stars sparkling in the sky, trying to think of some way to convince him that I could do this on my own, and not to bring in anyone else.

I followed as Jace showed me to my room. It was the first room up the left staircase from the living room, and to the right. He opened the door and showed me in.

"Remember, you have to look into the rooms to see what is holding you here. I will be with you, always. Call my name."

I nodded, "good night, Jace." He smiled warmly and pulled the door closed behind me.

Chapter 4 Discovery

I stood there a moment staring at the door. I didn't want him to leave. It had been so long since I felt so comfortable around someone. He felt like a friend I had known forever. Yet, when I closed my eyes, it was like I could still feel him there. I wondered if Jace was an angel, but I wasn't even sure I believed in that sort of thing. He was my subconscious, I was sure of it, he was part of me. If he was part of me then I could trust him, right?. *What am I talking about?*

I felt like that lonely old lady that talked too long with the check-out person at the grocery store. I was lonely and I knew it.

I am losing my mind. I thought. I had absolutely no resolve to keep my guard up with him. I blurted out whatever I felt in the moment.

I turned and looked around.

This room was exactly as I would imagine a room if I were to have designed it myself. Oh, and if I were very wealthy.

It was simple, yet beautiful to the smallest detail. The bed coverings were overstuffed and made of the finest fabrics. The bed had a tall, white leather headboard. Nothing too gaudy, but very elegant.

The floors were rich, hardwood with thick, fluffy rugs. In the corner was a lamp that I had seen in a very exclusive furniture store window a couple of years ago. It was expensive and I had wanted it then, but dared not spend the money, for fear Aden would be angry. It sat on a simple, bedside table along with a lovely, ornate book of fairy tales that my father had given me for my ninth birthday.

This room was modern, with electricity and lights, that sort of thing. A small clock radio sat beside the bed blinking 12:00 in red numbers. Off to the right was a bathroom with a huge tub and a separate shower. It was state-of-the-art with all the bells and whistles. Buttons for water temperature, heating and cooling the room, music, and fragrance. On the sink were a toothbrush and toothpaste and all the toiletries I may have needed. Shampoo and conditioner (the expensive kind), and even my favorite perfume.

On the bed lay the pajamas that I had seen on a TV show only a week prior, some soap opera. It had been playing in my therapist's waiting room. Light blue pants and an accenting tank top with vertical stripes of pink and yellow. The pajamas were my size and perfect. It seemed everywhere I looked was something that I had seen before and had been brought there, just for me.

I gazed out the window behind the bed for a moment before closing the curtains. The stars here were bright and unencumbered by city lights. I could see into forever, the forest, the mountain silhouette beyond that, and the Milky Way that splashed across the night sky. It occurred to me that this window could not possibly be where it was. There was a whole wing behind this room, but trying to work it out just made my head hurt and sparked a curiosity in me I hadn't felt in some time.

Smiling mischievously to myself, I crept back to the door and opened it wide enough to look out. I didn't see Jace anywhere, so I slipped out onto the balcony and looked over the edge. All was quiet, but the crackling of the fire.

Something came alive in me, and I giggled, and then slapped a hand over my mouth. I looked over the balcony again, but I was still alone. Nothing or no one moved. I crept quietly to the next door along the balcony and tried the doorknob. It was unlocked.

Slowly I opened the door and looked in. Inside was a blank room, devoid of anything but an orb of light that hung suspended in the middle of the room. I looked behind myself one last time and then stepped into the room. There was nothing, no walls, no ceiling, just a white floor and emptiness, and light, blindingly bright light coming from the orb.

It was peaceful, warm, and inviting there. The orb floated without strings or attachment, as I walked all around it and waved my arms over it, like a magician on a stage. It just hung there silently. So, naturally, I poked it. The moment my finger touched the orb, however, the light burst forth and I found myself suspended, attached by finger to the orb, and floating in the expanse of space. All around me space flew by, stars, planets, moons, light, and darkness. I gasped and pulled back my finger and found myself safe in the blank room standing by the orb once again. My heart hammered in my chest. The door was where it always was, strangely inserted into nothingness like a stage prop. I ran over and slowly opened it, and looked out. All was as it should be.

I let out a breath of air and held my hand to my chest, leaning back against the wall. "That. Was. Amazing." I giggled. "I am freaking out. This is not real." My mind flitted between believing I was having a mental breakdown, or I had hit my head when I fell and I was hallucinating. I giggled again, "May as well make the best of it."

I walked slowly back to the orb and studied it again, and against my better judgment, I poked it again. This time the orb burst into life and all around me was an undersea ecosystem of fish and plants, coral and anemones, plankton, and microscopic life. I could see it all as it swam around me, from the smallest organism to the largest shark. I could hear all the sounds and feel the chill of the water, but it didn't affect me adversely, I was just in it, breathing, living, watching. I pulled my finger away from the orb and, again, I stood in the blank room, dry and warm. It was amazing, but made me feel very tired, like trying to study all day makes you feel drained. I made a mental note to come back and then snuck back to my room and locked my door.

I took a quick shower to get the dust and plaster out of my hair. I didn't even bother to blow-dry it before crawling into my bed.

As I lay there, I thought of my grandparents and silently prayed they wouldn't worry. I wanted to sit awake and contemplate what all of this meant. I wanted to ponder all that had happened and wondered if I was still in danger from the Jester. I wanted to call Jace and ask him all the questions that weighed on my mind, for him to sit by my bed like my dad used to do when I was little; till I fell asleep. Which, frankly I found weird. I just met this person, but couldn't shake the feeling I'd known him forever. I didn't do any of these things anyway. Sleep took me quickly and I rested better than I had in a long time.

Chapter 5 Mr. Kort

I woke the next day, or what I would call the next day; the sun was shining through the impossible window. I woke to the sound of someone shouting and what sounded like someone rattling the gate outside the living room. I sat up and, for a moment, didn't know where I was. I blinked a few times and looked around the room. It hadn't been a dream.

Suddenly, I was very anxious and hoped my family was okay. They were sure to be beside themselves with worry. A sick feeling in my stomach told me that something was very wrong. Then it dawned on me that there was someone in the house; someone other than Jace.

I sat on the bedside, feeling the dread of my situation weighing down upon me. Someone was in the mansion trying to break in the gate! The mansion began to quake again, the same as it had the day before. My bed shook back and forth and pictures swayed from side to side. I pulled my blankets to my chin and squeezed my eyes shut. After a moment the shaking stopped and all was quiet again.

Kicking aside the covers again, I stepped out of bed. I walked to the door and pulled it open enough to see out, but I couldn't see over the balcony to the gate downstairs. Frustrated, I crept to the railing and looked over.

There, behind the gate stood a man. He was looking around the room with his hands gripping the bars, like a prisoner, trying to reach the lock. When he noticed me looking at him, he waved through the gate like he was happy to see me. I just thought he was odd, but upon closer examination realized it was my self-defense teacher, Mr. Kort.

What on earth is he doing here? I thought.

"Mr. Kort?"

"Zoey! Oh, thank God! Can you let me in? There's a really creepy guy outside with a huge, demon dog. Seriously! He isn't human!" Mr. Kort looked over his shoulder and grimaced. "He keeps rattling the doorknob and laughing. He's freakin' me out." Then he mumbled something about having to fight demons, unarmed.

Crap, the Jester! I thought. "Uhm, yeah. I'll be right down!"

I ran back into my room to get the key out of the pocket of my jeans.

Crap! What is the Jester doing here? How did Mr. Kort get in? Why isn't the front door locked? What is he doing here?

I had a million questions going through my mind while I frantically dug through my jeans pockets to find the key. It wasn't there. I unzipped my backpack and dug through every pocket I could find, the key wasn't there. I could hear Mr. Kort yelling from the gate.

"Zoey! Please hurry."

I started to panic, the mansion began to shake. I huddled against the wall, pulled my knees to myself and squeezed my eyes shut.

"Jace, where are you?!"

"I am here." I heard his voice say, but it wasn't my ears that heard, it was in my mind, or my heart. I don't know, it came from inside me.

The shaking stopped and the house settled. There were popping and creaking noises as the house settled, and then all was still again. I breathed a sigh of relief and opened my eyes. There, on the floor was the key and my compass. They must have fallen out when I hung my jeans over the chair. Quickly, I grabbed the key and ran out the door banging my toe in the process.

"Ouch!" I mumbled, and quickly limped down the stairs.

Mr. Kort was standing in the corner at the edge of the gate with his hands over his head. He was covered in plaster that had rained down on him during the quake. He looked over at me as I approached. Little pebbles fell off his head making crackling noises as they hit the floor. The look in his eyes told me he was not happy about his situation. Mr. Kort is used to being in control, he teaches self-defense after all.

I could feel fear like I had walked into a cloud of it, as if it were a tangible thing. I looked past Mr. Kort, through the tunnel to the door at the other end. There, in the open, front doorway, stood, whom I assumed to be, (it was pretty obvious) the Jester and The Wild Card. He was not what I expected. He was a man, a huge, tall man, and didn't look like a court jester at all. He was beautiful and terrible. His hair was silver and long and he had strong, sharp features. I couldn't see much detail from this distance, except that smile; Oh that nightmare of a smile.

He exuded fear and disgust; palpable and unbound.

The Wild Card was an enormous, wolf-like creature. A muscled, black, demon dog that looked as if it had a dire case of mange. Torn flesh hung in places and he had a hunched back. Drool hung in long ropes from his mouth and he breathed heavily and ragged. The scent of death wafted through the tunnel, putrid, and sweet on the breeze.

I stood there, petrified, stifling the reflex to gag.

The Jester laughed at me; mean, snarling, and cruel. He stood in the doorway with both doors swung wide open, watching. Though he never passed the threshold.

"Zoey!" begged Mr. Kort. "Please open the gate."

Mr. Kort stood there with his hands on the bars; eyes pleading with me. I had never seen him look frightened. I didn't think he could be afraid of anything; he had always been so calm and sure of himself.

I came to my senses and grabbed the lock, blinking away the silhouette of the Jester that the sun had imprinted on my retinas, and focusing on the lock. My hands were shaking and I was having trouble getting the key into the keyhole. Mr. Kort kept looking at me and then over his shoulder to the door on the other end. Fear was tangible, like a living thing. It made me jump at every noise and the hair on the back of my neck stood on end. I knew Mr. Kort could feel it too.

"Let me try." he pleaded, hands gripping the bars in front of me.

"I can do it. Hang on."

He looked over his shoulder again, but the Jester didn't move.

"Why is that Freak just standing there?"

"I don't know," I answered, finally getting the lock open.

Mr. Kort pushed the gate open and slammed it behind himself. He turned and took the lock and key from my hand and quickly replaced it on the gate with a loud "click." Then he backed away into the room. We both stood there staring through the tunnel at the front door.

The Jester blew a kiss, a very disturbing gesture from a man like him. Coupled with that terrible smile, it was a scene out of a horror movie. He took a step back and the doors slammed in front of him.

"Oh my God! Who was that guy!?"

"They call him the Jester. He wants to kill me."

"Why, what did you do?"

"I didn't do anything."

I don't know how long we both stood there staring at the door. Never daring to look away and at each other.

"That was weird," he said. "Almost like a fear... spell."

"Yeah, I felt it too."

When it seemed that The Jester wasn't going to bother us anymore, Mr. Kort turned and looked around the room. "What is this place?"

"I don't know. It's mine. My house... sort of. What are you doing here!?" I asked, finally looking at him.

"I don't know, I think I'm dreaming…" Mr. Kort mumbled and then turned his attention to the room.

He began wandering around touching things and talking to himself. For some reason, this made me inordinately uncomfortable and I wanted him to stop, and to leave.

"Mr. Kort…"

"Gabe."

"What?" I faltered.

He turned to me, with a small, steampunk box in his hand. "I'm only, like, a year or two older than you, and we're not in class. You should call me Gabe. My *name* is *Gabe*."

"Oh."

I walked up to him and took the box from his hand and set it gently back on the table.

"*Gabe*, why are you here?"

He went back to wandering around the room picking things up and setting them down.

"This place is amazing. It's like Wonderland meets Beetlejuice," he said, to no one in particular.

I followed behind him feeling nervous and agitated that I was not getting answers (again) and that he was touching my stuff. Stuff, that before yesterday, I didn't even know was mine.

The steampunk box was a trinket that I had seen when I visited Sarasota several years ago with Susanna. The 'dancing man' shaped candleholder was a gift from my friend Brandi when I moved from California. (I thought I had lost that. Actually, I thought Aden had thrown it away.)

He picked up a copper music box, which had belonged to my mother when I was a child, and wound the butterfly at the top to start the music. The little butterfly spun around the flowers and played La Vie En Rose. The tinkling little tune was a stark contrast to my growing irritation and I pulled the music box from his hand and raised my voice.

"Mr. Kort! What are you doing here!?"

"I told you, I'm dreaming. I went to sleep and woke up here. A man named Jace said I was supposed to help you open doors." he explained, staring off into space. Then he mumbled something about drugs and strange dreams. He had a confused look on his face and he shook it off and continued what he was doing.

"You met Jace?" I interrupted, stumbling after him. "Where is he?"

"Will you please stop calling me Mr. Kort?! My name is Gabe! Mr. Kort is my dad. Geeze, why are you so formal all the time?"

He turned to face me. "You do that in my class and it drives me crazy! Didn't you notice the others calling me Gabe?" he raised his eyebrows, questioningly, then turned to explore the room again.

"What am I telling you this for? It's a dream, *you* aren't gonna re-member this," he mumbled to himself, throwing his hands in the air for emphasis.

"It's not your dream, it's my dream! I was here first!" I shouted, and pulled yet another trinket out of his hands.

He looked at me, paused, and then snatched the trinket back out of my hands.

"That doesn't even make sense!" he shouted and then plopped the trinket back down where he had found it. Which made me worry and rush to see if he had damaged it.

"And why am I dreaming about you being like some sort of 'crazy cat lady'? You always seemed pretty cool in class. I swear this is the craziest dream I think I have ever had."

He rubbed his head and paced the floor. "Oh, and nice pajamas, by the way," he said, turning back to face me.

It was that moment that the tinkling music of the butterfly box stopped, and I stood there hugging it like a hoarder at an auction. I was staring at Gabe; completely dumbfounded. I looked down at myself and then over to the mirror leaning against the wall. I was a mess. My hair was disheveled and there I stood; bare feet and pajamas.

I took a deep breath and composed myself, lifting my chin slightly. I set down the music box and smoothed the wrinkles out of my PJs. I clasped my fingers in front of myself and turned back to him.

"If you will excuse me, I'd like to go get dressed."

Gabe started laughing and I blushed, but held my composure.

"Yes, of course, go," he said, still smiling broadly at me. I heard him chuckle as I walked calmly away to the stairs. Then I ran up and into my room.

Chapter 6 Where'd He Go?

I showered and dressed, basically going through the motions. I was preoccupied with my thoughts and in a slight state of panic.

What is Mr. Kort doing here? How did he even get here? What is he doing in Northern California?

He saw Jace. I wonder what Jace told him.

Then I remembered what Jace had said about bringing people to help me.

Of all the people he could have brought, he brought Mr. Kort? What, am I going to have to fight my way back...home...or reality... or whatever?

I imagined myself in full ninja garb, in a fight to the death with the Jester, and then shook off the thought; shuttering.

I thought about Mr. Kort as I applied mascara and then dried my hair. He wasn't the worst person who could have shown up. I had to admit I had always felt safe around him, although at the moment I was irritated with him showing up there. I didn't think he would try to take advantage of me and he could defend us if something bad happened, although I doubted he was any match against the Jester, maybe he could help me find the door that led home.

I could only assume he would want to get home as badly as I did.

Pretty soon he's gonna figure out this isn't a dream. I thought. *I wonder how he'll react to that.*

I tried to imagine his reaction and found myself picturing his face.

Gabriel Kort was, what some might call, striking. His hair was dark brown and longer on the top, leaving pieces to fall over his eye. He was usually clean-shaven and had bright blue eyes that were squinty in a very sexy way. He was tall, much taller than me, and was in great shape. Martial arts and staying in shape were what he did, and it showed.

I surprised myself a bit, I had never really thought about Mr. Kort that way. He was just someone I saw in class and that was it. I really hadn't ever thought much of him at all. After all, I hadn't been trying to make friends. I had been trying to escape.

I knew he was a nice guy and seemed very patient in class. He smiled easily and had a great laugh.

I remembered a time when he had been trying to teach us a technique in class and I couldn't seem to get it right. I was being a klutz again. He took the time to teach me, even when everyone else was ready to move on. I didn't know if I liked him, but I respected him.

Looking at myself in the mirror, I assessed my appearance. My outfit was one I'd recently seen in Elle Magazine. Besides I may as well take advantage of it, I couldn't afford to dress this way at home.

I sighed and resigned myself to going back out to meet with Mr. Kort. I figured I wasn't going to make up for my crazy lady performance, but at least I'd look good. I was careful to avoid the scrape on my side that seemed to be a bit more painful today. I put on some perfume and called it good enough.

When I emerged from my room I had intended to find out what Mr. Kort was doing there and get him going on his way. I composed myself as someone on a mission and walked right down to where I had left him. Let the confrontation ensue!

He wasn't there.

I stopped in my tracks, looking around the room. He was definitely not there. The gate was still locked and thinking back I remembered he never gave the key back to me.

He was roaming around my house, alone!

How dare he wander around without me! How rude! Who goes into someone else's house and just roams around without permission?

I looked around for any sign of him and which way he had gone.

I opened a large door to the far right and looked inside. It was a dark hallway that smelled like it hadn't been opened in a long time. The air was stale and warm. I closed that door and looked around again.

Then I opened the door to the dining room and looked inside. The smell of coffee and pastries filled the air and I breathed it in, suddenly wondering if Jace was in the kitchen.

Jace! He'll know what's going on. I thought, and headed through the dining room to the kitchen that I assumed was on the far side.

The dining room showed no signs of last night's dinner and was dimly lit and quiet. I felt as if I needed to tiptoe so as to not disturb the silence. I was on a mission, however, so I put myself in business mode and clomped through to find Jace and Gabe, and to see what was going on. My Prada heels probably sounded like a galloping Clydesdale on the marble floors and through the huge room.

I busted through the door calling for Jace only to find Mr. Kort sitting on the counter with a pastry in each hand.

"Zoey!" he mumbled with his mouth full. "This is the best dream I have ever had."

He held the pastries up to show me and then went on. "I've eaten four of these. I'd die if I did that at home." He laughed and took another huge bite of pastry. "Mmmm, surrr good!" he garbled, and then washed it all down with a big gulp of coffee.

I stared at him for a moment and then surveyed the room.

"Wow, this is something out of an episode of 'Real Housewives.'" I said, spinning around to take it all in.

Apparently Mr. Kort thought the same thing, because he did a terrible impression of a rich woman, yelling about not getting the scone she wanted. He crossed his legs daintily (as dainty as a man can) and pretended to adjust his fake breasts. I tried not to laugh, but it was just so ridiculous.

He seemed pleased with himself for that.

The kitchen was large with oversized appliances, dark marble countertops, and white cabinets with glass doors. The lights were inset except for the crystal chandelier above the eating nook by the floor-to-ceiling picture window. It was a cozy space with a small, round table adorned with a simple table cloth and flower centerpiece.

The window overlooked a beautiful garden with a high iron fence all around it. Outside were flowers of all kinds, and a maze of high hedges. Stone statues adorned sitting areas with elaborate benches, and a beautiful fountain sprayed water into a pool in the center of the garden. A large ornate, Victorian, glasshouse loomed beyond that.

Beautiful birds spotted the landscape with color, some blending perfectly with the flowers, and as I looked, I thought I spotted a rabbit disappear behind a bush. My mind went back to the boy that had been in the forest the day before. Carl.

How does he fit into all this? He can't be real. Maybe that is what Jace meant about some things being real and some not.

There was a huge island in the middle of the kitchen that was covered in glass plates filled with pastries and breakfast meats. On the opposite counter where Mr. Kort sat, was a fancy coffee maker filled with fresh coffee and an assortment of creamers and condiments. I was certainly wowed by it all.

Mr. Kort must have gone through every cabinet while I was getting ready. He knew where everything was and handed me a plate to fill with breakfast goodies. Meanwhile, he stuffed another pastry in his mouth and rolled his eyes with delight. I had never seen this light-hearted side of him and, although I was trying to stay aloof, I was losing my nerve. He was amusing, but the health nut attitude seemed a little overboard. Everyone cheated on their diet once in a while. *Get over it, Dude.*

"Have you seen Jace?" I asked as I helped myself to coffee.

"Not since this morning when I got here," he answered. "He's quite an interesting fellow, isn't he."

I turned around to look at him and he was looking at me like he was perfectly at home; unperturbed with the fact that he had woken up in a strange place, not to mention the Jester and Jace or even me being there.

I must have given him a strange look because he said "What?" and then picked up a napkin and wiped his face.

"Yes, he is an interesting person. What did he say to you?" I pressed.

He frowned at me like I had killed his good mood.

"Well, we talked about a few things and then he said that I should help you find your way home. He was all kinds of mysterious."

"Yeah, I know. What did you guys talk about?"

"About stuff." he retorted, glaring at me. "Why do you need to know?"

"Forget it." I snapped. "It's just that I've been here since yesterday and I'd like to know why you're here and if I should expect anyone else. This is my place, ya know!"

"How should I know if anyone else is coming? I don't rehearse my dreams. I just go to sleep and take what I get. Although this is the strangest you've ever acted in *any* of my dreams."

He set his coffee cup down on the counter and hopped down, folding his arms in front of himself in a pseudo face off with me.

"I… You...What?" I stammered."Listen, this is not your dream! I'm a real person, crazy as I might seem, but you have no idea what I have been through the past... however long I have been here! *You* are the one who isn't real and..What am I saying? I'm arguing with an imaginary person."

Gabe glared.

I stopped talking and decided to eat my cheese danish. If this wasn't real I sure didn't have to worry about my diet and especially about the feelings of an imaginary person.

I took the danish and my coffee and plopped down at the table trying to will Mr. Kort to disappear.

He didn't.

He walked over and sat down at the other side of the table and stared at me. Then he looked away, then he stared again. I tried vehemently to ignore him and enjoy my coffee and failed miserably.

"Well, Mrs. Jacobson…"

I rolled my eyes. "It's *Ms.* Jacobson. My husband died. And you *already* call me Zoey."

"Oh, I'm sorry." he replied genuinely. Referring to my husband's passing, I assumed.

I just smiled mockingly and sipped my coffee. I didn't feel he needed details.

I kicked off the Prada heels and pulled my legs up on the chair, taking a deep, calming breath. I figured I should loosen up a little. Getting to know him a bit wouldn't hurt. Besides, we may be spending some time together since I didn't know how to get rid of him, let alone get home myself. I supposed I'd have to call him by his first name as well. Although, I preferred to call him Mr. Kort. In my way of thinking, it kept him at a distance and I liked it that way.

I'd loosen up, but later. I had things to do.

Gabe sat quietly, and I finished my coffee and excused myself, not bothering to put the heels back on. He raised an eyebrow, but I didn't stay to explain or to let him think he was invited.

Chapter 7 The Museum

I left Gabe in the kitchen, determined to find a way out on my own. He was a useless figment of my imagination anyway, and frankly, an irritation. The only person I would need to be protected from in this place was the Jester and I didn't really think Gabe was going to win that fight, black belt or not.

I realized when I got to the living room, however, that the door leading to the first floor East Wing would require me to go through the gate.

I stood with my hands around the bars straining my eyes to see the double doors that sat recessed into the walls on either side inside the tunnel. "Looks like I'll be starting at the top." I mumbled to myself.

After a quick stop in my room and a change of shoes, I found my way up through the inner staircase and into the hallway to the East Wing fifth floor. The hall was dark and all I had for light were the candles that I had pilfered from the candelabra in the entranceway and some matches I had found in my room.

It's amazing how such a small amount of light can light up such a large space. The dancing flame made the old pictures on the walls seem to move as their eyes watched me pass. The silence only exacerbated the noise of my flats clicking on the hardwood. I was thoroughly creeped out by the time I got ten feet down the hall and stood in front of 501 E. The first door in the East Wing.

The door stood slightly ajar, not enough that you'd notice, but came open when I tried the knob. The room inside was brightly lit by another strange orb of light that hung, unimpeded, in the middle of the room.

I walked in and the orb of light began to grow and take shape, the room now resembled a museum. That was different, I hadn't even touched it.

There were statues on pedestals, portraits of all sizes that lined the walls, and little speakers by each of the exhibit's pieces and a button under each piece. The wall behind the pictures was covered in antique wallpaper.

I entered, blew out my candle, and walked to the first picture closest to the door. It was a picture of Aden and me where we had met, in the style of Monet, with slightly blurred images in soft pastels. There we were at the cafe, me walking across the street and Aden with his hand slightly outstretched, calling to me.

I pressed the button under the picture and I could hear the tinkling of spoons on cups, of people talking, cars passing by, and then I heard Aden's voice calling me. "Excuse me, Zoey wait… Zoey!" It sounded just as it had that day. I had ignored him in my embarrassing attempt to get away after spilling coffee all over him. I could remember the feeling of embarrassment as if it had just happened.

I moved to the next picture.

This painting was of my wedding, done in Michelangelo's style. I laughed at the absurdity of it. I looked so innocent, and Aden was captured as the Devil himself, in a tux with tails that his devilish tail stuck out between. I wondered who would have known Aden so well as to capture him in that way.

The button underneath this one only played the Midsummer Night's Dream Wedding March on the organ, just as it had in that giant church the day of our wedding. I often wondered how we were able to have our wedding in that beautiful church. We weren't even members. Aden probably gave someone enough money to look the other direction, so to speak.

The next picture was of Aden and me at one of his many social engagements. Done in a style I didn't recognize, nor was it written in the description. It simply said "Another Dinner with The Trophy."

I had been wearing a dress of Aden's choosing. I remembered feeling very uncomfortable in it and asking if I could wear something else from my closet. Aden said I couldn't wear something I'd already worn. "That would look wrong." And that it was too late to try and find something else. He had brought home that dress at the last minute, insisting that he had forgotten to tell me about this fundraiser and that it was important that we attend. He had "buzzed by" the boutique and picked me up that 'little number' on his way home.

I pressed the button beneath the picture. Aden's voice, soft and honey-laden came out of the speaker. "Zoey, Honey, you look sexy. There's nothing wrong with showing a little skin. What are you a Nun?" His laugh was loud and sardonic.

Anger welled up inside of me thinking about that day. He had made me feel like a piece of meat. The men he introduced me to looked me up and down with either lust or disdain. I had been embarrassed and angry. If I was being honest with myself, I had been hurt. Husbands are supposed to love and protect, that was neither loving nor protecting, and it certainly wasn't cherishing.

I looked back to the picture of our wedding and the Devil wiggled his eyebrows at me. I guess that should have shocked me a bit, but I just got angrier. I gripped my hands into fists and moved to the next picture.

The next picture was a Salvador Dali look-alike, depicting Aden yelling at me in the kitchen. It was one of a series entitled "What Is Wrong With You?" The images were distorted and strange, but recognizable for what they were. Each of the pictures depicted a cowering version of me and an angry Aden. I had been a weak person to have stayed with him. I didn't know why I had.

The button underneath the first one yelled: "Why didn't you do it how I told you to!?"

The next said: "You can't do anything right!"

The next: "You've never had an original thought."

"I didn't tell you to go that way!"

"Quit acting like an F-ing Child!"

I stopped pressing the buttons after that. I stood, shaking with my white-knuckled fists clenched; feeling nauseous and dropping bits of candle wax onto the shiny floor. I turned away from the last painting and stood face to face with a bust of Aden on a pedestal. The smug look on his handsome face sent me over the edge and I snapped. I pushed the heavy bust off the stand and watched it shatter onto the floor.

That felt good.

Poised to react, I waited for alarms to sound, lights to flash, or guards to come running; nothing happened. I walked back to the door to the hallway and looked out. Nobody there, all was quiet and dark.

Turning back to the museum room, a giggle escaped me. Nonchalantly, I sashayed back into the room and stopped in front of the vase that Aden had bought me on one of his "business trips." It was beautiful and ornate and expensive. "Oops!" I pushed it off the table and it smashed to pieces on the marble floor. I laughed again.

Then looking around the room at all the memories, all the lovely things that represented our relationship; I went into berserker mode. I smashed all the fragile gifts with which Aden had bought my forgiveness, or rather, my silence. Guilt tactics.

I smeared candle wax into the Devil Aden's face. I laughed and screamed at Aden all the things I had wanted to say in the past, but had held my tongue, either out of fear or out of need. The need to be wanted, to be cherished, to be loved. I tore the paintings from the wall and threw them across the room until I came to the last few paintings in the corner I'd not yet seen.

These were a series in the style of Johannes Vermeer, with his beautiful shadows and elements of sadness in his expressions. My face was painted with that sadness, I was sitting in the dining room of our home in Florida. It was late and I had been waiting up for Aden to come home.

I stood there, breathing heavily, with my hands on my hips. This picture caught me off guard and all the anger faded into heartache and pain. I pressed my hand to my lips and swallowed a lump that was welling up in my throat.

I mustered up the courage to press the button. "I know about her Aden, I want a divorce." My voice.

The next portrait depicted him flying into a rage and slapping my face. "I'm sorry Zoey, you made me do it." Aden's voice.

The last painting was of the officer that stood at my door. "I'm sorry Mrs. Jacobson, There's been an accident." The officer's voice.

I backed up and sat down on the bench sitting in that corner. Like someone had known that I'd want to stop and reflect on these last few depictions of my life with Aden. I stared. So much emotion welled up in me, I was overwhelmed. I felt the same as I did the day the Sheriff had come to my door. Sadness, loneliness, despair, guilt.

As I sat there gazing, I noticed a button on the wall next to the exit that didn't have a painting to go with it. I rose, walked over and pressed this last button. Whispers emanated from all the speakers around the room.

"It's her fault he did this." "She was never good for him." The voices of his parents.

"It's because you got boring, Zoey." "What do you need your daddy for? You've got me!" "I'm so sick of you." "Maybe if you weren't such a prude!" Aden's voice.

"He'd been drinking, Ma'am, his car hit a utility pole." The Officer.

"Did you know he was seeing someone else?" Aden's friends at the funeral.

"Zoey, you've just never been a great judge of character." Dad's voice.

A culmination of voices began to all talk at once, making it difficult to pick out any one separately. Voices of all the people in my life.

Accusations, excuses, explanations. Whispers.

The anger came again, and I screamed. I tore the remaining pictures from the wall and stomped them, breaking the frames and tearing the canvas. I picked up a cup from the tea set that sat on display by the Johannes Vermeer series and turned to throw it against the wall behind me. There stood Gabe, eyes wide and sad. I stopped and lowered the cup, feeling like I'd just been caught doing something terrible. Wondering how long he'd been there and how much he'd seen.

***

My life before Aden hadn't been all bad. I had lived in Pensacola, Florida for several years. Before that, I grew up in Burney, California, where my grandparents live. My father moved us across the country after my mom was killed in an accident. I guess he needed a change of scenery and, well, a place far away from snow and slick roads.

I met Aden in Florida, and we were married for a little over four years before he got himself killed.

We met at a coffee shop. It was a Monday, and I was having a terrible day. My car had broken down that morning and I had called to inform my job that I wouldn't be coming in. I worked for an insurance agency and went to school in the evenings.

Of course, Madison, from Human Resources gave me attitude. Sometimes I thought she believed she was placed on the earth to make me miserable. It was her solemn duty. She found pleasure in finding fault in everyone and had no trouble voicing her opinion, much to the chagrin of many of the employees at Gibbons and Thompson Insurance Agency. She was pretty and thin and made you want to hate her just for breathing the same air you had to breathe.

The fault she found in me, apparently, was that I was young and that, in her book, meant I was irresponsible and flighty. She wasn't even that much older than me and I had given her no reason to continue putting me into that category, until that day.

As I stood there in the mechanic's small waiting area, Madison told me how she "just knew" I'd show my true colors eventually and that I'd start making up lies to get out of work so I could party on the weekends. It probably wouldn't have mattered if I told her that I had graduated high school with honors and already had my AA.

When she finished her little rant, I hung up. My car hadn't even been released from the tow truck so I knew it was going to be a long morning. I walked across the street to the coffee shop, lost in my own world, irritated. I was going through the motions to get some coffee and wait for the bad news about my car.

I had never been to that particular coffee shop before; my apartment was on the other side of town and I just hadn't ever ventured down that way. Sweet Cakes was small, with only two tables inside, but had several tables on the large patio out front.

It's Florida, a heliophile's dream. Me, not so much.

It was, however, a beautiful, March morning. It was a little chilly, but to me, chilly is a treat before the hot days of summer set in. I purchased a coffee and found the last available table outside. People were working on laptops and chatting quietly among the other tables. On any other day I would have been content to watch people and enjoy the morning, but that day I was preoccupied with my heavy thoughts and I was still angry with Madison. Too distracted to notice, I had sat at a table that was already occupied by a man who had just stepped away to get something out of his car. His drink sat on the table along with his newspaper and his cell phone. I had been looking over at a lady that had laughed loudly at another table when he walked up. I looked up at him, still lost in my thoughts. It took a moment for me to snap out of it.

He was strikingly handsome, several years older than me, with blue eyes, blond hair and a manicured beard. He wore a suit and had a large briefcase. His eyes met mine and he smiled; warm and friendly.

"Hello, May I join you?"

"What? Oh, yeah, sure. Uhm." I stuttered.

I looked around. "Oh, I'm sorry. I took your table." I stood up to leave, completely flustered, and bumped my coffee against the table, splashing it up onto his tailored pants.

"Oh my Gosh! I'm so sorry." I looked around for a napkin. Setting the remainder of my coffee down, I quickly darted back into the shop to get something to clean off the coffee that I had spilled on this poor, gorgeous man.

"I am such a klutz," I mumbled. By the time I returned, paper towels from the ladies room in hand, he was sitting down, had already cleaned off the excess coffee and was blotting it with a handkerchief.

"Oh, uhm, here," I said, handing him the paper towels.

He looked up at me and smiled, took the towels from my hand and set them on the table. I felt like an idiot as I stood there, my brain was as foggy as pea soup.

"I'm terribly sorry. Here, let me give you my number. If you'll call me, I'll pay for your dry cleaning. Just let me know where you take it." I dug through my purse and found a piece of paper and quickly jotted down my name and number.

"It's no problem. You don't have to do that."

"Oh, no I insist." I protested, practically shoving the paper into his hand. I picked up what was left of my coffee and my dignity, and quickly walked away across the street, back to the Mechanic's shop. I heard him asking me to wait, but I acted as though I hadn't.

All I wanted to do was get away, I almost ran.

It had been the worst day, and sitting in the waiting room of Mick's Automotive and Tow didn't make it any better. My car was done around one and I had sat there all morning watching Days of Our Lives, a couple of shows on HGTV and Spongebob until they finally came out to tell me my car was finished. The bill topped the day off like the cherry on a Sunday. Four hundred dollars later and I was on my way to work. So much for saving for a vacation.

It was Saturday when he called. I didn't recognize the number and I had completely forgotten about the incident that had happened on Monday. So, I answered it.

"Hello?"

"Hi there, Zoey? This is Aden. We met on Monday, at Sweet Cakes."

"I'm sorry, who are you?"

"Aden. You spilled coffee on me."

Crap.

Crap.

Crap!

"Oh Hi, Aden, I suppose you want to let me know where you had your suit cleaned? Let me get a pen."

"Uhm, well, no, not exactly. I was wondering if I could take you to dinner. If you promise not to spill it on me, of course...haha... Hello?"

I'm not sure how long I sat there, dumbfounded. Long enough to make him uncomfortable I'm sure. I couldn't believe what was coming out of my mouth when I said, "Okay, uhm sure, that would be great."

"Okay, if you'll text me your address I'll pick you up, say around seven? Do you like Italian? I know a great place down on Palafox Avenue."

"Uhm, yeah, It's my favorite. Okay, see you then."

Pensacola isn't the prettiest city, but it has some nice places, especially the beaches. Unbelievably beautiful beaches; pristine, white sand spilling into the beautiful aqua-green ocean. Perfect for those who want to work on their tan eight or nine months out of the year. Again, not me. I have what most people call porcelain skin. I just call it white and freckly. And pale eyes are light-sensitive; frankly, I was born to live in the Arctic or a cave. God knows why I ended up in sunny Florida.

Over the years, The Historical Society and The Powers That Be had brought in some great artsy spots. museums, art galleries, opera houses, great restaurants, and a huge ballet studio and actors guild. Palafox Avenue was the up and coming place to be, and he was taking me to one of the most expensive places downtown.

My roommate and best friend, Susanna, asked a million questions and was enjoying my nervousness as I got ready. I thought she'd die laughing when I told her how we had met.

"After all that and you're still going out with him?" she giggled. "You're braver than I am!"

"I'm not brave, I'm stupid! I don't know what came over me." I held up a black dress for her opinion. She shook her head.

"I accepted before I knew what I was doing. It must have been his charm, or the fact that he is freakin' gorgeous, oh my gosh, you should see his eyes."

I held up another dress, this one red. She shook her head again, this time with a grimace.

"That's a winter dress," she explained.

I think I tried on every piece of clothing I owned and finally settled on a sundress and a light sweater. I would have rather worn something black and mysterious, but he already knew I was a klutz. Nothing mysterious about that. I wore my hair down and settled on some sensible flats. We decided if I couldn't be mysterious, maybe I could pass for sweet.

"He's here." Susanna yelled down the hall. "And he's hot! He's in a Mercedes, looks new."

"Shhhh, he's gonna hear you yelling." I answered, walking down the hall to get the door.

She closed the curtain. "He's just gotten out of his car, chill. He looks a lot older than you though."

I took a deep breath to calm my nerves. "Not a lot," I lied, and moved a curl out of my face. "Maybe five years?"

"Maybe ten." she argued.

"Then he's going to be mature. That's a bonus, right?" I offered.

"I hope he isn't a bore," she added.

The doorbell rang and I grimaced at her. My heart pounded in my chest as I opened the door. Aden smiled broadly. "Hi, Zoey. You look great."

"Thanks, uhm, so do you. Er, nice, you look nice." *I'm an idiot,* I thought.

I introduced Susanna to Aden and then we left. Aden took me to Valentino's, a new Italian restaurant that I couldn't afford, and required a reservation, unless you know the right people.

He was charming, funny and altogether amazing. He was a successful lawyer, having just made partner at a local firm. Susanna had been right, he was almost ten years older than me, but was anything but boring. He was well known among the elite. He was well read, bright and funny. And for the seven months we dated before we got married, he was the best actor I had ever known. I fell madly in love, and so began a tumultuous and very unhappy marriage.

I know I've skipped over a lot of details here, but the time we dated was the happiest part of our lives together. He introduced me to his friends and his family, and I Introduced him to mine. Everyone seemed to get along well. He soon whisked me away from everyone and acted as though he wanted to have me all to himself.

We had a short engagement, and I admit that the proposal was lackluster, but you see past those things when you're in love, right?

He appeared to be happy and excited, saying he didn't want to wait. We had an enormous wedding in an elaborate church downtown. The reception was full of many people I didn't even know. To this day, I honestly don't know why he married me. He said he loved me, but you don't treat people you love the way he treated me.

Not long before he died, I began seeing a shrink and taking antide-pressants. As I remember they didn't seem to help me feel better, just nothing at all.

When you need a pill to go to sleep, another to get out of bed, and something else to get you through the day, you've got a problem. I had many.

After the funeral I was determined to get my life back together. I suppose I may have swung a little too far to the other side in some ways.

My therapist told me that I needed to try to start feeling in control of my own life again. "Ms. Jacobson, give yourself time. You can't just walk out of a narcissistic relationship and feel in control when you have been controlled for so long," she would say. "We do agree that it was a narcissistic relationship?"

"Yes." I would say, but I wasn't convinced.

"You need to put yourself in places that make you feel safe," she would look at me with a kind, tender expression, like she felt sorry for me. "And surround yourself with people who are going to sup-port you."

Her pity just made me angry.

I joined a woman's self-defense class, figuring I could make my-self feel safe. I threw myself back into my schooling and took on too many classes at once. If I wasn't in school or studying, in self-defense class, or the gym, I was in church, trying to heal my spirit, struggling to trust God to take care of me. I believed, for the most part, that I could do a better job, alone.

I ate right; strictly healthy, and I exercised regularly. I essentially made myself too busy for most of my relationships and the people who actually cared about me took notice. After several months, I went to church, the gym, and self-defense less and less, and spent more time studying at home, avoiding social situations as much as possible.

My dad was happy to see me getting involved and seemingly en-joying life again, but he was worried.

"Zo, Honey, You're taking on too much," he was saying, as we stood by my car outside of church one rare Sunday morning..

"I'm fine Dad, I like staying busy." I looked down at my watch. I gotta go though, I have a paper to write by tomorrow."

"Okay, but Zo, consider going to see Grams and Pops. They miss you and I think you could use a break. You're gonna be off for Spring Break in a few weeks. The country will do you some good, and I'm sure your old friends in Burney would love to see you."

I was climbing into my car and Dad was holding open the door. "I'll think about it Dad." I replied, starting the car.

Dad nodded and closed the door, waving goodbye.

Susanna and her boyfriend, Andrew, had also been encouraging me to take some time to relax. It wasn't until I yelled at that poor fellow in the parking lot of The Fresh Market, that I was willing to admit that I might be a little stressed out. I'm sure he didn't mean to spill his drink on my car and the scene that I made over it was just embarrassing.

I called my grandparents that night and booked a flight. Two weeks later I flew out to spend spring break with Grams and Pops in my old home town; beautiful, Burney, California.

***

I stood in the Museum Room feeling caught, and watched Gabe silently walk over to me and put his hand out for the cup. Confused, I handed it to him. He smiled at me kindly, and I felt ashamed. I opened my mouth to try and explain my behavior, why I would destroy such beautiful things. I was silenced, however, when he turned away from me and chucked the cup against the wall on the far end. It shattered to pieces and my mouth fell open. He turned back to smile at me.

"HA!" I squealed and clapped my hands together. I grabbed another cup and threw it against the wall behind Gabe. Soon he was throwing saucers and sugar bowls as well, and we were both laughing. Me, because he didn't condemn me or tell me I should behave (and because I might have been a little crazy). Him? I'm not sure why he laughed. Perhaps at me, perhaps because it's just fun to be a bit wild. I didn't know, in that moment I didn't care. Maybe Gabe wasn't such an annoyance after all.

We sat quietly together on the corner bench and surveyed what used to be the Vermeer styled corner. There was nothing left on the walls except the beautiful wallpaper. Pretty much everything breakable was broken. The sad and angry feelings were gone for the moment and I felt refreshed.

Had these been real works of art I'd have been heart broken, but these were only depictions of my pain and memories; in beautiful style.

I looked over at Gabe, he was staring at a fixed space on the wall and I wondered what he was thinking. I wasn't sure I wanted to know, considering, but I asked anyway.

"How long had you been standing there, I mean, well, how much of that tantrum did you see?" I blushed in spite of myself.

He looked at me, his expression unreadable. "I saw enough." he answered, staring back at the wall. "It wasn't your tantrum, as you call it, that disturbed me though."

He must have been there long enough to hear the audio clips. I wondered how much he had heard. Pesky emotions. I was feeling ashamed and stupid. He must have wondered why I would have stayed with such a man. He probably thought me a weak minded person. *Oh my god, I hope he didn't see the picture with the dress.* I blushed again, and a queasy sensation welled up in my stomach, but I don't think he noticed.

I decided to change the subject.

"What about you? Are you married, Gabe?" I asked, looking down at his hand and attempting to be cordial.

Gabe half smiled and shook his head. "Nah, I'm not married. I was engaged once, but it didn't work out. She wanted to live together first and well… let's just say I'm old fashioned."

"You broke up with her then?" I asked, and then felt really nosy and wished I hadn't. Darn curiosity always got the best of me. "Oh, I'm sorry, that's none of my business."

"It's alright. It was a long time ago," he said, looking over to me. The corner of his mouth lifted in a sort of half smile. "No, actually I didn't break up with her. She found someone else, without bothering to break up. I assumed we were done when I found out she was pregnant."

"Well, didn't you assume it was yours?" I asked and, again, willing myself to shut up, it wasn't my business. Gabe didn't seem bothered, however, and simply answered, smiling shyly.

"Like I said, I'm old fashioned."

"Oh. Oh!... I'm sorry. Well that sucks!"

He raised an eyebrow and grinned, questioningly, tilting his head slightly.

I blushed again, realizing how that sounded. "I meant it sucks that she cheated on you!"

"Yeah, I know. I'm kiddin'."

"Well.., So." he said, changing the subject. "Tell me about this place. Let's find out why I'm here. That is what you wanted to know, isn't it?"

"Well, actually, I don't even know why *I'm* here. All I know is that the only way out of here is through one of the doors or something like that. That's what Jace said anyway."

"Yeah, Jace." he mused, making a thoughtful expression and nodding his head.

I smiled, and my heart felt a bit lighter at the thought of him.

"He also said nothing here is real, except the things that *are* real. Whatever that meant." I explained.

"Yeah, he told me that I needed to help you open some doors, I figured that was what you were doing when you left me."

"How'd you find me?"

"I thought you'd want to avoid the front entrance, that Jester guy is a freak! So, not on the first floor. I just chose a side and looked into the halls. I saw the light when I came into this hall, and then I heard the... commotion." he paused thoughtfully. "I think it will be kind of cool to explore this old mansion; it's huge."

Anxiety gripped me again. I wondered if the Jester was still outside. I imagined him standing there waiting for me, with that nasty smile, and that horrible dog. I shuddered, and the thought of Gabe wandering around my house made me cringe. Surely not all the rooms were like this one, but I didn't want him to look in the rooms. There might be somethings even more private. Suddenly, I didn't want to know what was behind the doors at all, and I found myself pulling my legs to my chest and closing my eyes. The mansion began to shake.

The ceramic on the floor rattled in tinkling noises and something behind us fell and crashed onto the marble floor. I squeezed my eyes tighter and hugged my knees.

"Jase, where are you!?" I screamed inside my head.

"I am here."

I felt someone put their arms around me and lean over my head in a protective stance. *Jace.* I thought, and sighed a relief.

The mansion began to settle and groan and then went still.

The arms loosened and I opened my eyes. There knelt Gabe looking at me with worry etched on his brow. I recoiled slightly and he pulled his hands away. Then I felt bad for making him feel like a creep.

"I'm sorry, I just…uh, Thank you," was all I could muster.

"It's you." he vouched, looking into my face and placing his hands on my knees.

I felt a bit like a zoo animal on display and looked down at his hands, hoping to break the staring game.

"What? What're you talking about?" I replied, looking back up into his relentless stare.

He backed away and stood up. "The quakes, it's you. You're making them happen."

"What? That's ridiculous." I put my knees down and tried to compose myself.

"Zoey, how did you feel when I mentioned The Joker?"

"He's The Jester! And well, frightened, I guess."

"Okay, and how did you feel when I mentioned exploring the mansion?"

I grimaced.

"What are you trying to hide Zoey?"

"I'm not trying to hide anything, but you see this cute little display of my life here." I made a grand gesture of the room. " I've never been here, remember."

"But you have."

"Okay, that's annoying. Are you going to contradict everything I say? Okay, well if you must know, I've been burying bodies in the crawlspace and running a drug ring from the back door!" I snapped.

"No, I'm sorry, I didn't mean…" He put his hand on the back of his head like he was trying to stay calm and sighed. "What I mean to say is, this place isn't yours; it's you."

Then he mumbled. "That's what Jace was trying to say."

Now it was my turn to stare.

"Zoey, I don't know how, but we are *in* you… God knows what *I'm* doing here." He trailed off and began to pace the room.

"Outside in." I remembered.

Gabe continued. "Jace explained that I needed to help you find your way out by opening doors, and said this mansion is yours, but he said it more like this house is *you*."

Then he began to pace the cluttered room and mumble something about the meanings in vivid dreaming.

Like so many times before, I felt heavy and lost. I could feel myself turning inward…

Inward! How is it possible? But, if I am inside myself then it's not a nervous breakdown, but something different. Something I've never heard of before. Why is Mr. Kort in my head? Why not my dad? or Susanna? or my therapist!?

I sat there and thought quietly for several minutes, staring at nothing.

Where am I? My body must be somewhere if I'm trapped inside my head. I wonder if I'm in a hospital somewhere. What if I'm dead? I don't believe in purgatory. Well, I guess it would explain why everything here is something I've seen or read about.

"I understand now!" he exclaimed. I was so deep in thought that his voice made me jump.

"Oh, sorry," he said, walking back over to me. "I didn't mean to startle you." He knelt down in front of me again. "Zoey, I'm sorry. I didn't understand. But I do now. I know you are afraid because you have to show me what is inside you."

I pulled my knees up and hugged them to me.

"Zoey, I think Jace brought me here. I don't know why. Maybe he thought you could trust me. Maybe he thought I could protect you. I don't know. I think this dream is supposed to teach me something." He stood up and ran his hand through his hair.

"You aren't real," I whispered.

He frowned defensively. "Yes I am!"

"Well, of course you're gonna to say that, you're a figment of my imagination and I am in the forest somewhere talking to a stump and eating bark, drooling; completely out of my mind."

I gripped my hair in handfuls at the top of my head, my gaze shifted around the room. None of this made sense and I was feeling like I was losing it.

Sympathy softened Gabe's expression, and he came back to kneel in front of me again.

"They're gonna find me out there in the forest and put me in a padded room. They'll throw away the key. Gabe, I'm completely nuts!"

"You're not crazy, Zoey."

"How do you know?"

"Well, because I know you, sort of. And Jace told me to help you, so there must be a reason, right?" he explained. "He wouldn't have brought me here if there was no hope for you, or me… We'll figure out why we're here."

"Jace is just a figment of my imagination too." I whined.

"I don't think so, Zoey. I think I may know who he is. If he is who I think he is, well, we can trust him."

I stared at him without looking away and he held my gaze.

"How do I know you're real?"

"Of course I'm real."

"That doesn't prove anything!"

I still had my hands gripped in my hair and I couldn't seem to wrap my head around any of this. Jace wanted me to find a way out by looking through rooms. *The rooms that I wouldn't let him in. If I wouldn't let him in, why would I let Gabe in?!*

I was in a place I'd never seen before but knew, somehow, it was mine, and now Mr. Kort was here and I didn't know why or how. He couldn't be real because real people don't get in my head, that's crazy, and against some law of physics or something.

"I don't know Zoey, You're just going to have to trust me."

"Okay, this is what I think." I explained. "You are a figment of my imagination and I'll prove it!"

"How're you gonna do that?" he asked, as he stood up and paced in front of me again.

"Because everything in this house is part of me." I jumped from my chair, convinced I knew the answer. "So, if I ask you a question I will already know the answer you are going to tell me."

"That doesn't make sense." he argued. "If you are dreaming of me, which you aren't, but if you were; dreams play tricks on people all the time. Dreams are weird." Then he mumbled about people sharing the same dream, his face was a mask of confusion.

I sat back down still sure my trick would work. "Just let me try." I pressed.

Gabe chuckled, "Fine. What's the question?"

"Okay, uhm, What color are my underwear?" I blurted.

The look of chagrin he gave me made me frown. "Really?" he complained. He closed his eyes and sighed. "Pink."

"See! I knew you'd say that!"

"Because I saw that old Superman movie too. The one with Christopher Reeves?"

"Oh... yeah." I grumbled.

"Lois Lane was trying to see if Superman had ex-ray vision though. I don't have ex-ray vision. Zoey, I'm real. I know you won't believe me, but it doesn't matter, because this is *my* dream."

"Why!" I yelled. "Why you?!"

I didn't want to cry, but the tears came anyway. I was frustrated, I was confused, and I didn't want Mr. Kort in my house, my life, my anything. I didn't want to let anyone in. The last man in my life hurt me badly. I had lost myself and I wasn't about to give anyone else that chance again. My mother died and left me, my Dad threw himself into his work. I'd been alone before. I was fine on my own. I could control my own life.

Gabe sat back down on the bench and thought for a moment. He didn't get angry, though I thought I may have seen a hint of hurt in his eyes, but it was gone as soon as I saw it. Now he looked more confused and, to add to my perplexity, compassionate.

"I'm sorry that you don't approve of me being here. It wasn't my choice to invade your house or mind or whatever. I believe I am supposed to learn something here, this is some sort of lesson and I would like to wake up at some point and the only way I'm going to do that is to go through one of these doors. God knows which one that will be. So, the way I see it, I need you and maybe you might need me."

"Okay."I whispered.

"Okay, what?" he asked.

"Okay, let's open some doors."

I was afraid and uncomfortable, but I wanted to go home. If Jace thought I could trust Gabe, then I guessed I'd be okay. I couldn't bring myself to believe Jace wasn't real; he was too real to me, but what could it hurt? Gabe was obviously a subconscious... entity that looked like a familiar face. If he was real he thought he was dreaming, so what could it hurt?

Gabe smiled and stood up, holding out a hand to help me up, when we heard a noise behind me. Gabe looked past me and I turned around. A man in a janitor's uniform was sweeping up the mess on the floor. He wore a great big pair of headphones and hummed loudly as he swept. His shirt had a name engraved above the pocket; "Carl."

I gasped and Gabe eyed me skeptically. "What?" he asked, looking back to Carl.

"Oh, nothing." I answered, "I thought I knew him."

Chapter 8 Preparations

We had no idea what to expect. I wondered if all the rooms were museums. We prepared as best we could. I could only assume that behind the doors were not just ordinary rooms. Why would I need to look through a mansion of rooms in order to find an exit? No, this was a test of some sort. Gabe believed it was for him; I knew better.

We tried all the doors in the living room, kitchen, and dining room first. We found closets, storage rooms, a gymnasium with a basketball court and several bathrooms. There was no back door, or any entrance to the back garden anywhere.

Next we looked into the doors along the balcony by my room. Those rooms were empty. Not just empty, but void of anything, just white nothing, with bright orbs of light floating in each of their expances.

We decided to start at the top; fifth floor West Wing. I didn't need a replay of the Aden museum from the East Wing and I didn't want to go into the tunnel to access the First Floor Wings. I was unwilling to go into the foyer, so those rooms were out as well. I didn't need to go running into the Jester, with or without Gabe.

Gabe asked me why there were no flashlights anywhere, and I could only assume it was because I was always kind of creeped out by them.

"My cousins used to tell me ghost stories when I was a kid. Long story."

Gabe just nodded and kept looking. We found a lantern, finally, and I remembered where I had seen it. It was my Pops's lantern. He had had it when he took me camping when I was ten. Gabe had found it in a closet off the main living room, and it would have to do, although it wouldn't fit in the backpack. We also had my water bottles, just in case; candles, matches and I found a first aid kit.

The mansion was huge and difficult to describe, because it was bigger on the inside, with impossible rooms and impossible windows. For example; I could see the garden from the kitchen, but the gymnasium was behind the kitchen, through a door off to one side.

The wings off to either side were pretty straight forward, however. They had five floors and two main staircases that went up from the foyer and the living room. There were rooms that wrapped around the foyer and living room, and also rooms that filled the hallways to the east and west of the house. In the inner hallway we could access the first floor hall without unlocking the tunnel doors. We planned to get to those last.

In the very center of the mansion, above the tunnel, was an enormous ballroom that's ceiling went all the way to the top with huge opaque windows. It had double doors on the living room side. They were locked.

We went all the way to the top floor and turned to the West Wing; into the inner hallway. The inner hallway went around the ballroom and then opened into a long hallway to the right. We could have walked all the way around the ballroom and came out the other side, above the foyer.

We turned into the long hallway to the West wing and all was dark. Gabe lit the lantern and it cast an eerie glow all around us. The hall looked endless beyond what we could see. It was at that moment that I wished I had never watched the old movie The Shining. It was reminiscent of a particularly scary scene, and we both stood there staring into the distance; into the darkness.

The carpet was tan, shabby, and worn. I wondered what aspect of my personality this represented; it was awful. The doors on either side were white with gold numbers on each one. The left door said 501 W and the one on the right said 502 W.

The white walls were adorned with golden framed portraits of people whom, it seemed, I had seen before, but couldn't name them. Each person portrayed was elderly and their gaze seemed to follow me as I moved. Gabe gave me a resigned look as we turned to door 501 W. I tried the knob, but it was locked.

"Well, what now?" I grumped.

I stood there thinking for a moment before Gabe reached into his pocket and pulled out the skeleton key that had been in the gate lock..

"Uhm, sorry, I forgot to give it back to you." he said, handing me the key.

"Do you think…?" I asked, looking at the door knob.

"It's worth a try," he replied.

I put the key in the lock and turned it. It opened with a "click" and I turned the knob. I turned back to Gabe, but he didn't seem nervous at all. He looked at me and smiled, while my stomach turned. I took a deep breath and pushed the door open.

We stood in the hallway and looked in. The room was completely empty. It was brightly lit with stark white walls. The light came, again, from a little, bright orb; it emanated from the middle and went out, casting a warm glow all around.

As I stood there, I realized I could hear voices. A child's voice and then, my mother's voice. I looked at Gabe, he had heard it too. He set the lantern down and listened. I am fairly certain that I had the same puzzled look on my face as he had on his. We just stood there, looking in. Eventually Gabe reached down and took my hand and squeezed. I'm sure it was meant to be a reassuring gesture. It made me nervous that he was touching me, but I didn't pull away. We looked at each other and then back to the room; we walked in.

It wasn't a room at all. It became a different place altogether, but as I looked back, there was still a door there. The dimly lit hallway looked very out of place through the open doorway, like a painting suspended in the middle of a forest.

We were standing at the edge of a stream, and there were trees all around. Beyond the forest everything was fuzzy. Like an unfocused camera. Other things were slightly blurry as well. I realized later it was because those were the things I didn't remember. We had stepped into a memory.

Gabe reached out to touch a leaf on a close tree, but his hand simply went right through it like a hologram. He looked at me thoughtfully.

Standing in front of us was a very young, beautiful Ellen; my mother. My heart squeezed a little too hard. Tears welled up in my eyes and I longed to run to her. Tears ran down my face as I watched.

She was sitting on a fallen log watching a little girl with curly brown hair; me. The little girl had on a pink, polka dot, bathing suit and was having so much fun playing in the stream. She splashed and giggled while my mother happily talked with her. She was telling her a story about a bunny. The little Zoey laughed and jumped up and down in the water, splashing water and squealing with delight. She had obviously heard the story before, and hopped at the parts when the bunny would hop, splashing Mom in the process.

"Zoey, it's time to go, you have presents to open."

She picked the little me up in a towel and carried me away. I reached out to touch her as she passed by, but my hand only went through her like a ray of sunlight. I pulled my hand back and felt a tinge of loss in my heart.

The scene changed and they were both at a campsite sitting on the tailgate of my dad's old, red pick-up truck. Family members and friends stood around talking and laughing. Fish was being cooked on a campfire.

I gasped. "I remember this! I was five and it was my birthday." I explained, wiping tears from my cheeks.

Gabe smiled. "You were cute!"

I realized I was still holding his hand and I let go. I smiled sheepishly and he chuckled. He seemed so put together, like nothing rattled him. I envied him, *but then again, he's just my imagination.*

The vision continued, though they could not see us. My mother had given the little version of me a plate of food and my younger self was crying. My mother asked the little me what was wrong. The little me explained that she didn't want to eat fish, she didn't like fish, but she knew she couldn't have dessert unless she ate her dinner. Over on a picnic table sat a lovely birthday cake with pink frosting and five birthday candles. The little me looked over at the cake and tears streamed down her freckled face. My mother laughed, "Zoey, you are the birthday girl. On your birthday you don't have to eat all your dinner."

"I don't?" asked the little me.

My mother shook her head and smiled, just as my dad came over and wrapped his arms around my mom and winked at the little Zoey. My younger self's face beamed and she quickly ate her potatoes.

The vision faded and started back over at the stream. I lingered there to watch my mother for another moment before Gabe and I turned and walked back out the door and into the hall. I closed the door and relocked it.

When I turned back around Gabe was watching me, smiling. My heart felt light and happy. I hadn't felt that light in a long time and I wanted to bask in it.

"That was such a good memory for me." I beamed. "I remember that day, although I don't remember being that little."

Gabe laughed. "You know it's funny. I didn't have that memory, but it feels as if I can feel what you felt in that moment. Like the emotion is real, but the memory is just a movie, or a story."

"How do you feel?" I asked.

"Really happy! Like all I ever wanted was cake!" Then he laughed loudly. His laugh was so genuine that I chuckled at him.

"Honestly, to me, that was happy and sad all at the same time. My Mom passed away several years ago, and I miss her terribly."

"Oh, I'm sorry." he replied, sheepishly.

We both sat down, leaning against the wall. I had put the backpack down and I wasn't sure I wanted to move on to the next door yet. The emotion was still strong and healing. I could remember how it felt to be free and joyful like a child.

Gabe and I talked and laughed; everything felt right with the world in that moment.

He told me of a memory he had when he was a child. His mother once let him throw cake at his father, like he had seen on a TV show, and started a food fight at his birthday party. He laughed as he told me.

"I wasn't allowed to eat sugar, and sugarless cake always tasted weird and gave me a stomach ache." Gabe smiled at the memory and stared at the ceiling like he could see his father's face before him in his mind. He sat against the wall with his head back. "I'll never forget the look on his face. He looked shocked at first and then he smiled at me, a mischievous look, and turned to glare at my mom." Gabe laughed. "He got her back for letting me do it, and then everyone was throwing cake. We had cake in the yard for a week, until we got a really good rain.."

I couldn't help but smile thinking about it. We sat in the hall basking in emotional childhood bliss for several minutes.

Gabe spoke without lifting his head, like he was ashamed to face me. "I uhm... I don't think this, me being here I mean, I don't think it's a dream."

Since he wasn't looking at me, I made a face at him as if to say " Durrr." but I didn't voice it. When I didn't say anything he opened his eyes to look at me.

"I don't know what I'm doing here though," he continued.

"Yeah, me either." I mumbled. If he heard me, he didn't say anything.

"Zoey, do you think all of these rooms are memories?"

"I don't know. Surely I have more memories than that. There'd have to be a billion rooms."

"Do you think that was a pivotal moment in your life?"

I thought about it for a moment. "Well, Maybe. It taught me kindness and that people can be flexible. I guess it taught me that I didn't always have to earn things. Sometimes things were given simply because I was loved."

Gabe smiled widely. "What is wrong with me? he laughed. "I'm giddy, and I just want to hug you. It's all so confusing."

I laughed. "The emotion is intoxicating."

I became very sober, however, as a thought occurred to me.

"Gabe, if that's how it felt to really relive a good memory? I mean, that room was very different from the museum room. The emotion was tangible. How is it going to feel if we come to a sad memory? Or a scary one?"

He had his head against the wall with his eyes closed. He lifted his head to look at me.

"I don't know Zoey, but we'll find a way. The good news is, we know they're just memories, even though they feel very real. How many scary memories can you have, right?"

I grimaced at that. He had no idea. "I wonder what we have to do. Opening that door didn't seem to get us any closer to a way out." I sighed.

Gabe stood up and stretched.

"I don't know. What do you say we get started?"

Resigned, I stood and walked to the next door, 502 W. I still wasn't sure I really wanted him seeing my private memories, but if he was just a figment of my imagination, it didn't matter. He seemed eager, but these weren't *his* memoires. I wondered if he'd be so eager if we were walking through his mind. I wondered if I had made him up because he was someone whom I felt could keep me safe. That would have been the only reason I'd have imagined him here. If he wasn't real, then everything would be okay. I'd wake up and he'd never know I'd been dreaming of him. He never needed to know that! *As a matter of fact, I think I'll quit self-defense all together when I get out of here.* I thought. *I don't think I could ever look at him the same way.*

He stood beside me as I unlocked and pushed the door open. I wondered if he was eager to see more of my life. He was a comfort at times, but mostly I felt exposed. I had to admit, I didn't want to do this alone. So, with conflicting emotions, I prepared myself to enter the next room.

This room was much the same as the last, except that the light was dim. We both stood and listened, wondering what to expect. It was very quiet, after a moment, we stepped in.

This vision was fuzzy, almost like stepping into dense fog. I could hear labored breathing and someone groaning incoherently. Gabe stood close behind me. The emotion in the room was starting to seep in, so to speak. Slowly, I began to feel uneasy, watched; paranoid. I began to hear a heartbeat that grew louder and louder, faster and faster; then a loud scream.

I took a protective step back and bumped into Gabe. I looked back up at him, and he put a hand on my shoulder, reassuring me that he was there, his gaze never leaving the glow in the center of the room. I didn't know how I felt about him being there, but at that moment I was content to stand close.

Slowly, a child's room began to come into focus. In the corner, on the bed stand, was a lamp. A ceramic Mary and her little lamb embellishment sat under the lampshade. Dim light flowed around the small room. The walls were covered in yellow wallpaper with white bows and cheerful pictures in white frames. In the middle of the room was a girl's canopy bed with lacy coverings; blue and yellow.

My heart thudded in my chest in response to the mounting emotion in the room. It built up like a crescendo in an orchestra. Soon we could see a child, around eight or nine, laying in the bed. She was tossing and turning, racked with fever. Beads of sweat covered her forehead and dampened her curls. Again, of course, it was me.

My parents sat at my bedside, placing cold cloths on my forehead and looking worried. My Mother was calling my name and shaking me gently. The emotion did not fit the vision and I realized we were feeling what the child was feeling, not what we were seeing.

"Do you remember this?" Gabe whispered.

"Yes, I was having fever dreams. I was very sick."

The vision changed and we were in the child's dream. Darkness and fire was all around, it was hot. The sound of the heartbeat was loud and distorted. From above came an evil laugh, high pitched and fast but then changed to a low pitch and slow, like turning a record too slowly. We stood in the center of a circus ring. High above us was a huge hammer. It began to drop, closer and closer, with the sound of each heartbeat it swung. Up and down, gears were grinding with each drop of the hammer and the heartbeat got louder and faster. It was going to crush us, the laugh was high pitched again. I was cold now; freezing. Young me was screaming and crouched on the ground, shielding her head with her arms. Terrified. We felt the emotion, gripping, I held my breath.

The vision changed again and we were back in the child's room. The younger me suddenly woke up, only to see her parents sitting beside her; Dad was holding her hand. She had been crying, and relief washed over her as she realized she was safe. We felt the relief as well, like a breath of cool air in a sweltering heat. I sighed, and the vision faded, becoming blurry again. We stepped out of the room and back into the hall and closed the door before the memory could start again.

The hall was slightly different this time. Gabe and I looked at each other. I wondered if it had been that way all along and I hadn't noticed. Along the walls were small sconces, casting light in the part of the hallway that we were standing in. The other end remained dark. The sconces were very modern and didn't seem to fit the drab décor of this part of the mansion. Gabe had the same bewildered look on his face as, I'm sure, I did.

"That's weird." I mumbled, "Were those there before?"

Gabe shook his head, picked up the lantern and blew out the flame. "No, it changed."

Soft yellow light filled the space of about four doors, ten or so feet between, while the end of the hall was still draped in shadow. I stood by 502 W. staring at the next door. The residual emotion of the last room was not as intoxicating as the first, but left me feeling tired. It felt like I had just cried for an hour, I was drained.

"Are you alright?" Gabe asked.

"Yeah, I'm tired. I feel emotionally zapped. Don't you?"

"I feel okay." he answered, then looked up at the ceiling and thought for a moment. "I feel like I have been advising a friend all day. Like I empathize with them, but in the end I am able to walk away. They aren't my memories, I guess they don't affect me as much as they do you. Although it is strange, feeling emotions that aren't mine. In the moment they're very strong and I think…" Gabe laughed before he continued. "I think I have an idea of what it feels like to be a woman."

I scoffed at that. "Why? Men feel emotions too."

"I know, it's different though."

"If you try to tell me men are logical and women are emotional…" I snapped, "I am just as capable of being logical as you are."

"No, no that's not it." Gabe stammered. "I'm not trying to start a fight here." He scratched his head and turned his back to me; thinking. I waited with my arms crossed. I knew I was being too sensitive, but for some reason I suddenly wanted to fight. I wanted him to know he couldn't belittle me. I could stand my ground. I could be logical and he couldn't stick me in the stereotypical role of an overly emotional woman.

"All I'm saying is…" he began again, turning to face me. "You aren't all bound up. You allow yourself to feel. It's just, men are often taught to suppress emotion; to hide it. I haven't felt that much emotion since I was a child."

"But I *was* a child in those memories!" I pointed back toward the door.

"I know, but you probably feel emotions that strongly all the time."

"How do you know!?" I shouted, I was angry. He reminded me of Aden when he would say I was just mad 'because I had my menstrual.'

"You don't know me! I'm an adult. I can contain myself!" I pointed at him. "You won't belittle me! I can be just as logical as you are. I'm intelligent, I bet I have more education than you do!"

"I don't want to belittle you!" Gabe shouted. "I think you're great, okay!"

Well, that shut me up. I stared at him, bewildered. I wondered if he was just trying to shut me up, like Aden would when he'd flatter me. Then he'd buy me something pretty or expensive. I used to think it was a nice gesture, until I realized it was just buying my silence. My anger fueled, I clenched my fists and glared at him. If there had been a tea set anywhere near me, it would not have survived.

"How dare you?!" I seethed.

Gabe looked confused and stared at me; like he was trying to read my mind. I stared right back, I was done being the "put together" woman behind the man, he wouldn't hurt me; I wouldn't let him. I don't know what came over me but I lashed out; and tried to slap him, completely forgetting, Duh! That he is my self-defense teacher.

Before I even knew what was happening he had grabbed my hand, spun me around and was holding both my arms across my body and my back was pressed against him. I struggled, but his hold was too strong. I squirmed to no avail.

"Zoey." Gabe spoke softly.

I struggled.

"Zoey, I will let you go as soon as you stop squirming."

I tried to stomp his foot, but he moved and his grip was like iron on my wrists. It wasn't long before I was just too tired to struggle any longer. My resolve was gone. The longer I stood there the more I realized I wasn't even mad at *him*. I was just so angry inside; angry at a dead man, at Aden. Angry that he never loved me. Angry that I was just an object to be used by him, angry that I had let him, and angry at who I had become because of it.

I had lost myself, forgotten who I was, and couldn't seem to get back.

I closed my eyes. His grip loosened. I stood still. He let go of my wrists.

"I'm sorry," I began, "I've just proven your point, haven't I?"

He placed his hands on my shoulders and turned me to face him. I couldn't look at him. I was ashamed and embarrassed, I had acted like a child.

"Zoey, look at me." He put his hand under my chin and raised my face to look at his. "I wasn't patronizing you. I don't think you're a basket case. I think you have a good head on your shoulders. I respect that you have deep emotions. I think you try too hard to keep it together. You've obviously been hurt, and I think you're afraid. Okay?"

He smiled gently, and a sob escaped me. Then he surprised me. He wrapped me in his arms and held me while I cried, and I surprised myself, when I let him.

Standing there like that, in his arms, it dawned on me. I hadn't let anyone hold me in a long time. Sure there was the quick squeeze and a pat on the back from my Dad. My Grandparents had hugged me when I arrived, of course, but to really let someone hold me; I couldn't remember the last time. Aden hated when I cried, he'd get so angry when I showed emotion. Towards the end, the only time he showed me affection was when he wanted something and by then I didn't want his attention.

What are you doing? I thought, *You're hugging Mr. Kort.* I pulled myself together and broke away from Gabe, wiping my face and smoothing out my clothes. He let me go and stood there waiting, he didn't say anything.

I was embarrassed, but I no longer felt angry. It's amazing how healing the touch of another person can be. I had been so hurt that I shut everyone out; held them at a distance. They couldn't hurt me, but they couldn't help me either. I questioned, for the first time, my decision to keep everyone so far away. It felt good to let someone in, but I was still afraid. Gabe was safe, he wasn't real.

I looked up at his chest (he was so much taller than me) and noticed the tears I had gotten on his shirt.

"I'm sorry," I whispered, reaching out to wipe at it, but then thought better of it. He looked down, pulling his shirt out by the seam to look at it.

"It's okay, it'll dry." he said, "You alright?"

I nodded. "I'd like to wash my face."

The only place that I knew of, that had a bathroom was downstairs. Apparently he was thinking the same thing, because he held out his hand, motioning to the exit. We walked in silence to the inner hallway and around to the balcony above the main room.

We stopped at the balcony and turned toward the stairs. I stopped, listening. I distinctly heard music. A piano accompanied by violin played a song called "Silent All These Years" by Tori Amos, from beyond the wall.

"Do you hear that?" I asked. Gabe nodded, and we listened.

Turning around, we faced the ballroom. We could hear music coming through the wall. I pressed my ear to it and I could hear the music and something else; voices. A voice was singing and other voices were talking. I put my back to the wall and pressed my hands to my mouth. I took a deep breath. Gabe looked at me like I may flip out again.

"Zoey?"

"There are people in there!"

"Don't freak out, Zoey, We'll find out what's going on."

The mansion began to shake, a violin screeched and conversation stopped. I heard glass break beyond the wall. The huge chandelier in the living room made tinkling sounds as the crystals hit together and it swayed slightly. I slid down the wall and hugged my knees,

Gabe knelt next to me.

He spoke softly. "Zoey, not everyone will hurt you. You have to let people in or you'll be alone. We aren't meant to be alone."

I looked up at him, he looked sad.

"That's what Jace told me." I replied.

"Well, it's true."

"The last person I loved destroyed me. I lost who I was. I won't let that happen again."

Thunder crashed loudly outside and I could hear rain beat on the roof. The house groaned loudly and the lights flickered. My insides were doing cartwheels. Anxiety threatened to crush me, I had no place to run.

Gabe looked around and then back to me. "Just because someone else hurt you, doesn't mean everyone will." he explained. "I was hurt too, remember? But you have to move on, and you have to heal."

"I don't know how."

Gabe was kneeling beside me, bracing himself against the wall.

"Well," he continued, "You're only causing yourself more harm by isolating yourself because of fear. You have to try to trust someone again."

"I can't." I whispered.

Deep within me I heard a voice; Jace's voice. *"Will you trust me?"*

I thought maybe I recognized the voice, I had heard it as a child. I closed my eyes and reached as far as I could reach within my mind, or rather within my spirit, and there, deep within me I found him. He was standing in a big room with large pillars all around, I could see him in my mind's eye. He was bright and shining and pure. Jace smiled and held his hand out to me. *"Trust me Zoey, I am doing a good thing on the inside of you."*

"But I'm afraid."

I must have spoken out loud, because Gabe answered. "I didn't say you wouldn't be afraid, but you still have to try."

Jace smiled at me and nodded his head. In my mind, I put my hand in his and opened my eyes.

The house settled with a loud groan and a crystal fell from the chandelier and crashed to the floor, shattering into a million pieces. Gabe stood up and looked around, all was quiet until the violin began to softly play another sad melody.

Chapter 9 Aden

We had taken a few moments to allow me to wash my face and pull myself together. I was feeling a little better, calmer anyway. We stood in front of room 503 W. I unlocked the door and we stepped in. The light slowly grew out of the floating orb and a hotel-like room appeared. I almost panicked.

"Oh, Crap!"

Gabe turned to walk out, but I stopped him, laying my hand on his arm. I realized where I was, and that it wasn't going to go anywhere that Gabe couldn't witness. Not a lot happened on our honeymoon cruise because Aden had booked a cruise that was a lawyers convention.

"Don't worry, I was wrong. It's not a private moment."

The room began to become more clear and I could see myself sitting in a chair. Aden sat close to the other me with my hands in his.

Gabe raised an eyebrow at me.

"I mean it *was* a private moment, but not like… *that*." I explained. Gabe just nodded and turned back to face the room.

Aden was talking to the younger me, but we couldn't quite hear what he was saying, yet.

"Gabe, meet Aden." I said, gesturing to the man sitting in front of the other me.

He stepped back up behind me and gave me a sad look that said, *"This is gonna hurt, isn't it?"*

The look confused me, but the scene began to play. I turned back to watch.

"You booked our honeymoon cruise for a lawyers business seminar?" the other me was saying.

"Zoey, sweetheart, you're beautiful. I like people to see you on my arm. And we're mingling, meeting people. This is good for my career, which is good for us, right? For you and me."

"It's our honeymoon!" her voice broke as she said it, and tears began to roll down her cheeks.

Aden stood up and his face began to turn red. "Grow up little girl! This is the real world. It's not all lovey dovey, gimme gimme. If we're gonna make this work, you gotta quit acting like a child!"

"But I…We.." she started, but was stopped by the look Aden gave her.

Aden sat back down and composed himself. "Listen honey, up until now I've let you be your giddy, silly little self, but you're my wife now and I don't want you embarrassing me."

The other Zoey's mouth dropped open and anger and hurt etched her features. She tried to talk, but Aden stopped her again.

"Listen, I gotta go down to the bar to talk to somebody for a bit. When I get back we'll get it on."

Her expression changed to disgust and she glared, but Aden seemed unmoved. He leaned over and kissed her and then chuckled as he walked out. "Hey, can you clean this place up a bit while I'm gone, Hun? Thanks." The door closed, and the memory faded and started over again.

Gabe and I walked out into the hall and I locked the door. Neither of us said anything for some time.

There were a few more lights in the hall now and the portraits were free of dust and cobwebs too. Things were changing.

Gabe didn't seem to notice, he didn't say a word. He walked back out of the hall and down the stairs with me in tow. He seemed angry. I wondered if I shouldn't have let him see that memory after all. I wasn't good with anger, it made me nervous.

I followed him quietly until we got to the living room. I plopped myself down on the couch and waited for him to say something, to yell at me, to say he was done, he was leaving. They all leave eventually.

He paced the room and when he finally stopped, he stood in front of me and stared for a moment before he spoke.

"What did you see in that guy?!" he spouted, eyes wide, with a look I could only describe as… hurt.

I felt like I was on trial. I felt shy and exposed; ashamed. "He was different when we were dating. He was nice. And I didn't do everything right either."

"You mean to tell me there were no bells and whistles going off in your head? No red flags? None of your friends or family told you he was an ass?!"

"Well, they…I…"

I had thought about it before. There were signs, but I had mistaken his loud behavior for him being strong. I didn't really see the signs as enough to leave. As for my friends and my Dad, they hadn't said much because I had never given them the chance. Aden swept me off my feet and isolated me away from friends and family. I didn't really see it until it was too late.

I wanted to be angry, I wanted to lash out and hurt him back, but I couldn't. He was right. I should have seen it, or I should have left. I stayed because I believed in marriage. I believed in trying to make it work. I believed in love, but Aden never loved me.

I blurted out, "I made a huge mistake when I married Aden. Okay. I'm not stupid. He seemed like a decent person. He stopped trying after I married him. I guess he didn't feel like he had to try anymore. He got what he wanted."

"Yeah, well as far as I can tell the only decent thing he ever did was die." he replied.

"Ouch, Gabe."

I looked up at him, surprised at his emotional state. Tears streamed down my face, and I stared through the blurr.

He sighed deeply and sat down beside me, it was several minutes before he spoke again. "I'm sorry." he whispered.

I hung my head. I was ashamed of Aden and of myself.

"I acted just like him just now too, didn't I?" he took a deep breath and rested his head in his hands. "I'm sorry."

I had nothing to say, so he continued.

"Zoey, Jace told me to help you, but how can I help you, protect you, if the damage is already done? It's so frustrating to watch that… man treat you like he did."

"He wasn't always bad." I defended.

Gabe just looked at me for a long moment and then he sighed. "Zoey, you deserve to be treated with kindness all the time. No one deserves to be treated that way." he finally looked back up at me. "Especially not you."

I dropped my gaze and looked down at my hands.

"You aren't leaving, then?" I asked.

"Leaving? Why would I be leaving?" he stared.

"Well, because you're ashamed of me. When people have enough of me, they leave."

"I'm not ashamed of you." he replied, looking confused. "I'm irritated, but not with you."

I gave him a confused look.

He ran his hand through his hair, and let it fall back down over his eye, as he bowed his head. "I'm the one who's an ass." he sighed. "You don't have to justify yourself to me. You don't owe me anything."

We sat quietly for some time before he spoke again.

"I know why you stayed with Aden."

I scoffed at that. "You do, huh? Enlighten me?" My tone was sarcastic, and I knew it. I didn't apologise.

"He was a narcissist, you thought it was your fault your marriage wasn't working. I bet he blamed you for everything."

I nodded, and that old familiar pain welled up in my heart. I pulled my knees to my chest and hugged them.

"It wasn't your fault, Zoey. Your marriage, his death, none of it."

"Oh, and how do you know?" I snapped.

"It's obvious. I bet if you ask anyone who knows you, they'd tell you the same. You care about people, he cared only about himself."

He was right and I knew it, but I couldn't shake the guilt and shame, knowing I couldn't fix it, that Aden hadn't loved me, and that I was never good enough.

"What makes you think I care about people?"

Gabe laughed at that. "Well, let me see. You're afraid you're going to hurt me in *my* self-defense class."

I giggled in spite of myself.

"And you are always going out of your way to help someone else and to give a compliment. You kept to yourself in my class, barely talked to anyone, but you helped Carolyn Anderson pick up her stuff when her bag broke and you offered to drive Mary Alvarez to the ER when she twisted her ankle. These are not behaviors of someone who doesn't care about others."

"Well, aren't you Mr. Observant." I jeered. "You're right though, I do care. I just wish I didn't. You don't get hurt if you don't care."

"When I was a kid, my mom told me something that made sense." he paused, looking a little sad. "I had this big dog named Smokey. He was such a great dog, We'd had him since I was a baby. Well, he got old and he died. I was heartbroken and questioning my mom. I wondered why he had to die, I loved him so much. 'Why do we love so much if the ones we love are just gonna die?'" he smiled. "She said 'If we didn't love, it wouldn't hurt to lose, it would just hurt all the time. Love is the price we pay to really live.'"

"I don't think I've been living for a while." I said, softly.

"You have time." he replied.

Piano music began to play in the ballroom, a female singer, an electric guitar, then drums.

"Is there a band in there?" he quipped. "That sounds like Evanescence."

"'Bring Me To Life.' Yeah, it just popped into my head."

"Is that why the music plays? Because you have a song in your head?" he asked.

"I don't know, I guess. I usually have a song behind my thoughts.

Don't you?"

"Yeah." he smiled. "I do."

I stood up and stretched. I didn't feel up to looking into another room. "You wanna go shoot some hoops?"

His smile widened. "Yes, I do!"

Chapter 10 Perfectly Charming

There were other changes, slight variations in the mansion that we began to notice. The main living room now had a window and the dome at the top was open slightly. The gate to the tunnel was now highly polished and there was a light in the tunnel. The pictures that were once cast in shadow were now visible. They were portraits of my family, or rather my ancestors. Portraits I'd seen in old albums at Gram's house. They were all beautiful, sepia colored pictures of people who resembled me, but whom I'd never met.

Also, there was a cat. Not a picture, but an actual cat; Figaro. Figaro had been my childhood cat. She was a female, and yes I know it's a boy's name, but the cat in Pinocchio was named Figaro and sometimes you just don't get to choose the gender of a cat. Besides, I was a kid when I named her. She was a big orange tabby with a white bib and white feet. She had been laying by the fireplace when we came down.

I had gone to my room to change. When I came back, I noticed Figaro had made a bed out of Gabe's lap. Gabe was absentmindedly petting her and staring off into space.

He'd apparently found a place to clean up too, as his hair was wet and he smelled of soap. I noticed as I walked by.

"I see you've met Figaro." I said, smiling at Gabe.

"Hmmm?" he mumbled, startled out of his daydream. "Oh yeah, he likes me, I think."

I scoffed, "Yeah well, *she's* feisty and can tend to be a bit mean. She does seem to like you though; weird."

Gabe chuckled. "Whadya mean weird? I'm likeable."

I smiled as I reached down to pet her and she bit at me, typical Figaro.

"Stupid cat."

Gabe laughed, "See, no wonder she's mean. You insult her."

"You called her a he." I replied, and made a face at him, taking a seat by the other end of the fireplace.

It was a high backed, purple chair that looped at the top. The seat was wide and comfortable. I threw my feet up over one arm and laid my head on the other. I was wishing my cell phone worked, but it wouldn't have had Wifi anyway.

I had looked at a few of the books on the shelves, but most of them were missing pages and incomplete. Some of them had pictures, but most of them were apparently there for show.

We sat in the main room watching the fire and listening to the storm outside. It was loud next to the gate and the tunnel. Rain splashed down on the floor in the foyer and echoed through the tunnel and muffled everything with a "Shhhhhh" sound.

I could no longer hear the music or the voices from the ballroom, though I knew they were still there. We had tried the ballroom door at the top of the first balcony landing after my freak out moment the first time I heard the music. It was locked up tight and my key didn't fit that door.

"The fire isn't warm." Gabe observed.

"Hmm? Yeah, I know, weird right?" I responded, coming out of my thoughts. "It isn't real."

I thought about it for a second, it was all so difficult to wrap my mind around. I suddenly wondered if it would hurt to put my hand in it, although I didn't want to try. Apparently, Gabe was thinking the same thing, because he put Figaro down and moved to kneel in front of the fire.

I moved to sit beside him on the floor, intrigued, yet alarmed. I wondered if he'd burn himself. I wanted to stop him, but I was curious.

"Be careful." I muttered, as I moved a bit closer.

Slowly he reached into the fire until his hand was right above the flame. He held his hand there for a moment and then pulled it out to examine it, holding it close to his body. I found myself squeezed in close, curious to see his hand. It was concealed by his body and his other hand. I got closer and he turned his body away from me. Finally I looked at him, wondering what he was keeping from me.

He grimaced and threw his hand up in front of me, with a mock look of pain on his face. I jumped, startled, and fell back on my butt.

He was fine; the fire hadn't left a mark. I reached out and took his hand, turning it over in mine. I examined it. I even smelled it, but it only smelled like Gabe's pleasant clean smell. I was amazed, his hair wasn't even singed. I looked up at him and he was looking at me, softly smiling. I realized how close I was, and I blushed. Gabe chuckled and I let go of his hand, and scooted back against my chair.

The storm had stopped and so had the music. The room was quiet save for the crackling of the fire and Figaro purring on the couch behind Gabe.

"Zoey, do you suppose any of it is real?" Gabe asked, looking again at his hand.

"None of it is real, except for the things that are real." I quoted.

"Yeah, but what does that mean?"

"I think it means that the memories are real, but the rest of it is just what my mind has made for me to make sense of this reality."

I thought about my room. How it was perfect for me and how this room was another aspect of my personality. It was all a part of me, whimsical, classy, bright, dark, happy, or sad, it was all there in the furnishings. I began to understand why the foyer was in disarray, or the drab carpet in the West Wing. The places that had been left alone, and untouched. Places I hadn't looked at for a long time. They became stale, old and drab; lifeless.

"What about me?" Gabe asked, taking me out of my thoughts.

"What *about* you?"

"Am I still just a figment of your imagination?"

"I don't know." I replied honestly.

"So, you've been thinking about me then?" Gabe smirked. "Because if *you* brought me here, you had to have been thinking about me."

"No! I mean…" I stammered. "I thought you said Jace brought you here."

"He did, but you don't believe that. So, if you don't believe Jace brought me here, then *you* did." he explained, smirking.

"You know, I have thought about that."

Gabe raised an eyebrow. "Oh? Do tell."

"Well, if I was capable of bringing anyone here, or if I made someone up to be here with me, I guess I would want someone who makes me feel safe."

"I make you feel safe?"

"Well, yeah. I guess so. I mean you teach me to defend myself, you're the safest person I know."

"But Zoey, nothing can hurt you here. It isn't real." Then he got a goofy look on his face and reached over and pinched me.

"Ouch!" I squealed. "What'd ya do that for?"

Gabe laughed. "See, I am real."

I laughed at him and rubbed my arm where he'd pinched me. "I don't think that if I made you up I would have made you to be mean to me."

Gabe laughed at that. "Oh yeah, how would you have made me?"

"Perfectly charming and helpful." I said, looking smug.

"I *am* perfectly charming and helpful." he replied, returning the smug look.

"You're right," I teased, "You're not real."

Gabe just laughed at me and it made me smile.

He laughed so easily. I remembered a time when I had been like that, when I just wanted to be light hearted, without pretense; just me. I found myself wanting to be that way again. Gabe made me feel safe in more ways than just physical self-defense. He made me remember who I liked to be. I tried to tell myself that I didn't care if he was real; I was glad he was there. Part of me really hoped he wasn't just a figment of my imagination. Mostly, however, I was terrified if he wasn't.

We sat quietly with our thoughts for a while. I still wasn't ready to face another room, it was too draining, and frankly, I was afraid of what I might see. I had some painful memories that I had spent years trying not to think about. Having to look at them now seemed overwhelming. In spite of Gabe's easy going attitude and good nature, I was on the verge of a serious mood swing. The more I thought about the rooms and what I had to do, the more I slipped into gloom.

Someone once said "The more wounded a person is, the more drama they will create." Unfortunately it's true. If you have ever had a sore thumb, you understand drama. Any other time you don't even think about that thumb, but when it hurts, you protect it. And unfortunately you will probably yell at anyone who bumps up against it, you may even lash out physically. Well, hearts work that way too, and mine was sore and tired of being bumped. I had built a wall around it and locked it up tight.

Now, I was faced with dealing with my demons in order to escape a place I wasn't sure I wanted to escape. I thought I was safe behind my wall, and now I wasn't so sure. There seemed to be cracks in it and things were getting through. *Gabe* was getting through, and it scared me.

Music began to play in the ballroom and I strained to hear what song it was.

"Pink Floyd's The Wall? Fitting." Gabe said, and smirked at me.

"Oh, geez!" I sighed, rolling my eyes.

I sat there staring into the fire, alone with my thoughts, when the song ended and the piano in the ballroom began to play again. Soon the violin accompanied Beethoven's Moonlight Sonata; beautiful and dark. I closed my eyes and let the music soothe me. Music, my melancholy friend, never disappointed. I swayed slightly to the melody, forgetting Gabe's presence and losing myself in the mournful song. My imagination took me through dark forests, through mists of fog and haunted oaks, forever searching, never finding what I was looking for. Not ever knowing what my destination might be.

The measure changed and I opened my eyes to see Gabe watching me. It startled me a bit, and I quickly averted my eyes and ran my hand through my hair. I was embarrassed that I had lost myself with him there to see. It seemed a private, vulnerable moment, and

I surprised myself for allowing it. I inwardly chastised myself and tried to turn the attention elsewhere

"You hungry?" I asked, finally allowing a quick glance at Gabe.

He was smiling softly at me. He paused for a moment before he nodded and got up, holding a hand out to help me up as well.

Chapter 11 Magic

Dinner was much like breakfast, all laid out for the taking. Breakfast had been miraculously cleaned up and gone. Lunchtime had come and gone, but I couldn't help but wonder if another exquisite meal had been there, even if we weren't. It was amazing there in the mansion, all of our needs were met without a finger lifted.

It was dark outside now, and fireflies flicked on and off in the night. Stars danced their reflection into the pond and somewhere in the dark an owl inquired of someone's identity.

"If time doesn't pass here, then why is it dark out?" Gabe asked, staring out the large kitchen window.

"Jace told me it's because I think it's the time that it should be." I said, shrugging. "I think he meant that time doesn't pass back home, or back in reality or whatever."

Gabe looked thoughtful and went back to eating his steak and potatoes. He poked at his potato for a second and then looked back up at me. "Do you think Jace is putting all this food out here for us?"

"Well, I thought so this morning. And he served me dinner last night, but honestly, I think it's me."

"You're doing this? How?"

"Well, I don't know. I think of what I would like to have and when I get here, there it is." I smiled and took another bite of my steak.

Gabe thought about that for a moment before he spoke. "You think you can make whatever you want just appear here in the kitchen?

"Yeah, I guess so." I shrugged, "It's all pretty new to me. Like, I didn't really think about the potatoes or salad. I just thought a steak sounded good. I guess somehow the details got filled in."

Gabe's eyes got wide and he smiled. "Oh, do you think you could get us a cheesecake, with strawberries?" His eyes darted around in his excitement. "No, no wait. How about a chocolate mousse, or red velvet cupcakes with cream cheese icing and ice cream?"

For some reason this struck me funny. To see a grown man so excited about dessert. It reminded me of my dad on Christmas. He would always roam around the kitchen, waiting to snag a nibble of this or that. I laughed out loud, a little bit more than the occasion warranted and Gabe looked a little sheepish. I think I embarrassed him.

"I'm sorry, I didn't mean to laugh at you… so hard." I smiled. "You sure like your sweets, don't you? I thought you were a health nut?"

Gabe smiled timidly. "Well, not by choice. I'm diabetic. Like, really diabetic."

That sobered me up. "Oh, I see," I said, feeling like a jerk for laughing. I wiped my face with my napkin and closed my eyes. I thought of all the things he said he wanted; ice cream, cupcakes, chocolate mousse, cheesecake. But as I thought about those things, it made me think about all of my favorites. Suddenly it was as if I could smell it all, delectable, sweet and rich.

I heard Gabe gasp and opened my eyes. There on the counter were all the things I had thought of. Honestly, I think I went a little overboard. The entire kitchen island was covered in desserts. Pies, cookies, cakes, ice cream with toppings, puddings and mousses and those beautiful tea cakes with the little flower designs on them. It was all laid out in a beautiful display of crystal bowls and cake plates, with flower centerpieces and accents.

 Gabe stood up and stared with the look of a child on Christmas morning on his face.

"Oh. My. Gosh." he gushed. Then he turned to me, grabbed my face, kissed my forehead and then turned his attention back to the banquet of delights.

I'm sure my eyes got huge and I probably blushed, but he didn't notice. He was too busy walking around the island, laughing.

"I'm gonna try everything."

"Are you sure that is a good idea?" I asked, chuckling at him. He really was quite a sight, walking around the island with a big dinner plate in his hand. "You do have to go back to reality at some point, ya know. Won't you miss it?"

"Well, the food that they serve at…" he stopped himself and looked at me. He had a look that I couldn't quite decipher, and then he shrugged. "Well, it doesn't matter... I'm here now and I'm going to enjoy it."

"I think I like that idea."

Gabe ate two platefuls of goodies and then leaned back in his chair, like a contented, fat cat. I had my share of desserts too, I admit it. How often do you get to eat whatever you want without consequences? That's everyone's dream, Right?

"Oh my, if I ate like that back home I'd be huge." I said, looking down at what remained of my cheesecake.

"If I ate like that back home I'd be dead." Gabe retorted, and then laughed. The laugh was a little too forced it seemed, though. I felt sorry for him, always having to watch what he ate and testing blood sugar all the time.

"How long have you been diabetic?"

"I was born type one diabetic. I almost died when I was a baby. I have been on a pretty strict diet all my life." he snickered, "I used to sneak sweets when I was a kid and got myself into trouble a few times. I spent a lot of time in hospitals as a kid" he paused thought-fully. "It's the whole reason I got into martial arts. My dad thought it would be good exercise."

"Exercise helps control your sugar?"

"Well, not exactly. It helps with circulation and keeping my heart healthy. And of course self discipline. Martial arts teaches self dis-cipline and respect. Being diabetic takes a lot of discipline if you want to be healthy."

He smiled a resigned smile and looked away. I wondered if he was bitter about having to deal with something like that his whole life. He seemed irritated about it, but I was still curious, so, like a child, I pressed it a little further. I never seem to know when to leave a subject alone.

"So, how did you know the pastries wouldn't hurt you this morn-ing?"

"I didn't," was all he said, and then got up from his chair and stretched.

"It's getting late, or, well, it feels late." he said looking outside. "Is there a place I can crash tonight? It doesn't exactly look like I'll be going anywhere."

I decided I had been too nosy and didn't press him on the pastries. "I don't know," I said. "Let's go see."

We went back to the living room to the door that was just down from my room. We had looked into this door earlier, knowing it was empty, I opened it anyway and looked in. There in the center of this blank room floated the orb.

"Come on, I wanna show you something." I pulled him in and over to the orb.

"Nothing happened. It didn't... grow... or turn into a memory." he said, looking perplexed.

"I know." I grinned. "On the count of three reach out and touch it."

"Okay." Gabe looked intrigued, his eyes lit up with excitement.

"One...Two... Three!" The room exploded into a blue sky and we were flying through the clouds. I could feel the wind in my hair and see for miles. We were over a city, I didn't know which one. I looked at our hands and they were both touching the orb, anchored together as we flew. Gabe's look of wonderful astonishment made me giggle. It caught his attention and he looked at me and then down at our anchored hands on the orb. It was like a safety line.

"How do we get back?" he yelled over the rushing wind.

"On the count of three we let go." I yelled back.

Gabe nodded.

"One...Two...Three." We were back in the stark blank room in incredible silence. I jumped, startled, when Gabe spoke.

"That was amazing!" he laughed. "Let's do it again."

I smiled. "Pretty cool huh. I think it's different every time."

We did it three more times, until we were both too tired to go again. We sat on the floor, laughing and chatting about how amazing this new little trick was. We went to a microscopic place, into a volcano, and another trip to space, although different from my first experience.

"I've always wanted to be able to fly." Gabe was saying. "But considering I rely on insulin, I can't get a medical certificate to get a licence."

"Oh, I'm sorry. That sucks."

We were quiet for a moment before Gabe spoke again. "Uhm, about that place for me to crash?"

"Oh, yeah, sorry." I got up and we went back outside the room.

"Okay, I have an idea." I said, pulling the door closed.

I closed my eyes and thought of all the things I knew about Gabe. He was a guy, so not too frilly. He liked martial arts and japanese influences. I assumed he had good taste, although, at this point I had only seen him in his Gi and jeans and a t-shirt, but with good looks like his, he had to have a sense of style, right? He was easy going and seemed to like to have fun too. I concentrated, willing the room to be perfect.

When I was done I opened my eyes.

Gabe was looking at me curiously. I smiled at him and turned back to the door. I almost opened it and he stopped me, putting his hand on mine.

"Wait, I want to try something," he said. Then he closed his eyes and smiled, taking a deep breath and then let it out slowly. Then he nodded.

"Okay, go ahead."

I looked at him inquisitively, but he didn't say anything. I opened the door and looked in.

The room had walls now and substance. The walls and furnishings were a simplistic design of black and white. There was a bathroom off to the left side of the room, but all I could see was a large shower with, what looked like river rock adorning the walls. There was a large platform bed against the wall of the room and paper scrolls adorned either side. They had japanese writing on them and I wondered what they said. I looked up at Gabe and I watched his eyes scan the room and stop at the scrolls.

"That one says Love and the one over there says Life." he said pointing to the scrolls. He smiled and looked at me like he knew something I didn't.

"You know Japanese?"

"Hiragana and katakana, actually. Japanese writing." he shrugged. "A little, yeah."

Still smiling, he walked into the room. He seemed a little smug to me and I wondered what that was about. It was a bit out of character for him, I thought.

Aside from a dresser and a small side table the room was sparse. Off to the right was a sliding door made of wood with small paper windows, like the kind you may see in a Japanese restaurant. Gabe walked to the door and slid it open and I walked over to see what he was seeing. The room was completely impossible and huge. It reminded me of the TARDIS from Doctor Who; it was bigger on the inside. The dimensions would have placed the room far into the East Wing hallway and into the adjacent room as well; my room.

I stepped back and over to my room and opened the door. All was as it had been. His room hadn't encroached upon mine in the slightest. *Weird.*

I walked back into his room and beyond the paper doors. Inside was an amazing game room. The walls were dark mahogany with large beams that made square patterns on the ceiling. The paper door on this side was a solid, polished wood, pocket door.

There were large windows that overlooked the garden on the far wall and a huge fireplace at the back of the room. There was a pool table, a card table, a bar with comfortable looking leather stools, and leather overstuffed furniture. The room was masculine in design and very classy. There were pictures of people I didn't know along the walls and each person was posing with Gabe. He walked back and forth looking at each one and then came back to stand by me.

I looked closely at one of the pictures. One in particular was of a lovely woman with blond hair and brown eyes. She looked nothing like Gabe, but postured herself like a mother. She was hugging Gabe and smiling. I found myself embarrassed by the picture. Gabe would see into how my subconscious believed his family to look. I glanced at him, and he too was studying the picture with an expression that I couldn't quite distinguish. He looked... amused.

Then I realized that if I *had* made Gabe up, then this *would* be his family. Ugh, this was confusing.

"Gabe I...."

"That's my mother, and that one over there is my sister, Anna." he explained, walking from picture to picture. He stopped with a sad look on his face and said, "This one's my dad." A tall, dark haired man in glasses stood beside Gabe in a graduation picture.

"Oh my gosh, this is my prom picture." he looked closely and then laughed sardonically and shook his head. "That's Brianne." he said, pointing.

I stepped up to get a closer look. She was beautiful, tall and elegant.

"Oh, this one is my family and our dog Smokey. The one I told you about!"

I looked at a few more, and watched as he looked down the row of people he cared about.

"But, how is this possible? I've never seen your family."

Gabe smiled, turning to me. "You didn't do it, I did."

"But how? This is my mind, remember?" I replied, pointing to my head. I was a little unnerved at the thought of Gabe being able to manipulate things inside my head.

"Well, I was thinking. Do you ever notice how when someone says something gross, you kinda picture that thing in your mind, whether you want to or not?"

This reminded me of all the times Aden would tell me terrible stories just to see my reaction. Aden would lie or embellish things just to scare me, or to manipulate me. When I was pregnant, before the miscarriage, he told me we couldn't get a dog because there was a time that a dog chewed the fingers off a baby while the momma was getting the mail down the driveway. He had made the whole thing up because he didn't want me to have a dog. I had nightmares about it for weeks. He thought it was funny. "You're so gullible, Zoey," he'd laugh.

He once told me about a case he was working on. He was defending a man who was accused of killing his wife. The man had told him how he'd done it, it was terrible. I begged Aden not to defend that terrible man and Aden laughed at me. He would say, "It's bastards like him who pay the bills, Sweetheart. It's all in the way you look at it."

After a while I learned not to give him what he wanted. I felt ashamed of my compassion for others, and foolish for being afraid. Instead of feeling sad or helpless, I just became angry. He said I was becoming desensitized, "Good girl. Don't let it touch you. It's a tough world we live in, Kiddo."

My mood was going south fast, and I thought Gabe had better explain himself.

Apparently, I had a disagreeable look on my face; Gabe frowned at me. "Zoey, it's not a bad thing. It's a good thing."

"How can *you*," I pointed at him, "messing with things inside *my* head, be a good thing?" I yelled.

"Because you let me." he explained, very much to my dissatisfaction. I thought about how 'I'd let' Aden put images of terrible things in my head with his stories and it just pissed me off. I'd never wanted those images in my head.

"I didn't *let* you do anything of the sort, Aden!"

Gabe had a look of surprise on his face and he raised an eyebrow at me. He opened his mouth to speak, but apparently thought differently and stopped.

I stood there, stunned for a moment, trying to pull myself together. I was so angry, but I knew right under the surface was pain and fear, things that made me vulnerable. He'd bumped up against my sore heart again. I clenched my fists and glared at Gabe.

"Look Zoey," Gabe began, "Maybe I gave you a bad example. All I was trying to say is that everyone in your life causes you to change in one way or another; everyone. It can be good or it can be bad. Some of it you can control and some you can't."

Gabe smiled at me, although he looked sad. "I didn't mean to make you feel out of control Zoey. Sometimes the things that people change in us are beautiful."

I was still standing there like a robot when he tried to take my hand. Of course, I just pulled away.

"Come here, I'll show you what I mean." he said.

Reluctantly, seething, I followed him to the end of the room, along the rows of pictures to one at the end. There hung a picture of the dojo where he taught self defense. As we got closer I saw that I was in this one. It was a picture of the day that Gabe had brought a friend of his in to help with demonstrations. Paul, a macho fellow with a pompous attitude. He was muscular and the type of guy that knew he was hot. I remembered not liking Paul.

On the day of demonstrations I was asked to participate in a dis- arming technique that I had actually been struggling with. Gabe had called me out of the circle and gave us a scenario. Paul was to be my attacker with a tire iron, and I was to disarm him. We started in a neck hold position, with him behind me. I had been angry with Gabe for calling on me for this. He was obviously trying to make me look foolish, I had even seen him whisper something in Paul's ear before we started.

Paul put his arm around my neck and held the foam crowbar in his hand. The other hand he put around my waist. Right before Gabe gave the signal to begin, Paul whispered in my ear. "You smell good, sweetheart." Gabe said go, and before I knew what had hap- pened I had flipped Paul over my back and kicked him in the ribs. I was holding the foam tire iron and breathing heavily. When I came to my senses I gasped.

"Oh my gosh, I'm sorry." I blurted, gripping the foam crowbar like a teddy bear, and grimacing at the man on the floor.

Paul shook his head at me and groaned, hugging his ribs. Gabe was laughing and clapping his hands as he dismissed the class. He helped Paul up and pat him on the back. I just stood there biting my nail and feeling terrible about hurting the man.

"Who took this picture?" I asked. The picture was of me in mid flip. The look on Paul's face was priceless and I couldn't help but chuckle a bit.

"No one took the picture, it's a memory."

"Your memory? Why did you put this picture in here? You made me look like an idiot that day!"

Gabe laughed and his smile beamed at me. "I was so proud of you that day, Zoey."

"What? Why? I kicked that poor guy in the ribs!... You called me out in front of the whole class. You knew I was having trouble with that technique!"

"You had been struggling with that disarm maneuver for weeks. You outdid yourself that day! Besides, Poor guy, nothing. Paul needed to be knocked down a few notches."

"I lost it, is what I did!"

"Well, I guess that is my fault. I told him to taunt you a little. I don't know what he said, but it worked."

"You told him to taunt me! Why?" I snapped, feeling a bit hurt.

Gabe had his arms crossed in front of himself. He had this way of looking me straight into me with those gorgeous eyes. It always made me want to look away, but at that moment I was mad. He had intentionally made me angry to accomplish something, and I wanted to know why. I didn't look away.

"Because I knew you could do it. You're just too nice, too reserved; guarded." he explained, and then he laughed at the look I gave him.

"Look! You are the strangest mix of goofiness and class I have ever met. I have never met someone who was graceful and incredibly clumsy all at the same time."

I glared.

He smiled at me and continued, paying no attention to my attitude. "You are sweet and shy and always have something nice to say. But you're strong and brave too, you just don't know it. I was just trying to show you how to bring those things out a bit."

"I yelled like Mister Miyagi and kicked the man in the ribs!"

"Yeah, well… I didn't know you would do that, but you disarmed him." Gabe said laughing. "He was okay. Besides Paul's a better man because of it, and he speaks highly of you."

I couldn't help but laugh at that, and I realized what Gabe had been trying to show me. He had been someone who brought something out in me; caused a change that good or bad, controlled or uncontrolled, made me a little different than I was before. He had manipulated me, but in a way he believed was for my betterment.

I thought about Aden and how he thought he was doing those things for my betterment as well, but he was trying to make me like him. They both were. I had to realize that if I am to let people in, they had better be someone I want to be like, because people will try to make me like themselves. People reproduce what they believe. In themselves and in others.

I looked closely at the picture now and realized it was ridiculous. My hair and facial expressions were perfect, like a model; my hair blowing in the wind and a sparkle on my lips. The exaggerated look on Paul's face was hilarious. It dawned on me that the picture was how Gabe saw me in that moment and I was flattered, and completely amused. The more I looked at it, the more I couldn't help but laugh. He had such a different perspective on things.

"What?" he said, looking at me and back at the picture. "What's so funny?"

I know I was blushing, but I was laughing too hard to say anything. I guess Gabe realized what I was laughing at, because his ears turned red with embarrassment.

"What can I say? It's a perfect memory." He said, chuckling to himself.

I looked round again and saw more of his influence on the creation of his room, and realized why he had looked smug. "You added the scrolls."

"Maybe," he smiled.

Chapter 12 Unreal

The next morning I woke with my side hurting. The sun was shining brightly through the impossible window and birds were singing outside. I sat up slowly and hung my feet over the side of the bed. Gingerly, I pulled my shirt up and pulled away the bandage to examine the wound. It had bled in the night and seemed to be infected, with a red ring around it. The whole area felt very sore.

I got up, showered and readied myself for the day. Standing in front of the mirror I could see the wound entirely. It was longer than I had realized and slightly swollen. I wondered if there may be some tylenol in the house somewhere, and hoped something would take the edge off the pain.

I didn't know how that would work because I didn't know if the pain was real. It was like trying to wrap my brain around a time travel movie. If I changed something here, would it change out there? Was it a mind over body issue? Maybe it was like being in the Matrix and if I just believed hard enough my mind would heal my body. I didn't know. Was I really hurt out *there* or was this wound only in my mind? Was my body out there or was I really "*inside out*?" It was all very confusing, but common sense told me I needed to clean it before the infection got worse.

The thought occurred to me that I may be lying in the forest, bleeding and unconscious. Maybe someone had found me and I was in the hospital. Maybe I was dying and this was my mind's coping mechanism. I didn't know, but I decided to concentrate on getting out. Which meant opening more doors; more memories.

Gabe and I had stayed up late the night before. We played several games of pool, and I refused to go to bed until I won at least one. I am fairly certain he let me win the last game so he could get some sleep.I was so exhausted by the time I went to bed I didn't bother to change into pajamas. I brushed my teeth and crawled into bed. I knew he would be tired, so I quietly opened my door and crept out onto the balcony.

The piano played from the ballroom, an instrumental piece, soft and beautiful. Then I heard breathing, or rather, loud exhales.

I looked over the balcony to the living room below and saw Gabe standing in front of the gate. He was shirtless and statuesque, in only his Gi bottoms and bare feet. He was practicing his Kata; a choreographed pattern of movements and positionings in martial arts, almost like a dance. His graceful movements only emphasised the beauty of his body; fluid and adept. He would breathe through the movements, making kiai sounds at the appropriate moments in the choreography. I watched, spellbound by his skill and, hey, I'll admit it, he looked amazing.

Resting my elbows on the balcony, I found myself thinking about how much fun I had had the night before. I forgave him for manipulating my mind, or whatever I had believed he was doing. I felt stupid for being so angry about a few innocent pictures.

Gabe was funny and even a bit flirtatious. I found myself being able to let my guard down a bit. I didn't think he was leading me on or trying to get me into the sack. He was just Gabe, thoughtful, funny, intelligent, amazing, gorgeous, Gabe.

I don't know how long I stood leaning over the balcony watching him. I was off in my own little world. When he finished, he held the last position for a moment, his eyes fixed forward. When he relaxed, he addressed me.

"Good morning, Zoey." He turned to look up at me and smiled warmly.

I straightened, and I'm sure I blushed. "How long have you known I was here?" I stammered.

"I heard you come out of your room," he answered, picking up his shirt and putting it on. I was glad for that; the thought of trying to carry on a conversation with him shirtless was way too distracting and I felt I needed to avert my eyes. I had seen a million men shirtless, I lived in Florida for Pete's sake, but for some reason I was a nervous wreck thinking I'd have to spend time with him like that.

Geez, Zoey, get a grip. I thought.

"Oh. Uhm, I didn't want to disturb you." I said, walking down the stairs to join him in the living room. "That was really beautiful."

"Would you like to learn?"

I laughed nervously, "Uhm, no. I'm about as graceful as...Well, I'm not."

Gabe laughed. " I know how graceful you are. Come on."

"Ugh." There was that anxiety again.

Gabe had me stand an arm's length away from him and asked me to do what he did. He began with a bow and then into a fighting stance. From there he stepped and turned, very gracefully, then he did a punch move and then a block with a turn. He did them very slowly so I could follow. I kept up fairly well for a little while, until I bumped my tender side, and winced. I was caught.

"Why'd you do that?" he asked, looking concerned.

"Do what?" I put my arm back over the wound, trying to act natural. It throbbed and ached.

"You're hurt."

"No, I'm okay." I faked a smile.

"Let me see."

"No, It's fine."

"What's fine?" he questioned. By now he is trying to lift up my arm and I am trying to turn away from him so he won't see the blood that has stained, yet another shirt. We spun in a tight circle with Gabe holding my hand away from my body as we argued.

"Oh my gosh, you're bleeding."

I rolled my eyes. "It's nothing."

He reached out with his other hand and touched the stain on my shirt causing me to wince again. He pulled his hand away and looked me in the eye, still holding my hand away from my side.

"Zoey, let me see it. I can help." he pleaded.

"But you can't. This isn't my body."

"What?" he asked, gaping at me, still holding my hand up in the air, trying to get a look at my side, that I kept pulling away from him, so he kept turning with me. It was like a crazy dance.

The look on his face struck me funny, and to think about what I had just said made me laugh even harder. As we spun, I laughed and Gabe continued to bend over, with my hand lifted up almost above my head with the most bewildered look on his face, till he finally let go of my hand and stopped to stare at me; hands on his hips.

"Whose body it is then? That's the weirdest thing you've said since I woke up here and, trust me, you have said some pretty strange things!"

I continued to laugh; a mix of nervous laughter and comic relief. I was hugging my side, trying not to look at his bewilderment so that I could quit laughing. It was hurting to laugh, but I couldn't seem to stop.

Gabe's expression went from concern, to confusion and then he just stood there with a big, stupid grin on his face, crossed his arms, and waited for me to stop.

Had I laughed like that with Aden, he'd have yelled at me, told me I was being childish and, probably stomped off, plotting some way to get me back for making him feel foolish. That thought sobered me and I composed myself to explain. I didn't want Gabe to be angry with me.

"Okay, how do I put this?" I began. "I didn't steal this body, it's mine, but I'm inside my own head, so everything here is just my imagination. If I was really, *physically* inside my own head I'd be inside out. Right?"

Gabe furrowed his brow.

"Therefore, this body that you see isn't my body. My body is… Well, I don't know where it is. In the forest where I left it, or in a hospital or a mental institution, I don't know. So, you can't help me. Get it?"

He stood there staring at my side, concern etched on his face, deep in thought. Finally, he scratched his head and spoke.

"*I'm* obviously not really here, not physically, but how did you get here?"

"What makes you think *you* aren't physically here?" I asked, trying to change the subject. I wasn't going to tell him about the bridge and Carl. No way! Besides, I assumed that incident was just some psychological pathway to my inner self. I had no idea where I really was, although it felt like I was really there, so much more than a dream. It felt real.

"Where were you before you got here?" I asked.

He looked up, and I was surprised to see fear in his eyes for just an instant.

That was weird. I thought.

"I was, uh, sleeping." he confessed, dismissively, and turned it back around on me. Genuine concern etched on his face. "Then, you're alone somewhere, unconscious and wounded in a forest?"

I shrugged. "I guess."

"Where?"

"California." I smiled sheepishly.

"Huh, well, I don't like that little fact." he said, and then paced across the room and back, mumbling something I didn't catch. He ran his fingers through his hair like he always did when he was frustrated. Then he paced the room again for a few minutes. I took a seat. He was obviously not going to let it go.

When he finally turned back to face me, he still had his hand in his hair. "One thing at a time." he began. "We have established that nothing here can hurt us unless it is each other doing it. Like when I pinched you yesterday."

"Well, not exactly. I stubbed my toe on a chair yesterday morning when you woke me up screaming for me to open the gate. That hurt."

"I was not screaming." he defended, with a wounded expression that made me stifle a grin.

"You were screaming."

"That Jester guy is a huge freak. Did you see his teeth? I was like four feet away from that guy when the doors opened! Did you smell the dog... thing?" he mocked a shutter. "Okay fine, we *can* get hurt. So why didn't the fire burn me?"

"Maybe it was because we had time to be logical about it and notice it wasn't hot. It didn't burn you because you believed it wouldn't. When I stubbed my toe I wasn't trying to be logical or wondering if the chair was real, I just kicked it. What's your point?"

He paced away from me and then back. "Well, it's like this. Either you're going to have to believe you are not hurt, or do the most logical thing and clean your wound and believe that will help."

"Or we are going to have to get us out of here so I can get out of the forest and to a clinic." I said, sounding much more snappy than I had meant to.

Gabe nodded and then stared at my side again. "You're right. Now will you just let me look at it?"

I rolled my eyes. "Fine." I conceded, standing up and carefully lifting my shirt to my ribs. The fabric was stuck to the wound and caused me to suck air through my teeth.

Gabe knelt down and studied it. It was seeping yellow liquid along with watery blood, and looked much worse than it had when I had first noticed it in the forest. It was ringed in red and warm to the touch. The whole matter worried me, but I wasn't about to tell him that. Not that he could do anything about it anyway.

"I'll be right back." he said, and ran up the stairs to his room, taking three stairs at a time. When he came back a few moments later he had a first aid kit.

"Where'd you get that?" I asked.

"In my medicine cabinet."

"There was one in the backpack."

"I don't know where the backpack is."

"How did you know there would be one in the medicine cabinet?"

"I didn't, but I wanted it to be."

"Right." I furrowed my brow.

I realized he had made it appear there. He was quickly getting the hang of living here. I wasn't sure how that made me feel, considering "here" was in my head. Then the thought occurred to me; if it were possible for him to manipulate things in here maybe he wasn't real after all. I found that thought comforting. Especially considering he was touching my midsection and was way too close for my peace of mind.

"But, it isn't gonna help."

"Yes it is, because you believe it will."

"I just told you it wouldn't, so obviously I don't believe it will."

"Yeah, but you're a logical, educated person and you know modern medicine works, so you *do* believe it will, whether or not you believe consciously." he explained, dabbing hydrogen peroxide on the cut with a cotton ball.

"Okay, that didn't make sense. Ouch, that burns."

"See, I told you it would work." he remarked, smirking, but not making eye contact.

Gabe was gentle, but thorough. By the time he finished, the wound was cleaned and had a sterile bandage over it. I admit, I felt a little better about it, but I didn't tell him that.

Before long we were back on the fifth floor, West Wing hallway, standing in front of a door marked 504 W. It was eerily quiet in the dark hallway and smelled of stale air and dust. The stately portraits stared unwaveringly, giving us the feeling we were being watched. We stood in the small illuminated space and unlocked the door, pushed it open and waited.

The same orb of light that the other rooms had, floated in the middle of the room, casting a warm glow in the empty space. Soon we could hear children's voices laughing and talking loudly. Gabe looked at me inquisitively, as if to ask if I remembered this one. I just shrugged. I had no idea. I stepped in.

Slowly, a classroom began to appear. The door we walked through became the classroom door and chaos ensued all around. Children were running everywhere playing tag, laughing and squealing loudly. Several teachers, the Principal and a couple of police officers stood around talking in hushed tones, neither of which were watching the children.

The classroom was laid out with desks in rows by a wall of windows. Under the windows were shelves of books and art supplies. At the back of the classroom was an art station with several easels set up for finger painting, and a large sink for hand washing. A can of blue paint had been knocked from a small table and was slowly spreading across the floor. In the space in front of the door there was a large, colorful rug with squares for children to sit for story time.

Gabe pointed to a curly haired, little girl in a blue dress, sitting at a desk. She wore a worried expression and watched the commotion with big intuitive eyes. She and a little boy, who also looked worried, were the only ones sitting. I nodded to Gabe, the little girl was me.

The emotion of the memory began to set in and I could feel anxiety and fear well up in my stomach. I looked at Gabe and he too wore a stressed expression.

The Principle finally walked to the front of the classroom and attempted to regain order, clapping her hands and yelling, "Children, Children! Take a seat please. Kaden, now you know better than that. Hands to yourselves. Quiet please!" She waited until everyone was settled and relatively quiet before she spoke again.

"Hello Children." she began. "I'm sorry for the confusion this morning, but I'd like to introduce you to your substitute teacher, Mrs. Morris. She will be teaching your class today." She looked at the other teachers like she wasn't sure what to say. One of the teachers frowned at her and nodded. She took a deep breath and continued. "Children, Ms. Mitchell didn't come to school today and we can't seem to locate her. I'm sure she is just fine." she wavered, clearing her throat. "These police officers are going to be looking for her for us. So, we are going to have a good day with Mrs. Morris. Okay?" she clapped her hands and motioned for Mrs. Morris to approach the class.

The room faded and another vision started to take shape around us. We were now standing in a playground. The anxious feeling faded and everything felt normal and calm, but sad. We looked around and spotted the little me by the slide. She was waiting for two little boys to climb the tall ladder. She wore a pair of pink, flowery pants and a white blouse; it was a different day. She finally got her chance to climb the ladder behind the two boys who were talking as they climbed. The first boy, who sat at the top, was talking, "My mom says she was murdered," he said, and then went down the slide. The other boy sat at the top and yelled down at the first boy, "My mom says that's bologna!" Then he slid down the slide. The young version of me sat down at the top of the slide and cried silently. The emotion permeated the memory, and I felt heavy with sorrow.

The vision faded and began again in the classroom. I realized I had tears streaming down my face and I quickly wiped them away before I stepped out into the hallway. Gabe closed the door and we both stood there in silence and waited for the sadness to fade.

Gabe took a deep breath, leaning his back against the wall. "Well, that was unpleasant," he sighed.

"Yeah, that sucked."

"What really happened to your teacher? Was she murdered?"

I nodded. "Yeah, they found her body by the lake a few days later."

"Did the people at the school tell the kids what happened?"

I shook my head. "No, my mom told me. She didn't keep things from me, she believed truth was easier to live with than me coming to my own conclusions. Besides, I would have heard it from someone. It was a small town and everyone had been talking about it."

"What happened?"

"It was awful, she'd been tortured and then strangled. Come to find out, her killer was her son's friend. I think he wanted money and she wouldn't give it to him. He was some sort of addict; a drug buddy of her son's."

"Wow, that *is* awful." he grimaced. He stood against the wall for a few silent moments staring off into space. I too, was quietly contemplating what we had just experienced. I wasn't sure what made this memory pivotal except that it shattered the safe belief a five or six-year-old child would have lived in; the world I lived in. The world is not safe, people hurt people. Monsters are real.

"You were a beautiful little girl." Gabe said, smiling softly.

I knew it was supposed to be a kind sentiment, but it made my stomach turn and I wasn't sure why. I smiled at him, as best as I could muster, because, of course, that is what you are supposed to do when someone compliments you.

I wanted an excuse to change the subject, but couldn't think of anything. I wasn't ready for another room yet, and I wasn't hungry. On the contrary, I had lost my appetite. I felt a little sick.

Gabe had slumped against the wall and was sitting on the floor with his arms resting on his knees. He was deep in thought and I was thankful for the silence. It gave me a moment to compose myself and look around a bit.

There were even more sconces in the hall now, and the floor where we were was now polished hardwood. It looked very odd butting up against the old drab carpet just beyond the newly lit area. I walked over to where the wood ended and the carpet began. It was as if the wood morphed into carpet. There was no dividing marker, no break from one to the other. I wondered if the old carpet just depicted memories that hadn't been looked at in a long time. Like we were bringing new life to an old place.

I bent down to touch it, running my fingers along the contours of the wood where it changed into fabric, when I heard footsteps and saw Gabe's shadow come up behind me."

"That is weird, isn't it." I said.

"What?" replied Gabe, from back where he was sitting against the wall.

I whipped my head around and the shadow was gone, but it hadn't been Gabe's. My heart pounded in my chest and I caught eye contact with Gabe. His eyes went wide and he was up on his feet faster than I thought possible, looking around. Then he rushed to my side, and looked beyond me into the darkness. I was a statue of fear, pleading to him with my eyes. I was terrified. There was someone else in my mind; in my house. I stood, holding my hands to my mouth to ward off the silent scream.

"Zoey," Gabe said, holding my shoulders. "What is it? What did you see?"

My heart raced and adrenaline threatened to make me sick. "There's someone else here." I whispered.

"Who? Where?"

"I don't know, but they walked up behind me, I heard footsteps and saw their shadow. I thought it was you."

"I didn't see anything, are you sure?"

I nodded, and Gabe took my elbow and led me back into the light. Then he held me by my shoulders again and looked me in the eye.

"I know you're scared, but remember, nothing can hurt us here. Nothing here is real."

"That felt real to me."

"Let's get outta here for a while." he suggested, offering a smile.

I nodded and we walked back towards the inner hallway to the main room. Before I walked around the corner, I looked back towards where I had been standing by door 506 W. The door was ajar and a small stream of light flickered through the opening.

I threw my back against the wall around the corner, and looked up at Gabe.

"What? What'd you see?" he asked, looking around.

"Look back down the hall. There's an open door. I didn't open it."

He stepped back to the doorway and peered down the hall. Then stepped back by me, moving me away from the opening. "Yeah, I see it. That's disconcerting."

I thought that was a stupid thing to say and my fear was quickly turning to anger. I suppose that was a fight or flight response, but I was about to take it out on the wrong person. I wanted to run, I wanted to hide, I wanted Jace to come and make it all okay.

"Uhm, okay. I'm going to go back to check it out. You stay here." he said, stepping away to go back down the hall.

"No!" I squealed, grabbing his arm, my anger alternating back to sheer panic. "Don't leave me here."

He looked down the hall and then back to me, uncertainty etched on his face. "Okay?" he paused to look back down the hall. "You don't think we should just leave it that way, do you?"

I leaned my head back, bumping it against the wall. Indecision and fear threatening to be the death of me. "I don't know, I'm scared. I don't know if anything could... Or did come out of there."

"Nothing can hurt us here, right?"

I just stared at him.

"So, let's go check it out and I'll keep you safe. Okay?"

There went that angry feeling again. Always right at the surface. Always covering for my fear, my insecurity, my pain. I wasn't about to go down to the living room alone, and I didn't want to stay there, and there was no way I was going to be able to relax if I didn't find out who had left that door open. He was right. *Crap!*

Resigned, I nodded and he smiled at me and stretched out his hand for me to take. I put my hand in his and we slowly walked back into the West Wing hallway to door 506 W.

The hallway was as quiet as ever, and there was no one there as far as we could see. We approached the door and Gabe slowly pushed it open, nudging me behind himself with his other hand. I looked around his body to see into the room. Light shone brightly from the center orb, just as it had in the other rooms. Gabe turned and looked at me and I shrugged.

"I smell popcorn." he whispered.

I could smell it too, along with a strong musty scent of mildew and old cigarette smoke. It made me want to gag.

"You ready?" he asked.

I nodded and clung to his hand with both of mine. We stepped in.

We let the vision appear around us and found ourselves standing in an old, decrepit, movie theater lobby. There was a small concession stand and a man standing by the door to the theater room. He wore a red suit and fez, and had a gold name tag that read "Carl."

I realized my fingers were hurting from the death grip I had on Gabe's hand and I loosened my hold. Gabe smiled at me and then led me over to Carl.

"Tickets please." he announced. "Oh, my apologies, Ms. Zoey, go right in."

I nodded and started to walk in, when Carl stopped Gabe and asked for his ticket. Gabe looked at me.

"Oh, he is with me." I explained.

"I'm sorry, Ms. Zoey, but he can not get in without a ticket."

"Where can we get him a ticket?" I asked.

"I'm afraid there aren't any. We're sold out."

Gabe smiled at the man and led me away, out of earshot of Carl. "Will you be okay to go in by yourself?"

"I could go in and see if I can get someone to give up their ticket, or something." I suggested.

Gabe nodded and reached up to tuck a loose curl behind my ear. "Yell if you need me, I can take care of Carl." he said, grinning.

His smile was genuine and made me feel better, although I was still uneasy. I took a deep breath and walked back to Carl. I nodded and he opened the worn velvet rope divider and the accordion gate for me to enter the theater.

This room was different from the rest. I passed the threshold and stood in an old theater room with a large screen at the front, and filled with rows of old, faded, theater chairs. The walls were covered in long, black curtains and reeked of mildew, a sickly sweet smell that I couldn't quite decipher, and old cigarette smoke, a smell that always brought up terrible memories. There wasn't a single person there and the projector was flipping the end of the reel over and over, making a bar go up the screen repeatedly, and causing a tic tic tic noise.

I walked in and instinctively wrapped my arms about myself in a protective hug and looked around. The carpet was faded red with pictures of popcorn and candy embellished in the fibers. The chairs were once red as well, but time had worn holes and stains in the fabric from years of use and neglect and were now more of a copper brown.

Carl had said that the movie was sold out, but there wasn't a soul there. I scanned the floor for a discarded ticket, but there was nothing but old wrappers and popcorn. *Maybe there's a reason Gabe wasn't allowed in,* I thought.

I decided to take a seat at the end of the middle row closest to the door marked with an exit sign. Dust filled the air as I settled into the old chair, and the lights dimmed. It was as if the whole theater had been waiting on me to find my seat. Fuzzy black numbers began to flash on the white screen, 4..3..2..1. The film began.

The film was about me. It started with my childhood in a memory that was so painful, so shameful, that I had never shared it with anyone. The first time I had been molested.

The movie opened with scenery, the forest, the abandoned train tracks, the steep grade that was too steep for a five year old to climb down; too steep for the child, me, to get away. Then I see him, with his cigarette and his boots, the trusted family friend. It was a silent movie.

A subtitle appeared across the bottom of the screen: "Please don't do that!" As I watched, my breath caught in my throat and my stomach began to churn. I felt as though someone had punched me in the gut. The confusion and disgusting feelings began to permeate the room. Shame threatened to crush me.

A new subtitle appeared: "It's not my fault that you're so beautiful."

No! I can't watch this! "NO!" I said aloud, as I threw my hands over my eyes and shook my head. Anxiety welled up inside me and I thought I may throw up. I couldn't escape for fear of seeing the pain and awakening an anguish that I could not face. I couldn't scream either, Gabe would come in, he'd see my most shame-filled memory. The pain and disgust that was being displayed on the big screen.

As I sat there, racked with sobs, I heard someone sit down behind me.*" Oh no, Gabe came in anyway. How did he get past Carl? He can't stay here.*

Whoever it was smelled of popcorn, cigarette smoke, and the reeking smell of decay. Before I could even turn to see who was behind me, I felt it; the fear that grips. The fear that swallowed me up like dense fog. It wasn't Gabe, it was The Jester.

I was cornered, alone. I was going to die. I was helpless. The emotion was strong and real.

I tried to stand, inching to the edge of my seat, but as I leaned forward to get up, the Jester put a hand on my shoulder and gripped tightly, pulling me back to sit in the chair, his nails digging into my collar bone. I squeezed my eyes closed tighter and hugged myself. His hand was hot and moist and smelled like blood. I gagged.

"No, stay." he said, in a voice that was sultry and sickening in my ear. "You're going to love this part." he laughed, loud and obnoxiously. Bits of chewed popcorn flew at me as he guffawed and slapped his dog.

"Helpless little baby, HAHAHAHA, and the best part is, I told him to do it! HAHA!"

He blew smoke at the back of my head and flicked the cigarette across the room. The Wild Card growled, sounding something like death throes, low and guttural. My fear was palpable and I could taste bile in my throat.

I dared to look up for a moment and the scene had changed. I was a young girl at the circus, somewhere around ten years old. Young me was walking through a tight crowd trying to find my friends. We had gotten separated. I had been walking close to one of the tents when a man grabbed my arm. He was pulling the younger me into the tent with a big nasty smile on his face. His teeth were yellow and black and I remembered how he smelled like booze. Thousands of people surrounded the young me and no one would help me, no one noticed or cared. I watched my younger self silently scream on the screen and there was fear in her eyes. I watched, feeling the exact feelings as I had felt that night. No one heard me scream. I could see the man's mouth moving and the words across the screen read, "Just come 'ere, I'm not gonna hurt ya, little girl. You sure are purty." The young me was shaking her head and looking around for someone to help.

Again the Jester laughed behind me. "Still helpless! HAHAHA, you're a joke!" he yelled, laughing loudly and tossing popcorn at the back of my head. I covered my ears and sunk as low as I could in my seat. The scene continued and just before I had been pulled completely into the tent, someone grabbed hold of my other arm and yanked me back. Then they shoved the young me to the ground and disappeared into the tent. I could only assume it was the man's girlfriend or his wife. I couldn't see her on the screen, but I remembered how she had gone in and started slapping him. She was yelling profanities about how she was tired of him messing around with little girls.

The scene changed again, this time the younger me was in the house that I had shared with Aden after we had gotten married. I recognized the scene from the beginning. Tears streamed down my face there in the theater. I was a mess, completely helpless to do anything to stop it. I was trapped, tormented to watch the most painful memories of my life played out before me.

The scene started in the bathroom. I had been 12 weeks pregnant and there was blood in the toilet. I watched as the woman on the screen silently called to Aden as she bent over in pain. My heart was breaking all over again, just as it had that day I lost my baby. The scene moved to the hospital where the doctor was telling the younger me that my baby's heart was no longer beating and that my body was miscarrying the fetus. The woman on the screen was sobbing and Aden was sitting on a chair, rubbing his temples with his elbows on his knees.

The scene changed again. The young me was lying in bed with Aden pacing the floor, yelling. He was so angry. The subtitles on the screen read "You can't even do this right, can ya! What the hell did you do? You wanted this to happen. Did you drink the baby to death? Well, screw it, it was probably a girl anyway!" Then he left the room and younger me was left there in the bed alone.

I was sobbing, the pain was the same there in the theater as it had been that day in my bed and I remember feeling like I could do nothing right. There was something wrong with me. I wasn't even a proper woman, able to carry a baby to term. I was helpless and alone.

The Jester laughed again, and I could feel the Wild Card breathing on my neck, loud, raspy, and hot. I was terrified, gripping the arm-rests, willing myself to run, but unable to move.

Memory after memory reiterated my helplessness, my failure and my shame played out for what seemed all the world to see. And each time the Jester laughed and spit and I was helpless to stop him; to even get up and leave. I was petrified. I watched the light dance off the screen and make eerie shadows around the room as I tried to avert my eyes.

I had to get out of there, I needed to be rescued. Add anger and self-reproach to the growing list of emotions I was feeling, and it's a wonder I didn't burst. *So much for being able to take care of myself, I can't even get out of this theater.*

"Jace," I whispered.

Then I heard Jace speak, his voice clear and sure in my mind; peace rushed over me like a breath of fresh air in stifling heat. "It's a lie Zoey, they are all lies. See for yourself."

I looked up at the screen and it started over at the beginning, the same scenery, the same man. Me, the abandoned train tracks, the wretched family friend. But this time I could see Jace there with me. He cleaned me up and held me and began to speak. The subtitles from the original version were blurred, unreadable, irrelevant. His was the only voice that was audible in the movie and I wondered if the Jester could hear it too.

"You are not shameful Zoey. The shame is his and his alone. He used his free will to do this to you, but you were not alone. I was there, I felt your pain." The scene didn't change, but I was able to see how Jace saw it.

He continued to show me an added scene of me, as I was there in the theater, a strong woman capable of taking care of myself and standing up for others. No longer helpless.

"Your enemy is the bringer of lies and deceit," he said. "The door had been left open for him to come in and bring lies to your thinking. I have come to bring truth and set you free."

The Jester was yelling at the screen now. "Hey! What is this Bull...?" I realized he could not see or hear what Jace was saying to me. He punched The Wild Card and it yelped an awful sound, while the Jester yelled profanities and spat. I was terrified.

Jace spoke calmly, "I give you my authority, use it to command your enemy to leave. You are not helpless."

"But, I'm afraid," I replied.

The Jester laughed again. "Of course you're afraid, Stupid, You're helpless."

Jace spoke again in my mind. "Trust me. Tell him to go."

I was still afraid, but I stood on shaking legs and turned to the Jester, who still had a smug look on his face. The light danced off his chiseled facial features, accentuating his sharp cheekbones and sunken eyes. His eyes were black and lifeless and his grin was full of pointed teeth. He raised a questioning eyebrow.

I had made a choice, I was no longer helpless, so I reached deep to find my voice. "I choose to use the authority given to me by the Master and I command you to leave!" I blurted, with fear in my voice and shaking hands.

Rage lined every inch of his expression as he stood, towering over me. He threw the bucket against the chair beside me, making popcorn fly into the air. Snarling at me, frightening and grotesque, he lowered his face to mine in mock laughter once more, loud and mirthlessly. His stench was indescribable and I held my breath and tried not to panic or be sick. Then both he and the Wild Card disappeared.

I plopped myself back in my chair and took a deep breath. I was shaking and exhausted. The movie continued to play and I watched my younger self on the big screen.

I was at the fair, I was being pulled, I was looking around, screaming. And then I saw him. Jace was there. He tapped the lady on the shoulder and pointed to me. She was furious and marched towards me. Jace smiled at me and nodded his head. The woman does as she always had done, and threw me to the ground. The memory hadn't changed, but my perception had. I wasn't helpless after all. Jace was there, he saved me.

The movie changed again and I saw the blood and then the hospital scene playing again. The memory was the same, yet this time as I looked around the scene I saw Jace. He was standing in the doorway of the hospital room holding my baby. She was perfect, small and beautiful, with brown curls and an adorable little nose. Jace smiled at her and then to me, and kissed her forehead. He saved her from an abusive father, his mercy had been beyond my understanding.

The scene changed and the younger me was back in bed while Aden was yelling, but it didn't hurt anymore. There was nothing wrong with me. I didn't do anything to hurt my baby. She is in good hands now and she is perfect, in the arms of the Master.

Memory after memory played, all exactly the same, except that Jace was there showing me truth, dispelling the lies and healing my heart.

The scent of jasmine filled the room and it felt like someone had turned on the air conditioner. I could no longer detect the cigarette smell or the must, just clean air and fragrance. The last memory played on the screen and I watched without fear. The memories were still unpleasant, but they no longer caused me pain. They're just memories. At the end of the reel I saw something new. There was a door, like the ones in the hallway of the West Wing. It was open and the camera panned closer to watch the door slam shut and bolt, locked. My enemy was no longer allowed inside to torment and cause pain. The only thing left are the memories, the lies are gone.

I walked out into the lobby and turned to lock the accordion gate by where Carl stood. "You can go now Carl," I said, he nodded with a smile, and faded away.

Gabe watched and waited for me to approach him. I smiled at him and his expression relaxed, worry fading into a sigh of relief and he smiled, gesturing me out the door to the hall.

"You okay?" he asked.

"Yeah, I am now."

"And the shadow?"

"I think it was the Jester, but he's gone now."

Gabe nodded, "Good."

He pulled the door closed behind him and we heard it latch. Locked, just as the movie had shown.

The mansion was quiet and the hall was brightly lit as we walked back down and around the ballroom to the living room. I noticed some of the pictures were crooked and one had fallen from the wall. I wondered if the house had quaked in my moments of panic and had been unable to feel it whilst in the theater.

"Quakes?" I asked, looking up at Gabe.

He nodded. "Yeah, it shook out here pretty badly while you were gone. You didn't feel it?"

I shook my head.

"I was worried about you. The doorman refused to let me in. He assured me that you were in no danger. I had to brace myself and pray. I wanted to take Carl out," he chuckled nervously and then smiled at me. "I'm glad you're okay."

I smiled back, I felt like a weight had been lifted from my shoulders; a weight that I had been carrying for far too long.

I picked up the portrait and placed it back on the nail in the wall. It was my great aunt Mildred, whom I had only met once. Her features were much like mine, and she had kind eyes. I smiled at her likeness and then moved to plop myself down on the couch. I was exhausted and just wanted to rest.

I laid back and closed my eyes. Gabe didn't ask questions, he just let me rest. I fell asleep within minutes and slept soundly with pleasant dreams.

I don't know how long I slept. It's difficult to tell when time doesn't pass as usual. I woke to the smell of bacon, which by the way, is one of the best smells to wake to. Gabe wasn't around so I figured he was in the kitchen. I stretched and went to go find him.

When I got there, he was cooking and the kitchen was a mess. There was a radio on the countertop and it was playing a popular song, although it sounded a little off, I couldn't quite put my finger on why. Gabe was humming along while he flipped bacon and checked a waffle iron off to the side of the stove. When he turned around to put something in the sink he saw me and startled, dropping the spoon on the floor.

"You startled me," he said, picking up the spoon.

"I could have gotten the drop on you, Mr. Martial Arts Man," I said, smirking.

He chuckled. "Yeah, what would you have done if you did?"

"Eaten your dinner, I guess."

"Well, I made it for you anyway, so you don't have to knock me out, okay."

I looked around. He had set out two trays with juice, syrup, and one of the trays had a white rose in a small vase. I looked back at him and he smiled at me.

"You made this for me?"

He nodded. "This is what my mom used to make me when I had a rough day. It's like a do-over; breakfast for dinner, minus the sugar-free syrup."

"Thank you. That was very thoughtful. But couldn't you have just made it appear? Like you did the first aid kit and the pictures."

"I don't know. I came in here with the intention of making it, and all the stuff was here. I figured it would be a nice gesture if I put some effort into it."

It didn't seem to me that he wanted anything. I wondered why he was being so nice to me. I tried to believe that he would just do something like this because he was just a nice guy, but I was suspicious and I wasn't going to let him manipulate me into anything. I know what Aden would have wanted, but he'd never have put that much effort into it.

"Thank you." Was all I could think to say.

Another song came on the radio, but the words were garbled, only the chorus seemed to be playing correctly. We both stopped to look at the radio, and it dawned on me why it sounded that way. I gave him an apologetic look.

Gabe just smiled crookedly. "It sounds weird doesn't it," he said, with a bewildered look on his face.

"Yes, but I know why," I said, blushing. "That's the only part of the song I know."

He looked confused and opened his mouth to ask, but it must have dawned on him because he started laughing.

"Ha, that's hilarious. Zoey, That song by Adele?" he chuckled, "it says *Chasing Pavement*, not *chasing penguins*. That song came on earlier and I thought it sounded weird."

"No, really?" I smiled, "I always wondered what that song was talking about, I thought it was a metaphor."

"Well, it is, but..." he smiled, "Nevermind."

We ate our dinner on the big fluffy rug of the living room floor. The fire popped and glowed brightly in the dim room, casting dancing shadows all around.

There were several more impossible windows in the living room now. Windows that should be looking into the dining room, but somehow had a view of the gardens outside and the forest beyond. The dome at the top had opened a little more as well. The sun had just set, and the stars were beginning to sparkle in the night sky. Figaro was purring loudly on the back of the couch, and the ballroom was quiet this evening.

I told Gabe what had happened in the theater, although I didn't give details about the movie. I told him about the Jester and his dog and how Jace had come to save me. I explained it had been the lies that had made them so painful, and once they were dispelled the memory was just a bad memory. The pain was gone.

"I can't believe you were that close to that guy!" he said, "He's repulsive, and that dog…"

"Yeah, I thought I was gonna die. He seems to have an aura of fear about him, but when Jace spoke, he didn't seem so frightening."

He nodded, "Perfect love casts out fear."

"What?" I asked.

"It's in the Bible. Love is the opposite of fear. Like light and darkness, they can't both occupy the same space."

"I didn't know you knew the Bible," I said, finishing off the last of my waffle. "I used to go to church when I was a kid, but we stopped going when we moved to Florida."

"Why?"

"My dad used to say preachers are like car salesmen, they're just selling something. I guess after Mom died, Dad just got too busy.

"Do you believe that? What your dad said, I mean," he asked, then he stole the last of my bacon and popped it in his mouth.

"Thief!" I accused, with mock surprise.

He smiled unapologetically.

"I don't know, I think it's just never been really real to me; not since I was a kid. I've been going to church lately, but I'm not sure if God is really listening. I have questions. "

"Maybe I can help. My father was a preacher."

"Oh, I never took you for a preacher's kid."

He laughed. "Oh yeah, why not?"

"I don't know. Preacher's kids are either stuck up from being in the 'elite club' or they are completely out of control."

"Yeah, I've seen that a lot too. I think It happens when pastors get so involved in their churches that their families come second."

"Was your dad that way?" I asked. "Wait, you said 'was,' did he quit?"

Gabe shook his head, with sadness in his eyes. He pulled on a loose string hanging off the hem of his shirt. "Nah, he, uh, died."

"Oh, I'm sorry."

"Yeah, me too," he said quietly.

Uncomfortable silence. I was never good with that. *Do I say something else? Do I ask how he died? Do I change the subject?* I stared at the floor wondering what I should say.

"He had cancer."

I looked up at him, but his gaze was distant. He stared up at the ceiling, but I knew he wasn't really looking there, but somewhere in the past; somewhere painful.

Chapter 13 Sadness

The next day we started at 507 W. I unlocked the door and we walked in and waited for the light to grow and the memory to begin. Loud music roared around us before the orb had even stopped growing outward. Club music, fast and full of bass, emanated from large speakers on a raised platform. The room was full of people dancing and crowded in tightly below a DJ on a platform. The DJ was speaking loudly into a mic inviting the throng to dance. I looked at Gabe and he looked uncomfortable, he was frowning with his brow furrowed. I wondered what that was about.

"What?" I asked.

"Brianna brought me here once. It wasn't my scene."

"Oh," was all I could think to say. I was glad he wasn't upset with me. I looked around trying to find the slightly younger me; this memory hadn't been that long ago.

The memory soon focussed on another version of me. She was sitting at a hightop table, alone. We watched as this version of me sat nervously sipping a drink and trying not to make eye contact with anyone. She wore a conservative blouse and slacks and very little make-up. It wasn't long before Susanna came to the table and sat down. She was breathless and smiling.

The emotion of the memory began to settle in and a feeling of panic and anxiety gripped me as I watched.

"You should come dance with us! It's fun!" she yelled over the music.

The version of me faked a smile and shook her head. "No thanks." she yelled. "I think I'll call it a night. I have a lot to do tomorrow."

"No, you don't," Susanna argued, and took a long chug of her drink.

"I do," she argued. "I have to..."

Susanna sighed, looking sad and resigned. "Come on, I'll take you home."

The memory changed, the club faded away and I saw my not so younger self at the dojo. She was sitting on a bench tying her shoe and listening to conversations going on around her. She looked so sad, and the same feeling of anxiety permeated this memory, but this time it was mixed with loneliness. I looked around the memory and realized Gabe was in this one. He stood against the doorframe of his office and watched as his students packed up their stuff to leave. The others were laughing and making plans for the weekend and one of the girls walked over to younger me.

"Hey, Zoey, do you want to join us for a movie tonight? There are a bunch of us going. It'll be fun." She smiled and waited for a response.

The emotion reached a crescendo of anxiety and panic and I hugged myself protectively as I watched. I felt ashamed to look at myself making another excuse to not join them when all I wanted to do was join in and be accepted. Before the memory changed I caught a glimpse of Gabe shaking his head before stepping back into his office, he looked sad.

I didn't dare look up at the Gabe standing beside me.

Memory after memory played. People reached out to me and I had made excuses, the feeling of panic, anxiety, and loneliness was so heavy in the room that I finally turned and walked out into the hall. I got the message. I had seen enough.

Gabe came out behind me and closed the door. He looked sad and tired. I stood there, holding myself, staring at the floor. The next thing I knew I was engulfed in Gabe's arms. He held me tightly and rested his head on mine. I don't know if he would have let me go if I tried to break away, but I don't think so.

"I always knew you were dealing with stuff. I'm so sorry you felt so alone." he pulled me tighter. "You don't have to be so strong anymore. You aren't alone."

He kissed the top of my head like my dad used to do and I could feel myself relax. I felt loved. Not a boyfriend thing, or a sexual thing. A human thing. It felt like connection. Someone cared. It was a friend thing, and I felt safe. I pulled my arms from around myself and wrapped them around him and we stood there until the emotion of the room subsided and we exhaled a sigh of relief.

We both had to take a break after that one. We went down to the kitchen for a glass of iced tea before we began again. I wasn't sure if it was the emotion of the memory room that caused Gabe to be sullen, or if he was dealing with his own emotion. I caught a lingering glance a few times while we were sitting on the countertops in the kitchen.

If I was to believe that Gabe was dealing with his own emotion, then I'd have to believe he was actually there, actually real. I wanted to believe he was a figment of my imagination. It was safer that way, but didn't seem probable, unless my imagination was better than... well... than I imagined. It was a paradox.

I finished my tea and put the glass in the dishwasher. Gabe chuckled, watching me.

"What?" I defended, "It's a good habit."

We made it all the way to the end of the fifth floor West Wing that day. I was feeling a bit more confident knowing some of my most shameful and painful memories were guarded, like the one with Carl in the theater. I hoped that trend would continue. It was nice to know I didn't have to open all the rooms alone however, and I was happy Gabe was with me. Doing all of that alone would suck!

The rest of the rooms were mostly awkward childhood memories that taught me something along the way. One of the rooms was the death of my next-door neighbor, Charles, a man who was like a grandfather to me. He had battled cancer for a long time.

We stepped into the room and as the light grew outward we found ourselves standing in a street, watching an eight-year-old me walking home from school. My mom met little me at the door and there were tears running down her face. The emotion filled the room like a punch to the gut. The little me ran to her and she held me and told me that Charles had passed that morning. She led me in and set me on her lap and we cried together.

The sadness was overwhelming and I cried like the pain was new. I think I may have even seen a tear in Gabe's eye in that room.

We watched as my mom told the little me about how Marylynn, Charles's wife, had come over a few days prior. She had come over to tell us that Charles had loved hearing the laughter from our BBQ the day before.

"She said that we had made a bunch of noise and laughter." My mother was saying. "I told her I was sorry, we didn't mean to disturb Charles. Marylynn explained that she hadn't seen him smile like that for a long time and he lay there in his bed just listening to our fun for hours."

The little me smiled as tears ran down her little face. The light faded and the memory started over in the street.

That one caused us to take a break for a while. We went downstairs so I could wash my face and blow my nose.

We were in the living room trying to recover from Charles's room. I was on the couch with my legs over the back and my head upside down, looking into the fire. Gabe was laying on the floor.

"That one was brutal," said Gabe.

I nodded.

"I'm sorry." he was thoughtful for a second. "Hey, what do you say I share a memory with you between each room? If I'm gonna see all your memories, it's only fair that I share mine with you."

I thought it might make him feel less awkward about this experience being so one-sided. I thought it was nice too, although I still wasn't sure if he was even real.

"Yeah, I like that idea." I said, and I smiled.

***

I unlocked door number 519 W. and pushed it open. The orb of light floated in the middle of the stark white room and we could hear a small dog barking and the delighted squeal of a young girl. We stepped into the room and the light from the orb began to grow outward in all directions.

As the light filled the space we found ourselves standing in my childhood living room. My mother and my six-year-old self were standing in the middle of the room watching a tiny, black, toy-poodle spin and hop. The young me was giggling and squealing.

The emotion of the room began to set in and suddenly I felt giddy with childlike excitement. I looked over at Gabe and he was bobbing up and down like a child receiving a present. His eyes were wide with anticipation. I giggled at him before turning my attention back to the room.

"Zoey, don't get too attached, we can't keep him. We are only fostering him until we can find him a forever home," explained mom. The little me wasn't really listening as she watched the little dog bark and beg.

"What is his name, Momma?" the little me asked.

"His name is Petey. They were going to put him down. I couldn't let that happen." Mom explained with a distant look in her eyes. "I'm so glad Becca called me before they… " she caught herself. "Well, I'm glad she called." She paused, thoughtful for several moments before coming back to herself. "Petey's last owner taught him lots of tricks, apparently," she said, smiling sadly. "I wonder why he was given up." she mumbled mostly to herself.

The little me laughed again and picked up the tiny dog and hugged him while he licked her cheek.

The scene changed, going through a rapid procession of scenes depicting the young me playing with and caring for the little dog. Gabe and I watched in wonder as the emotions flitted from delight, to love, and then to confusion. When at last the scenes stopped, we found ourselves sitting in the back seat of a mini-van with the younger version of me. She was crying softly while staring into the large window of the house in front of which they had parked.

The stark emotional change of the memory settled in and made my stomach roll. I felt overwhelming sadness and loss. I wrapped my arms around myself in a protective hug. Gabe was breathing deeply and trying to gauge what was going on.

"Did someone die?" he asked, I could hear the sadness in his voice.

I shook my head. "Mom found a forever home for Petey." I explained.

"Oh," replied Gabe. "No happy ending for you, huh?"

I shook my head and we turned back to see Mom getting into the van. She turned the ignition and gripped the wheel tightly, as she sobbed. The young Zoey climbed over the seats and wrapped her arms around Mom. They cried together for several minutes before Mom instructed little me to sit down and put her seatbelt on.

The scene changed again and we were back in the living room of my childhood home. Mom was holding the little me in her arms trying to explain that she didn't mean to hurt her, but that the little old lady needed Petey. The emotion was heavy, but slightly better than it had been in the van. The lump in my throat persisted nonetheless.

"Zoey, Petey is going to have a good life there. Mrs. Mason lost her poodle last month and he was like her child."

Little me wiped her tears and sniffed, thinking for a moment before she spoke. "Mrs. Mason doesn't have kids? But she's old."

Mom chuckled softly and helped little me blow her nose. "Zoey, not everyone gets to have children. Sometimes people live their whole life and never get to have kids. Mrs. Mason never married, and never had any kids. Her children have been pets, so to speak, and when her little poodle got hit by a car, well, it broke her heart."

"So, we had to give her Petey so her heart could get all better?"

"Yes, Love. We saved Petey so Petey could save Mrs. Mason's heart."

"Momma, frostering animals is hard and it makes me sad."

"It sure is Baby." Mom agreed, and held little me tightly. I felt a twinge of jealousy as I watched, but it wasn't the emotion from the memory, It was my longing for my mother.

The scene changed again and started over at the beginning. Gabe and I stepped back out into the hallway and I locked the door.

Gabe stretched and took a deep cleansing breath, as to clear the emotion from his system. "You never told me you had a dog."

"Technically, Petey wasn't my dog, he was just a foster, but I fell in love." I chuckled to myself.

"Your mom was a neat lady." he said. "I see where you get your big heart."

My heart felt lighter at the thought of being like her, and I smiled. "Come on, we're almost done with this floor." I motioned toward door 520 W. the last door of the West Wing. It had been a long day and we had gone through what felt like hundreds of rooms. We were both tired, emotionally drained, and just wanted to be done with this hall.

I unlocked the door and we looked in. Inside was another club, loud music played and colored light beams danced around the room. A large man sat on a stool checking Id's at the door. He wore a sleeveless shirt and had a tattoo on his neck that said "Carl" in big black letters. This Carl was burley and huge, with arms so muscled that he couldn't put them down at his sides properly and he had a long scar on the left side of his bald head. He stood up from the stool and took a toothpick out of his mouth.

"Hello, Ms. Zoey, Aden's been expectin' ya."

"No." I whispered. And began to back away. I knew this wasn't a memory, per se, but a recurring dream. It was always different, in that Aden would have blood on his hands, or he'd be with another woman. It was always Aden, the mob boss, always expecting me, and I always tried to make him happy.

"Ms. Zoey, Aden don't like to be kept waitin'."

I stared at him, anxiety welling up inside me. I had no choice. I had to go see what he wanted. I was the doting wife, always who he wanted me to be… He was expecting me.

Gently Gabe pulled me back, I stepped willingly, in a daze. He closed the door and we were alone in the hallway again.

I reached to open the door again, but Gabe stepped in front of me. "Zoey, he doesn't have that hold on you anymore."

"But he's expecting me… I"

"Zoey, he's dead."

I stared at him, searching for words to match the feelings that welled up inside me. *Be a good wife and he will love you, but he didn't love you. Why didn't he love me? What's wrong with me? There's something wrong with me.*

"What's wrong with me?" I whispered. Staring into nowhere.

"There's nothing wrong with you Zoey. Aden was a narcissistic jerk!"

"What?" I asked, barely hearing what he was saying.

"Your ex-husband, He was a jerk."

"How do you know? He wasn't always bad!"

Gabe looked angry and it scared me. Anger meant pain. Anger meant I had done something wrong. I recoiled, hugging myself in preservation. I expected rejection, I expected humiliation, I felt small and helpless, just like I did with Aden.

Gabe balled his hands into fists at his sides, and he yelled. "I know because you're wounded! I know because you feel you need to run to his beck and call. I saw the memory of your beautiful honeymoon, remember."

He pointed towards the door where Aden was. "I know because of the pain in your eyes, your tears! I know because for four months you were in my self-defense class trying to defend yourself against a dead man!"

He stopped and ran his hands through his hair, turning his back to me. His voice softened. "I know because I've watched you, even before the memory rooms."

I was still hugging myself, hot tears streaming down my face. I stared at him.

He turned to me, "Zoey, I didn't mean to scare you. I know better than to raise my voice to you. I... Dangit! Zoey, there's nothing wrong with you!" he took a deep breath and exhaled. "There is nothing wrong with you."

I stood there for a moment and made my decision. "Get out of the way please."

He opened his mouth to argue, but thought better of it, exhaling exasperation, and stepped aside.

I stepped up to the door and opened it. Carl sat on his stool picking at a fingernail. He looked up at me with a bored expression. "Aden don't like to be kept waitin' Ms. Zoey."

"Tell Aden I won't be coming."

Carl stood up with a cocky expression and pointed at me, opening his mouth to argue. I slammed the door and locked it for good measure. Then I stuck the key back in my pocket and stood there staring at the door. A window appeared at the end of the hall. Moonlight shone down from above in bright streams of blue in the night.

"Atta Girl." I heard Gabe whisper behind me.

Chapter 14 Mom

The next several days dragged on. It turns out that the 4th floor West Wing was full of very young memories and partial memories. I was too young in most of them to make real sense of what was going on. Those rooms were mostly confusing feelings and a lot of crying. The weird thing about those rooms was that we mostly felt hungry until we came back out into the hall, then the feeling would fade.

"I didn't know hunger was an emotion," Gabe said, coming out of the third or fourth room that day.

"I didn't either. Man, I was an awful baby. My poor mother."

Gabe chuckled. "You were cute, I guess it made up for all the crying."

"You mean they didn't kill me because I was cute?"

"Yeah, pretty much."

"You're terrible!"

He smirked, "Good thing I'm cute."

I laughed.

Our friendship was light on the surface, but I knew it was getting deeper. I often wondered if the reason we got along so well was because he was my creation. My imaginary friend.

"My mom said I was a pretty easy baby, although my parents didn't get me until I was a few months old." Gabe recalled after a moment. "I spent my first few months in the hospital, before I was given up for adoption."

"I didn't know you were adopted. Have you ever met your birth parents? I mean, if you don't mind me asking." I asked.

"Nope, never really felt the need to," he replied. "My sister struggled with that a little when she was younger, she was adopted too, but her birth parents died."

"Oh, how did they die? Do you know?"

Gabe shook his head. "The agency never said."

***

The third floor West Wing was different in that Carl was in a lot of them. Each time the same name, but different appearance, different build, a different attitude. Some rooms I was given a choice to take Gabe in with me. These were the rooms that I may have considered private. My first kiss, certain conversations and private matters that would have been inappropriate to invite him into. Carl was discreet in the rooms that I was given a choice. He was firm in the rooms where I wasn't given a choice. He was odd, but I began to appreciate Carl.

Gabe always waited for me and never complained about hurrying to find the right door. I began to wonder why he was being so patient. Surely he didn't want to spend any more time there than he had to, stuck inside my head. He was, however, generous with his stories and sharing his memories with me in return for a shared memory room.

Could I have made up all of his memories too?

We stood in front of room 304 W. and I unlocked the door. Bright fluorescent light flooded the hallway and the strong smell of antiseptic wafted out. We stepped in and were standing in a waiting room of a hospital. The receptionist was an older gentleman who sat with his feet up on the desk, chatting on the phone.

"Room 631, you're welcome. Have a nice day," he said into the receiver, and then hung up, turning his attention to us. He had a lanyard around his neck that held his badge, his picture, and his name. "Volunteer, Carl Williams."

My heart sunk. I knew where I was and this one was going to hurt, bad.

"Good evening Ms. Zoey. Will you be giving Mr. Kort your family's permission to go in with you this evening, or shall I escort him to the ICU waiting room?"

I looked up at Gabe. His eyes were darting from me to Carl, concern etched on his features.

"Uhm, excuse us for just a sec," he said, holding up a finger and then taking me by the arm and leading me back toward the empty chairs. Carl only nodded.

Gabe looked almost panicked as he put his hands on my shoulders and looked into my eyes. "Zoey, we don't have to do this one. We can walk right back out into the hall and go shoot hoops or play pool or something."

I didn't know what to say, but I wondered why he thought this one would be any worse than all the other rooms we'd been through, and I realized his hands were shaking.

"This is where my mom passed away." I explained.

"Yeah, I know. I figured that." he remarked, looking into my eyes. He furrowed his brow and looked anguished.

"Gabe, are you okay?"

He stepped back and ran his hand through his hair, sighing deeply.

"I'm not sure *I* can do this one, Zo."

He looked pale, and I didn't understand. I took him by the hand and led him back out into the hall.

"What's wrong?" I asked. "Is this about your dad?"

Gabe was pacing and had his hand on his stomach. He didn't look sad, he looked... Scared.

"I uh. I just don't like hospitals."

I remembered what he had said about spending so much time in the hospital growing up and I thought I understood his apprehension, but the fear in his eyes seemed unwarranted. There was something he wasn't telling me.

"Okay, I understand." I watched him, back up against the wall and lean his head back, taking deep breaths. "I'm gonna do this one solo then."

He nodded, never opening his eyes.

I stepped back into the hospital room and up to the reception desk. "Hi, Carl. Gabe won't be joining me."

Carl nodded, and stood to escort me to the elevator.

"Wait, Carl."

He stopped and turned around, genuine concern on his face. "What's wrong Ms. Zoey?"

"I uhm, Can I ask you a question?"

"Well, certainly Ms. Zoey."

"Who are you?"

He looked a bit confused. "I'm Carl Williams, a volunteer here at Mercy General." Then he raised an eyebrow as if to ask if there was more that I needed to know.

"I mean, who are you in terms of, well… Why are you in my head?"

Carl smiled. "I am your guardian, I work for the Master." he whispered, and then winked at me.

"I thought so." I said, smiling at Carl.

Carl smiled and then turned and led me to the elevator. "Second floor, room 223."

"I remember, thank you."

Carl nodded again, and I got into the elevator. There, in the center of the elevator, was the light orb, and as the door closed the orb began to grow into a memory.

I stood at the entrance to room 223. My fifteen-year-old self stood over my mother's bed. They had already taken the tubes out and her body lay still and lifeless. Young me was saying goodbye.

The machines were quiet, and as the emotion began to fill the room I was gripped by a physical sensation that squeezed my chest. Grief, abandonment, heartache, devastation, void, emptiness, loss. I pressed my fists to my chest as I watched the fifteen-year-old me watch my mother lie there on the bed. I had forgotten how much it hurt standing there that day, and it almost took me to my knees.

I leaned against the wall and braced myself, taking a deep breath. I watched my younger self sit on the edge of my mom's bed. The younger me looked numb, she looked stoic, she looked broken. She was broken.

I was broken.

"Goodbye, mom. I wish you didn't have to go," she whispered, reaching out to touch Mom's face. But Mom wasn't there anymore. She'd passed an hour ago.

Dad walked into the room and over to where the younger me was standing. His eyes were swollen and his hand shook as he reached for her.

"Zoey, it's okay to cry," he said with a shaky voice.

The younger me just shook her head, never taking her eyes off Mom's bruised and swollen face.

The room began to change and suddenly I stood in a vortex of pictures, memories and emotions. The room spun like I was in the eye of a tornado. All around me were movies of myself and the hours, days, and years that passed as I dealt with the passing of my mother. Emotions came through every memory like a storm blowing into my heart. Fear, numbness, pain, void, anger, loss, acceptance, missing pieces of myself, healing.

I watched as my dad was there for me, my grandparents, my friends. I watched as I grew up, as we moved to Florida and made new friends. I watched as I used the things my mother taught me about life. I watched how she influenced my choices in the things she had told me, I watched as I grew to look so much like her, and I watched my relationship with my dad grow into a strong bond.

The memories played through my pain and into a happier time. As the end of the vortex raced towards me a saw my reflection in front of me, and everything stopped. I found myself sitting with my arms wrapped around my knees on the floor of the elevator, looking into the mirrored surface.

I pulled myself up and braced myself against the railing of the elevator. I felt dizzy and disoriented, but my heart was light. I felt refreshed. The pain of my mother's passing was just a memory. That part of me was healed. I had healed a long time ago and she was a happy memory.

I missed her terribly, but she was a part of me. She helped shape me into who I was meant to be. Strong and able, stubborn and tenacious, caring, and loved.

I stood up, and the door to the elevator opened with a "Ding," and there stood Gabe, wringing his hands, looking nervous.

"Are you okay?" he asked, looking sheepish and concerned.

I felt like I'd just been washed on the inside, I felt clean and re-freshed. I felt healed. I beamed at him and threw my arms around him. I don't know what came over me. I felt so free. I had… hope.

He stumbled back a step and then firmly returned the embrace.

***

The next few doors were uninteresting until we stood in front of door 313 W. I unlocked the door and pushed it open. There, right inside the door sat Carl. This time he had a face I recognized. Carl had the appearance of Aden's paralegal, Kenneth. I walked in and stood in front of the receptionist's desk, unsure of how to address the person standing in front of me, but he spoke before I had to figure it out.

"Oh Hello, Ms. Zoey." he sputtered, and then proceeded to stack files and arrange the mess that was on the large reception desk. "I'm sorry, uhm, Candy, the receptionist, she isn't here today, she's out sick." He rolled his eyes before he continued. "I'm trying to get my work done and do her job too," he laughed nervously. "The Christmas party is across the street at the banquet room of the Hilton." He pointed around the corner and down the hall to a door that went out to the street. Then he bumped a stack of files and dropped papers all over the floor. He sighed. "Are you sure you want to bring a date?" he asked, from under the desk.

The Christmas party, I knew this memory. Carl was trying to ask me, nonchalantly, if I wanted Gabe to go into this memory with me. Good ol' Carl.

I looked up at Gabe and he looked curious. "Look, I'm gonna let you make the call on this one," I said. "It's embarrassing."

"If you're gonna be embarrassed, I don't have to go in." he said.

"Well, it's…" I fumbled for the right way to explain. I took a deep breath, "I was trying to fix our relationship, so, I had read a bunch of articles on how to… well, keep things interesting in a marriage."

Gabe raised an eyebrow at me.

"I made a bunch of naughty notes and stuck them all over the house." I blurted, blushing.

Gabe laughed. "You were married, Zoey, that's not embarrassing."

"Let me finish," I said, holding up my hand.

He crossed his arms and waited.

"When he found the notes, he said I was immature and shoved them in the top of his briefcase."

"O-kay?" he said, questioningly.

"Come on, you're gonna like this one." I snickered.

We walked down the hallway past the receptionist's desk and out to the street. The Hilton had been across the street from Aden's office building, but we were in the banquet room as soon as we went through the door of Aden's office. There, in the banquet room, was the orb. Light emanated out from it, as the memory began to grow outward. Soon we were standing in a huge room full of people dancing, and decorated tables surrounding the dance floor. There was a large Christmas tree off to one side of the room and an orchestra on a stage in the back. The other me was dancing with Aden, looking irritated.

People waltzed by and through us as we stood watching. Aden was trying to talk the other me into acting like she was having fun. "People expect to see you at your best, Zo. Put your personal stuff behind you, and smile." he was saying. "Ouch, and stop stepping on my foot!"

"You are my 'personal stuff,' Aden. And you were late, again! I had to talk to Mrs. Willington for half an hour. She is a horrible person." The emotion of the room settled in and I began to feel irritated, Gabe was looking irritated too, as his jaw tensed like he might be gritting his teeth.

Aden laughed. "Well, I'm sorry, Sweetheart, I couldn't get here any sooner." he twirled the other me around and danced past a row of tables.

The other me saw a briefcase sitting open on a table and gasped, noticing the notes that she had written and placed all over the house, were falling out of the briefcase and exposed on the table.

"Aden, is that your briefcase, there on that table?" she asked as they danced by.

"Hmmm? Yeah, why?"

The other me stopped dancing and stood, looking shocked.

"What's wrong now, Zoey?" he snapped.

"Aden, your...your... things are falling out." she spouted, lacking the words to explain, inconspicuously, what she meant as she tried to gesture towards the briefcase.

Aden, not understanding what she was talking about or noticing where she was gesturing, gasped and looked down at his crotch and then back at Zoey. "What?" he asked. "What did you say?"

The look on his face was sheer panic. The look on her face was shock, and then pure amusement. She giggled, realizing what she had said, and how he had reacted. The emotion suddenly changed from irritation to pure amusement.

Aden, on the other hand, was not amused. He was panicked, as he thought "His *things* were falling out."

Gabe started laughing as he watched the memory play out, and I couldn't help but giggle too.

The other me, however, was laughing hysterically, and Aden now had her by the shoulders and was shaking her saying, "What did you say, Zoey?!" People danced around them and even bumped into them. Some even stopped to stare. The other me continued to laugh and Aden's face got redder and he continued to shake her.

The room began to blur and the dance started over. Gabe and I walked out, past a very busy Carl, and back into the hallway. Both of us were still snickering.

Gabe was talking as I locked the door. "I see what you mean about it being embarrassing. That was a terrible thing to do, ya know."

I turned around to face him. "I didn't mean to!" I laughed, "I was flustered!"

"What happened later?" he asked, soberingly.

I shook my head. "Well, I left him on the dance floor and went to go clean up the papers that had fallen out of his briefcase. Aden stomped out and didn't talk to me for a few days. When he did, there was a lot of yelling." I smiled, "It was kind of worth it."

Gabe shook his head at me, but he smiled. "You're devious."

"I am not."

***

We found ourselves in the living room again, sitting in front of the fire, bored and lost in our thoughts.

"We still have two floors in the West Wing and five floors in the

East Wing. We're bound to run into something that will get you outta here." he declared, breaking the silence.

"I kind of thought that last room might be the one," I said, thoughtfully. "I don't know why, wishful thinking I guess."

I had learned a lot about Gabe in the days that slowly passed. I felt we were getting close and gradually I began to trust he wasn't going to manipulate me. I believed he was really trying to help me. I just didn't know why.

Through his sharing of memories, I learned he was adopted, as well as his sister. His birth parents had been from Indiana and Anna, his sister's, adoption was from Romania. His adopted mother had been in an accident as a teen and it caused her to not be able to have children. He didn't elaborate on the accident, and I didn't pry.

He didn't go to college, but started the dojo instead. His father died shortly after that. His grandmother was deaf and he was fluent in American Sign language, and I learned he had a rottweiler named Skittles.

"Skittles huh?"

"Yeah, well, my sister named him."

"Him?"

"She was seven."

I just smiled, and he threw a pillow from the couch at me.

"What?" I asked, laughing.

I had also learned that Gabe had missed his father's death by moments. He had been in a quarrel with his fiancee when his mother called to tell him time was short. He tried to leave and go to his father, but Brianna didn't believe his excuse for leaving and thought he was making things up to get out of their discussion. He admitted that he had done that before. His father's illness had been an easy out.

"She just always wanted to talk about our problems, even if I didn't even think we had problems," he explained. "I just got tired of always fighting."

"If you don't mind me asking, What were your problems?"

Gabe sighed. "Mostly money. She didn't like the dojo and wanted me to get a 'real job.'"

"Don't you do well with the dojo?"

"I do now, but it wasn't always that way. I was just starting out and only had a few students in the after school program. I hadn't even started the fitness and self-defense classes yet. That came later."

"If you were so unhappy, why did you stay with her?"

Gabe laid back on the floor and looked up at the dome in the ceiling. "We'd dated since we were in high school. I loved her, I guess, or I loved the thought of what I wanted to have with her. Besides, everyone expected us to get married."

"Do you still feel bad about, well, missing your dad's passing?"

Gabe nodded. "I don't suppose he would have been coherent anyway, but I would've been... It would just have been nice to be able to say goodbye."

"I'm sorry."

Gabe nodded. He was quiet for a few minutes. "I found out she was pregnant with another man's child a week later."

"Oh my gosh!"

"Yeah, that was a rough year. I threw myself into the dojo and didn't do much else for a while. That was three years ago"

"Sounds familiar."

"How long has it been since Aden died?"

"It's been a year and two months."

"Wow, I didn't realize it had been that long."

"Yeah, well, I've been pretty screwed up," I admitted, picking at some imagined speck in the rug.

Gabe sat up. "Ya know, I hadn't even looked at another woman since Brianna and I broke up. I just didn't see the point. The dojo was doing good, I had my friends, my church, my mom and sister, I didn't feel like I needed to be in a relationship and well, nobody caught my eye, really. Until, well..." he glanced up at me and seemed suddenly sheepish. "Well, there was one woman. Ah, nevermind."

I could see he didn't want to elaborate. I realized the words "there was one woman" sent a twinge of jealousy through me, so I had no desire to hear more details. I forced a smile of interest anyway. "And?" I prompted.

Gabe just shook his head. "Nah, nevermind."

I smiled at him, glad to change the subject. Gabe was a great guy, he deserved to be happy. I also realized that I was beginning to believe that he might not be a figure from my imagination after all. I didn't think I could just think up someone that amazing, someone so out of my league.

The heavy feeling of insecurity crept in and I knew I wasn't good enough for Gabe anyway. He had things together. He was ready to move on and begin again. I was stuck inside my head, literally. I was so messed up that I was in limbo, paralyzed. My mood was taking a dive and I sat quietly with my thoughts for a while, until he broke the silence.

"Let's do something fun!" he blurted out.

"Like what?" I mumbled.

"If you could go anywhere, where would you go?"

I thought for a minute, "Ireland, Scotland, the Caribbean..." *anywhere but here, alone with you, feeling sorry for myself.*

"I think it may have to be somewhere you've been before."

"What are you talking about?"

He stood up and pointed over to a room on the other side of the living room. "That's just another empty room, right?"

"Yeah, I think so."

"So, where do you want to go?"

I slowly stood up, understanding. "Oh, I get it." The thought was intriguing. At least it would be different than sitting in the living room or walking through old memories. I just didn't know if I was in the mood to try and create someplace entertaining.

We walked up and stood in front of the last room on the balcony floor across from our bedrooms. We had opened it to see what was inside and were confident that this was just another blank room. I had been standing there thinking for several minutes and Gabe was impatiently watching me.

"You're making me nervous," I said sheepishly.

"Oh, sorry. What's wrong?"

"I don't know, I can't think of anywhere that would be good enough."

"Good enough for what?"

"Nothing, nevermind." I tried to think of all the theme parks I'd been to in Orlando when we first moved to Florida. I thought of all the rides and the shows and squeezed my eyes together in concentration. When I opened my eyes Gabe was looking at me with anticipation.

I opened the door and we peered in. It was no longer a room inside, but a doorway to a place outside; a giant theme park, or what used to be a grandiose park that had seen better days.

Directly over the threshold was a brick road lined with old rundown shops. Candy shops, bakeries and clothing boutiques, all having displays of cartoon characters and movie themes in their windows. The rooves had missing tiles and the roof gutters and window shutters hung at odd angles. The paint was faded and chipped. Beyond that was a castle that stretched high into the sky, overgrown with climbing vines and weeds. The portcullis was up and the place overall was uninviting and grayscale.

Towering roller coasters lined the landscape beyond that, silent and still. Thunder clouds threatened a storm above and the whole place smelled of rain and soil.

We could hear music playing. The song may have once been a happy tune, but it was playing too slowly and gave an ominous feel to the already gloomy place. The park was empty as far as we could see and nothing moved except leaves being blown in the wind and a creaking door swinging on its hinges. There hadn't been a soul there in years, or perhaps souls were the only thing there. It was eerie and bizarre.

Gabe looked at me and raised an eyebrow. "Haunted theme park?"

That embarrassed me and tears welled up in my eyes. The truth was I couldn't remember having fun in a long time. The only fun I could remember was playing pool in the game room off Gabe's room a few nights prior or playing with the orbs, or basketball with Gabe in the gym. I had gone to clubs and social events with Susanna, but I had been a fly on the wall. I lost myself when I was with Aden and I didn't know how to come back.

Life had been a struggle of carrying the guilt of Aden's death, and the overwhelming weight of insecurity. I dove into school, and bettering myself, and ignored anything that touched me.

Aden told me I needed to grow up. My childlike spark had died a long time ago and I surmised my imagination had gone with it. Looking out over my creation of "fun," I was gripped with shame, regret and loneliness, and now Gabe saw me for what I really was and I couldn't do anything about it. It seemed to me that this was more revealing than any memory room he had seen yet. My years with Aden planted a firm belief that there was something wrong with me, and looking out over the expanse of my park only further nailed the coffin shut on that.

"Let's go!" gushed Gabe, and he stepped to enter the park.

"Are you crazy?"

He looked at me, confused, and stopped. "Uhm." Then he noticed the tears in my eyes, looked around confused and put his hands on my shoulders. "What's wrong?" he asked, looking deep into my eyes. "Are you scared?"

I shook my head, not daring to speak, knowing my voice would squeak with the huge knot in my throat. I looked into the park and a tear escaped my lid and rolled down my face.

"Talk to me, Zoey. Why are you upset?"

Anger welled up inside me. That whole defense mechanism rearing its ugly head again. I glared at him and stepped out of his grasp. He let his arms fall, bewilderment etched in his features.

"I'm going to bed," was all I said, and I stomped off to my room. I didn't look back to see if he was mad, I just shut my door and sat down on my bed.

That room...that place...was a picture of me. It was desolate and sad. Lifeless and horrible. I was so ugly. Seeing that place that I had created made my heart sick. *That is who I am.*

I laid in my bed and felt sorry for myself until I finally fell asleep. Gabe never disturbed me.

I woke the next morning to sunlight shining brightly through my impossible window. I felt heavy and depressed. I wished I had a pill to make me feel better and tried, to no avail, to go back to sleep. My muscles ached and the wound on my side was oozing and sticking to the bandage. I ignored it. A small songbird sat near my window, singing loudly when Gabe finally came knocking on my door.

"Zoey? Are you okay?"

I groaned. "I'm fine!"

He came back a few hours later. "Zoey, can we talk?"

"Go away!"

"What did I do?"

"You didn't do anything! Go away!"

"I'm coming in, Zoey. I'm bored out of my mind, the mansion is dark and gloomy, the candles out here have all gone out and the fireplace won't light."

"It's the middle of the day!" I looked out my window and the light was shining brightly, to my dismay. I would have welcomed the gloom to match my mood.

"It's pitch black outside and frankly your house is freakin' dismal out here alone. It's depressing."

I got up and opened the door. Figaro jumped in past him and up onto my bed. Gabe stood holding the lantern, casting eerie shadows around the large room behind him. He looked sad and worried. He glanced past me into my brightly lit room and then back to the dark living room.

"Weird," he said, and then focussed on me. I must have looked a mess. "You okay?"

I shrugged.

"You hungry?"

I shrugged again.

"Come on." He took my hand and led me to the kitchen and sat me down at the table. Then he started ladling out chicken soup into a bowl with fresh slices of bread. I could see the yard behind the table was dark and gloomy, and a thick fog lay on the garden floor.

"I'm not sick, ya know," I said, picking at a large noodle with my spoon.

Gabe sighed, and sat down with his soup. He ate quietly while I sat there and watched. Lethargic.

He stopped eating and looked up at me. "I wonder why your room is bright and sunny, and the rest of the mansion is like this." he thumbed towards the window.

"Probably just to piss me off." I scoffed.

"Boy, aren't you a bundle of sunshine," he mumbled and went back to eating his soup.

For some reason, that struck me funny and to my own surprise, I giggled.

Gabe looked up at me, straight-faced, and blinked. I laughed a little harder. He raised an eyebrow, and put down his spoon, sitting back in his chair. I know he thought I was losing my mind. He just sat there and watched me crack up. His lip began to twitch on one side and he stifled a chuckle.

When I had composed myself he asked if I was okay.

I nodded. Feeling a bit lighter.

He pushed his dish back and put his forearms on the table, watching me worriedly, until I finally started eating. Then he got up and took his bowl to the dishwasher. He put his hands on the edge on the counter and spoke, facing the wall.

"You ready to talk?"

I took a deep breath and blew it out. "I'm sorry."

He turned around and leaned against the counter. He looked frustrated and tired; sighing. "What are you sorry for? I don't even know why you got so upset. I was about to step into the coolest place I'd ever seen and all of a sudden you implode and run off."

I looked at him like he was an alien. "That place is horrible!"

"Are you kidding me? That place looks awesome!"

Again, I stared. He stared back. After a few moments, he moved back over to the table with me and sat down. I poked at my soup.

"You didn't mean to make it a haunted theme park did you?"

I shook my head.

"What did you mean to make?"

I shook my head.

"Come on Zoey, talk to me."

I dropped my spoon and looked him in the eye, defiant. "A fun place, okay. A happy theme park with rides, and shops, and the happiest place on earth! Okay."

"And that's why you were upset? Because it didn't turn out right?"

"No!" I snapped. "I was upset because I can't make anything fun, because I'm not fun. I don't make things beautiful or happy. All the things I try to make beautiful are just me acting like I have it all together! Just like I did with Aden. I did it all right, acted right, said the right thing, wore the right clothes! I was still wrong, It's all a fake. I'm a fake! He didn't love me either way. *I* am a haunted theme park."

He mumbled something under his breath, but I didn't catch it.

"What?"

"Nothing. Listen, why does everything have to be beautiful? Why can't you just be you?"

"Gee, thanks!"

"Crap! That's not what I meant." He stood up and paced across the floor, obviously frustrated. "Why can't you get it through your head? Aden didn't love you because there was something wrong with him, not because there was something wrong with you!"

"He was a lawyer."

"Oh, that explains it." He looked at me incredulously. "What the heck does that have to do with anything, besides further proving he was a heartless jerk?"

"He was educated."

"He was an idiot."

He plopped himself back in his chair and crossed his arms. He tipped his head back and closed his eyes, sighing deeply.

I just sat there feeling small, vulnerable and frankly, like I was on trial.

He rubbed his eyebrow and calmly tried again. "What I am trying to say is that not everything has to be everyone's idea of beauty. Why can't mysterious be beautiful? Why can't you just be haunting? That's interesting! If I had met you when you were with Aden, I'd have probably thought you were a flake."

"You're kind of insulting when you try to be nice."

"Ugh! Can we please just go into the park now?"

"You really want to go in there?"

He grinned. "Oh yes."

"Fine, but it might be scary."

Still grinning.

"Can I get a shower first?"

He rolled his eyes. "Hurry up." he said, smirking.

I got up, put my bowl in the dishwasher and headed out of the kitchen.

"Oh and Zoey."

I turned to look at him.

"For the record, I think you're fun."

I don't think I smiled. I don't think I believed him, but it did make me feel a little better. I turned and walked out of the kitchen.

Chapter 15 Haunted

When I came back out of my room, Gabe was sitting in the living room. The candles were lit again and the fire was burning brightly, although the sun had not come up. When he saw me he grabbed the old lantern and bolted up the stairs to the door to the park. He was a kid in a toy store; giddy with excitement. I shook my head at him, I was willing to try this, but I didn't understand his enthusiasm.

He let me open the door and he stepped in, taking my hand as he did. I pushed the door shut as I entered. We stopped just inside and looked around. The silence was palpable save for the sporadic music that played from hidden speakers and a breeze that blew through the trees and buildings.

Gabe never let go of my hand and, for now, I was content to hold his. I was nervous like I'd be if I was going to watch a scary movie. I didn't necessarily feel unsafe, but I felt uneasy. Gabe, however, was a firecracker of energy, with permagrin.

I turned to look back towards the door. The door and the frame were there, right in the middle of the entrance of the park. Like someone had brought in a prop and left it there, an oddity in that space. Beyond the door, the park went back for as far as I could see. A line of ticket booths filled the foreground and then beyond that was a lake and forest in shades of gray.

The thunder clouds had cleared and the sky was bright, though gray, like a painting of a summer day done in black and white.

"You ready?" he asked. His voice seemed odd in the silence and as I looked up at him I realized he looked odd in that place. His complexion looked pink against the drab backdrop and his clothes were bright and colorful. He stuck out like a sore thumb.

I nodded.

We walked down the middle of the brick road, slowly taking in the macabre surroundings. As we passed the shops, we could see inside open doors and into large shop windows. They were dark and ominous.

We passed the hidden speakers along the way, usually in some kind of fake rock or tree stump; all playing the same tune a little too slowly, a little too quietly.

We came upon a candy store and Gabe stopped and turned to me smiling. "Ya wanna go inside?"

I gave him a look as if to say, "Are you sure it's a good idea?"

Apparently, looks don't communicate well, because he whooped out a "Yes!" and pulled me towards the candy shop.

We crept inside and I looked around while he fiddled with the lantern. There were large shelves that lined the walls. Each shelf was full of dusty old jars. The jars looked to me like medical specimens of black and gray substances. Upon closer examination, I could see they were full of old candies of all kinds. From chocolate kisses to jelly beans, all varying shades of black, white, and gray. The color was odd, not as if it was cast in shadow, but actually in grayscale, void of color like an old movie.

The display counter was dusty, as was the cash register and the shelf behind that. There were still bars of, what looked like, fudge, and cookies in the display counter. It was as if the employees just went home one day and no one ever returned.

I could hear Gabe mumbling frustration about a match as I walked along through the isles. They were only about four feet tall and filled with boxes of assorted candies, chocolates, and licorices.

"Finally!" he blurted, and stood up holding the lantern. Light flooded the room and everything it touched came into color. Not only color but life, newness. He turned around and I screamed. When the light hit the counter, I saw a man standing there. He was in a striped apron and he was smiling. Gabe froze, poised to defend.

"Good evening folks! What can I get for you?" asked the man behind the counter.

The shelves were a myriad of colors. The jars were clean and polished and full of fresh candies and treats. The room filled with sweet fragrances and the music caught up to the correct tempo.

Gabe held the lantern out in front of himself and moved over to me, neither of us acknowledging that the man had spoken and never took our eyes off of him.

As Gabe walked between the aisles, the light was blocked and the man disappeared, lost in shadow; the counter returning to black and gray.

Gabe looked at me. "What just happened?"

I pointed to the shelf where the light was shining. The candy labels were brightly colored and fresh looking. The shelf was free of dust and I could still smell chocolate where we stood.

"That's the coolest thing ever!" he gushed.

My heart was still pounding in my chest. "That was frightening."

Gabe smiled. "I'll protect you from the horrible candy man," he said, winking at me, and lifted the lantern.

I wanted to scoff at him, but I was too freaked out to have an attitude about his pseudo-macho behavior.

As the light lifted, the man reappeared behind the counter. He lifted his head and smiled warmly. "Oh, hello, Ms. Zoey. So nice to see you again. Was there something I could get for you? A marshmallow treat, or a chocolate-covered strawberry?

He looked friendly and unassuming. Just a man working in a candy shop. Nothing scary about him, except that he disappeared periodically. *I think I could go the rest of my life without seeing another person disappear at will. It's just not normal, or polite.* I thought.

We walked around the shelf and over to the counter.

Gabe looked at me for approval and I shrugged. Gabe smiled.

"I've never had a chocolate covered strawberry before!" Gabe answered.

"Ah, good choice Mr. Gabe, good choice." He handed Gabe the strawberry in a dainty little bag and Gabe handed me the lantern, lifting the berry to his mouth.

"Wait!" I said, clutching his arm. "Won't it be dark in your stomach. I mean, well, won't it be rotten in the dark?"

We both looked up at the shop keeper.

"I assure you they are fresh, made just this morning." he boasted, proudly.

Gabe hesitated. I watched as he mulled it over in his mind. Clearly he wanted the berry, but the thought of ingesting rotten fruit didn't sit well, considering the look on his face as he contemplated eating it.

"It'll be dark in my mouth, if it's bad I can spit it out!" he objected. Smiling, he bit into the large berry and closed his eyes with delight. Savoring the delicious treat.

The shopkeeper beamed. "See, Mr. Gabe, delicious!"

Gabe nodded, and I let out the breath I hadn't realized I'd been holding.

"Can I get something for you, Ms. Zoey?"

"Uhm, no thank you. I'm fine."

"Suit yourself." he replied, and began to wipe the spotless counter with a cloth and hum along to the happy tune.

Gabe finished the strawberry and we waved our goodbyes and walked back out into the street. I lowered the wick on the lantern so as to not use our fuel too quickly, and we began walking on towards the castle.

"That was the best thing I've ever eaten!" Gabe said, as we walked down the road that alternated from gray to red as the lantern swung.

"I thought you said red velvet cake with cream cheese frosting was the best thing you've ever eaten." I teased.

His eyes got big and he smiled at me. "Oh yeah!"

I laughed. I loved his childish pleasure in all things sweet, but I worried that he wouldn't be able to go back to his strict diet once he got out of here and I realized I might be beginning to believe he really was Gabe Kort from Pensacola.

"What are you gonna do when you get back to reality and can't have this stuff anymore?"

"I haven't died yet." he said, with a strange half-smile that didn't reach his eyes.

I stared at him, thinking that response was rather morbid. I felt bad that it was such a bitter subject to him. I guessed that going back to a sugar-free life was going to be difficult. I knew I couldn't do it, I had been fairly strict recently, but I'd have to live without my occasional danish. That wasn't gonna happen. I didn't realize he was that bitter about it though. *Touchy subject.*

We chatted as we walked and I found myself at ease among the drab backdrop. The lantern only lit a small portion of the road as we walked and caused the music to distort from too slow to unnervingly happy as we passed the hidden speakers along the path.

As we neared the castle we came to a fork in the road. The castle looked locked up tight so we decided to go left, towards a large roller coaster and a haunted maze.

We stepped through an arched walkway with broken light bulbs and missing letters. The "S" in "Snake" swayed upside down on the sign, making a sharp screeching sound as it swung in the breeze; a few other letters lay already on the ground. Vines, dried and gray, had grown up and overtaken much of the entranceway. The original pathways were overgrown with weeds. The smell of dust filled the air.

"This is so cool." Gabe said, grinning.

I had to admit, it had an intriguing quality to it. I felt a spark of curiosity; of childish wonder ignited within me and it felt good. I lifted the lantern and turned up the flame, shining it up at the sign and the entrance to the coaster. Colorful bulbs blinked over the archway and the word "Snake" was lit up in red. A plaster serpent coiled itself around the pillars and over the arch. It's gaping maw showed huge fangs and a green light glowed inside its throat.

I lowered the lantern and turned down the wick. The scene returned to drab, gray, and lifeless. The Snake's head had broken off and was lying on the ground near the left side pillar. Gabe was nudging it with his foot, trying to turn it over for a better look.

Next, we walked further along the road and came upon a haunted house. The sign above the door had said Chamber of … I couldn't make out the rest, but it looked like horrors. Through the doorway was an entrance to a large maze. I looked back at Gabe and he gave me a nod that seemed to say "let's do this." I just smirked and decided to go right.

I walked straight down a long hall. There were doors that lined the hall on each side. It reminded me of the halls in my mansion, but this hall was dark and had bloody handprints on the walls and fake spider webs throughout. A draft seeped in from somewhere and caused the webs to blow eerily and the floor would creak as we walked. At the end of the hall, I had to go left or right, so I went right. I came out of the first turn when I realized I had hit a dead-end and had to turn around, only to find Gabe right behind me looking up at something above.

"Oh sorry," I said, bumping into him, but his momentum had him tripping over me and I found myself between him and the wall, his arms bracing himself against the corner. I looked up and he smirked, but held my gaze maybe a little too long. I averted my eyes and he backed away, nervously.

"Sorry, uh, I wasn't paying attention." he turned away, blushing. He ran his hand through his hair and then pointed back the way we had come. "I, uh, saw a spot right back there that looked like it might open. Let's check that out."

"This is kinda fun, ya know. In a creepy sort of way."

He smiled, "I told you!"

We backtracked about ten feet and, just as Gabe had said, there was a section of the wall that had a seam and when he pushed, it came open to the inner workings of the maze. Gabe looked back and smiled, then walked in and held the door for me.

It was dark, and dust covered everything. Long desk control panels with switches, bulbs, and levers took up the majority of the front of the room. Two desk chairs sat pushed up under the desk. There was a large screen that covered the wall in front of the panel. It had a spiderweb shaped crack that split across the entire screen. It looked as though it had been hit with a sledgehammer.

Gabe took the lantern from me and turned up the wick. The room came to life with beeping noises and blinking lights. Two technicians sat in the chairs in front of the panel and watched all the screens that flashed different sections of the maze. The people on the screens crept through corridors and mirrored rooms, laughing and screaming. It was fascinating.

The two technicians would manipulate the maze by pulling levers and pressing buttons. They seemed to enjoy their jobs and would occasionally laugh at someone whom they had successfully frightened. Doors would open and either something would pop out and scare the passerby or there would be glowing eyes in the darkness of an open doorway. There was also a soundtrack playing scary noises and chilling music. After a few moments of watching, Gabe turned the lantern back down and we walked back out to the road, having never even been noticed by the two technicians, busy with their tasks.

We walked and talked for a long time. Gabe threw a baseball and knocked down all the bottles in a game called the "**Base all Hall of Fa e**", and I managed to do terribly at a ring toss game.

Gabe was chuckling at my disappointment. "The games are rigged Zo. You aren't supposed to win."

"You did," I grumbled.

"Well, yeah, but I've thrown a baseball before, and I knew how the game worked too." he explained. "You gotta hit the bottles at just the right spot. The ring toss is a different story and pretty much just a game of chance."

A little later we came across the Bumper Cars. There, we turned the lantern up as bright as possible and spent at least half an hour chasing each other around the big ring and bumping our cars into everything. I laughed more than I could remember laughing in a long time. We probably would have stayed longer but the lantern ran out of fuel and everything faded back to black, white, and lifeless.

My side was hurting where the bandage was. In the excitement of the game I hadn't felt it much, but now that it was over, it burned and felt bruised. Bumper cars probably aren't the most merciful game. I really hadn't realized how competitive I was, but Gabe brought it out in me.

Gabe maneuvered himself out from all the stopped bumper cars and hopped over the guardrail. I was leaning on the railing, poking at my side. He noticed me wince.

"Crap!" he spouted. Then gave me a look like it had been his fault. "Let me see."

He lifted my shirt just enough to see the wound and pulled the bandage away to look around it. "Yeah, it's bleeding, but not too badly. You wanna get going back?"

"Nah, It's not hurting that bad and I'm having fun."

He smiled at me and then gently pressed the bandage back down.

"I'm sorry. Bumper cars might have been a bad idea. I forgot about your…"

"I wanna go see what that huge building over there is." I spouted, and pointed down the lane.

Gabe looked up and then back to me. "Ice skating? Won't that just make it worse?"

"I haven't skated since I was a kid. It'll be fun."

Gabe nodded, "Yeah, I remember, the memory with your mom in that beautiful place with all the stars."

I beamed, and picked up my pace towards the giant building. Gabe had no trouble keeping up with my short legs.

At the end of the road was an enormous black stadium with an opaque dome at the top to let in light. It had glass entrance doors all along the front. Tattered flags flapped in the breeze from long poles that stuck out perpendicular to the building. A sign read "The Ice Palace Skating and Games" in huge letters above the entrance.

The glass was broken completely out of one of the entrance doors. The ticket booth had large metal shutters that were pulled down and padlocked, and there was a "closed " sign in the window.

We went in.

All around the inside wall of the enormous building were booths for food vendors. Dull gray signs read Elephant Ears, Ice Cream, Hotdogs, and all kinds of carnival fare. They were covered in cob-webs and dust.

Between the rink and the vendors were rows and rows of benches for people to sit and put on their skates. There were also areas with tables for eating and socializing. On the far end was a large arched doorway that said Arcade Room. I could just make out the shape of an arcade game inside the doorway. The rest was lost in the darkness

The rink itself was set up for hockey and had a high plexiglass wall all around it, with gates on either side. A big scoreboard came down from the middle of the ceiling and a big Zamboni was parked off to the far end of the rink.

The plexiglass dome at the top gave the expanse enough light that everything except the game room was visible, although drab.

There was a long booth for skate rentals with a counter where the salesperson would stand. Gabe hopped over the counter and asked my size. There were shelves and shelves of all sizes of skates. He soon returned with a pair for each of us. We sat on a bench and laced up.

I laced my skates up tightly, excited to get onto the ice. I hadn't ice skated since I was a child and was anxious to try my skills. Maybe it would be like riding a bike, or maybe I'd break my arm.

I had good memories connected to the sport; memories with my family on a shallow lake that froze over every winter in Northern California. Gabe and I had observed the memory a few days prior. In the memory it had been nighttime and I was about ten years old. It probably hadn't been all that late considering it was winter. The stars were shining brightly and casting their sparkle on the frozen lake. My mother had been there, all bundled up, watching me skate. It had been a beautiful memory. Gabe had left me alone after the first play through and I stayed and watched it play over and over, just so I could spend time with my mother.

I opened the gate and stepped down onto the ice, letting the gate slam behind me. The loud "bang" echoed through the expanse of the large building, unnerving and loud. I looked back at Gabe and grimaced. He casually looked up from lacing his skates and shook his head at my response.

I skated out to the middle of the rink to test my skills a bit. I skated in a circle and then did a spin and stopped. I smiled in spite of myself. *Like riding a bike,* I thought.

I didn't know the technical terms for the spins, or for coming out of a spin, I was just having fun.

"What's taking you so long?!" I yelled to Gabe. The space was so large it almost seemed to swallow up my words. I barely heard Gabe's response.

"I... these... too small... another pair." He pointed back to the rental counter.

"Hurry up!" I yelled.

I decided to get up some speed and take a good lap around the rink. After my first lap around the rink, I turned my body so that I was now going backward; surprised that I could still do it without falling. The wind blew my hair in my face and stung my skin, exhilarating. I felt like a child again. I could almost picture my mother standing across the ice watching me.

I was coming around by the gate on my third lap, backward, trying to peer over the divider to see what was keeping Gabe, when my foot struck something and I fell. I hit hard on my butt and then my momentum flattened me on my back, coming down hard, I hit my head. Then I slid across the ice till I finally came to a stop.

I laid there with my eyes closed, hands on my aching head and my knees pulled up. My tailbone ached and I was sure that I had split the wound in my side wide open this time. I could hear Gabe skating up next to me. I just laid there waiting for the pain to subside.

"Always so clumsy, sweetheart. Tisk tisk tisk."

My eyes flew open! That wasn't Gabe's voice!

It was Aden's.

Aden stood over me with his arms crossed in front of him. "Who's the other man, Zoey? I always knew there was another! Who is he?"

His face was destroyed on one side. There were pieces of bark and glass embedded in his skin on his left side and he was missing an eye. His left arm was broken and cocked at an odd angle right below the shoulder. What looked like oil dripped from his chin and made tiny puddles on the ice.

I quickly sat up and tried my best to wiggle away from him, stealing a glance over my shoulder. Where was Gabe? My head throbbed.

I caught a glimpse of Gabe by the gate, he was yelling incoherently and banging on the plexiglass. My ears rang loudly and I couldn't hear what he was saying. He ran towards the gate.

There in front of the gate stood the Jester, leaning against it and laughing. The Wild Card was guarding the gate on the other side of the rink.

I was alone. Helpless.

Aden stepped forward and grabbed my wrist. I resisted, but he was too strong, impossibly strong. Then, from somewhere in his chest, he pulled out a chain and manacle and clasped it on my wrist. Black blood coated the length of the chain in sticky repulsive goo. Like congealed rotting blood.

He pulled me to my feet and slapped me hard in the face, just like he had the night he left. "You made me do it, Zoey, You made me do it." My vision blurred and stars danced before my eyes.

"Aden, please." I cried, pulling away from him, but again he was too strong and he clamped another oozing chain to my other wrist.

"Unchained hearts." he chortled and then laughed loudly.

Gabe had gone to the gate and was kicking and shoving against it, trying to push it open, but the Jester was leaning against it, laughing. Gabe ran around the outside of the rink and was trying to break the plexiglass with the blade of his skate. He was yelling, but I couldn't make out what he was saying.

"We're going home, Zoey!" Aden snapped. "You'll get back to your place and we'll be happy again." He began to pull me across the ice towards the Wild Card's exit.

"Gabe!" I yelled. "Help!"

Aden turned and hit me again. "You two-timing whore!" Then he pulled another chain from his chest and clamped it around my neck. The iron was cold and bit into my skin. He began to pull me along again, the bone in his arm grinding with the effort. Black blood ran freely down his tattered shirt and left a trail on the ice.

"Aden, it's not like that," I pleaded. "He is a friend, that's all."

I didn't know what to say. I was defenseless, completely disarmed. He was too impossibly strong for me to resist. My head ached and my eye was beginning to swell. He was going to kill me.

Aden yanked me forward and I fell to the floor. Sprawled out on my hands and knees. I struggled to get back up, only to fall again with each yank of the chains. The cold bit into my raw skin.

Where was Gabe?

Then I remembered, *I'm not alone*, and I cried out to Jace.

"Jace! Where are you? Are you here?"

The room exploded with light and color, and there, a few feet away, stood Jace. He was majestic and kingly. He wore a crown and a white suit.

"I am!"

Light flooded from him and grew outwards, covering everything in brilliant newness and color.

Aden was no longer a torn, rotting man. In the light of truth, he was a boy; a teen boy. He had pimples on his face and he was skinny. He wore large rimmed glasses and he had a bloody, swollen lip. He still had the chains in his chest, but his expression was fearful and lost.

Gabe was pressing his hands against the glass, watching in awe. The Jester and the Wild Card were still guarding the gates, acting bored.

Aden sat down on the ice and was mumbling something about not wanting to play sports. "Mom, tell Dad I'm just not good at base-ball, I wanna read. Please don't let him hit me again. Please, Momma."

I pulled on the chains that had gone slack. I was still connected to Aden's chest. Aden was a whimpering teen, sitting on the floor, crying. The chains were red with blood and pulled at his rib cage as he breathed. Disgust rippled through me and I gagged, dropping the chains, they clinked on the floor.

"Jace, please, set me free."

"I have already given you the keys to your chains, Zoey. I bought them for you at the cross. Use them."

Gabe was pounding at the plexiglass again, but I still couldn't make out what he was saying. He was miming something behind the glass and pointing to his heart. Then he held up his fist and opened his hand. "Let go," he mimed.

I looked down at my hands and I wasn't holding the chain. "What does he mean 'let go'?"

I looked over at Jace and he stood there in all his glory, hands to his sides, waiting. Then I saw them, the scars on his wrists and his forehead. My mind suddenly had a picture of Christ on the cross. Jace, Ja-Ce. JC! I remembered. I had been in Sunday School and the teacher had written the initials JC. I didn't know what initials were, so I read it as Jace.

Jesus Christ. *Jace is The Christ.*

My eyes flew wide and I understood. *What did Jace, Jesus, buy for me at the cross? Forgiveness.*

I looked at him and he smiled, nodding to me in approval.

"I forgive him!" I yelled.

The chain from my neck fell away.

"I forgive him!" I yelled again.

The chain from my wrist fell away.

Aden looked up and pleaded with me. "Zoey, don't let me go. We can be happy. Just get back to your place, be a good wife."

He was a man again and he was pleading with me, arms stretched out, beckoning me to come to him. His face was handsome again and I remembered how I felt before he had changed, when I believed he cared about me. How I loved him. He reached for me and I hesitated.

I was distracted by loud banging and looked to see Gabe pounding on the glass once again. He was shaking his head and yelling incoherently.

I looked back to Jace and then to Aden. His cruel eyes glared at me with complete disgust and hatred. Then his face became askew; a mask began to slip, like a morbid overlay of someone else's skin. He smiled morbidly and I could see his teeth, sharp and pointed. Then he reached up and pulled the mask off, laughing; a mocking, sick laugh.

"You're an idiot, Zoey." he spat, and held the mask up in his fist, blood dripped from it onto the ice. "You're never gonna be free of *this* demon. HAHAHA. He's a dead man; still pulling the shots! You worthless moron."

My stomach rolled over and I thought I'd be sick. But even seeing the mask come off, I still believed him; all the things Aden had said over the years, over and over, reverberated in my mind. *I can't have an original thought, I am stupid, who is going to love me? I can't do anything right, I'm such a klutz. There is something wrong with me. I am worthless.*

I looked up at Jace and he shook his head. Kindness radiated from him.

"I gave my life for you Zoey. You are priceless."

Gabe had run over to the other gate and had finally wrenched it open. The Wild Card growled and lowered his huge muzzle, ready to pounce on Gabe. Gabe stopped and faced the demon dog, looked it in the eye, and pointed. "Sit!" he yelled. I think all of us, except Jace, were astonished, when the dog sat, whimpering. Then Gabe was running to me, slipping and struggling to keep his balance on the ice.

I looked to the Jester who was sitting on the floor, nonchalantly yanking on his end of the last chain, pulling it from himself, just to watch the blood spurt from his chest with each pull. He looked bored. I gagged again.

I looked back at Jace and made my decision. I set aside my repulsion, it wasn't the Jester I was giving it to. It was Aden.

"I forgive him." I whispered.

The chain fell away from me and the Jester cursed me with a sneer. He got up, turned his back to me, and walked over to the Wild Card. "Stupid mutt!" he spat, and then kicked the dog.

The Wild Card yelped and then bit angrily at the Jester, growling like a psychotic beast. Then they both disappeared.

Just then Gabe reached me and pulled me up and into a tight hug, I winced at the pain in my side. He spoke in my ear. "I'm sorry, I couldn't get to you."

I held him tightly, he was holding me up. My legs were shaking and felt like jello. Laying my head against his chest I looked over to Jace. He nodded to me and faded away.

"Wait!" I yelled, pulling away from Gabe. "Don't leave me!"

"I will never leave you, Zoey." I heard him say, and then the stadium was silent once more.

I wrapped myself back into Gabe's embrace and stood there for a long moment with my eyes closed. When I pulled away and looked up at him he was gazing at me tenderly. He ran his hand through my hair, and grimaced at my swollen eye.

"Are you okay?

I nodded. "I will be."

As we stood there in each other's arms we began to hear noises, voices; music. Looking around we realized we were not alone. The stadium was filled with light, color and sound. Skaters chatted and spun around us on the ice and the air was filled with the aroma of corn dogs, popcorn, and fried funnel cakes. Children giggled as they passed.

"Two little lovebirds sitting in a tree…" they chanted and pointed.

I chuckled and pulled out of Gabe's embrace. He smiled at me and took my hand as we walked off the ice. "Let's go home."

I nodded.

We found our shoes and left through the now intact, glass doors in the front of the building. Outside, we were bathed in sunlight and warmth, the sky was a wash of orange and red in the coming sunset. The street was teeming with life. Brightly colored birds were singing in the trees, and everything looked clean and new. The grass was manicured. Flowers, every shade of the rainbow, bloomed, and the topiaries were trimmed in shapes of whimsical animals.

There were people everywhere. All nationalities, all ages, walking, talking, laughing; full of life.

The aroma of roasting meat and baked goods filled the air, and my stomach growled loudly. The sound attracted Gabe's attention and he turned to look at me. He grimaced again at the sight of my swollen eye and he reached out to touch it gingerly.

"Does it hurt?" he asked, still touching the side of my face.

"A little." I whispered. Closing my eyes against his touch.

His lips pressed to mine and his hand moved to cradle the back of my neck. My pulse quickened and I breathed in his scent. My hands made fists in the back of his shirt and I stood on my toes. The world around us seemed to disappear as his lips moved with mine. I was surprised to realize that I felt safe.

Fireworks exploded above our heads and I felt Gabe's mouth smile against mine and he slowly backed away. He was laughing softly.

Insecurity welled up in me and I suddenly felt shy, I'd done something wrong. I backed away and his arms loosened around me, but he didn't let go. Fireworks popped in the sky and rained color everywhere. People all around us stopped to watch the show.

"What's funny?" I asked, trying not to let the hurt show in my voice.

He blushed, and ran his thumb along my jaw. Then he pointed to the sky. "I uh… I think I did that."

I looked up, trying to understand what he was talking about.

"The fireworks?"

He nodded, smiling sheepishly. "Your lips taste sweet." He ran his thumb over my lips and looked into my eyes tenderly. "It struck me, you could be the one sweet thing in my life that wouldn't kill me, and well, It was just such a perfect moment, I..." He was smiling, but there was a sadness in his eyes that I didn't understand.

"You want me in your life?"

"Very much… I..."

I threw my arms around him, ignoring the pain in my side, and kissed him again. He braced himself from tripping backward, and then wrapped his arms around me firmly, stifling what it was he was going to say. The fireworks blazed above us and the crescendo of the 1812 Overture played loudly through the speakers. I laughed in spite of myself at the wonderfully ridiculous gesture, as confetti began to fall from the sky and all over everything.

He pulled away to look at me and smiled. He had confetti in his eyelashes. He kissed my forehead and rested his forehead against mine.

"You have no idea how long I've wanted to kiss you." he whispered. "You caught my eye the day you walked into my dojo."

I looked up into his eyes. "Me?"

He nodded.

I smiled sheepishly. "I've been jealous of myself."

"I'm sorry I never told you. You seemed so unapproachable, and you still wore your ring...I..."

"It's okay. I wasn't ready anyway."

"Are you ready now?"

"I want to be."

"That's enough for me." He wrapped me in his arms again and the world passed around us, unnoticed.

Chapter 16 Freak Out

The next day I woke up late, or at least I believed it was supposed to be late, so it was. The sun shone brightly through my impossible window and Figaro purred softly beside me.

I sat up and stretched, my breath catching with the pain at my side. I groaned and turned to look at it. Gabe had rebandaged it the night before, but for some reason, it didn't seem to be healing. It didn't seem to be infected anymore, just an open wound. I figured I'd been in this place for about a week now, it should be healing. I wondered what it meant.

Then I heard Jace's voice in my mind. *"Some scars are worth the sacrifice."*

Well, that didn't make sense.

"What sacrifice?" I questioned, but heard nothing in response. That was frustrating. Maybe I wasn't listening. I concentrated...Nothing.

"Jace?"

Silence.

What sacrifice? Was he talking about his sacrifice? Was I going to have to make a sacrifice?

I thought of my dad, wondering where he might be. I wondered if he might be hurt somewhere and I wasn't there for him. I couldn't bear the thought of anything happening to him. I had already lost Mom. Tears welled up in my eyes at the thought.

I got up with renewed resolve. I was going to find the door to get us out of there. Gabe deserved to be free and so did I.

Gabe.

The thought of him made my stomach flutter with butterflies and I smiled in spite of myself. I was surprised at how anxious I was to see him; to be in his arms again. And then, of course, the insecurity hit. What if he was just caught up in the moment? What if he just wants to keep it casual? Maybe he doesn't feel the same way I do. But he said he wanted me in his life, then again, so had Aden.

My butterflies turned to anxiety and my stomach felt sick. I wasn't ready for this after all. I didn't want to be that one chick that was always "working on the relationship" and drilling him with questions because of my insecurity. It wasn't right to put Gabe through that. He needed someone who could love him without drama, without hesitation. I didn't want to be another Brianna to him.

The fact was, I did love him, I adored him. He was kind and patient. He was gorgeous and athletic. He had helped me without complaining. He never even talked about going home.

Wait! He had spoken about getting me home, but had he spoken about getting home himself? My heart was pounding and my breaths were coming faster. My head hurt.

I stopped brushing my hair and concentrated, leaning on the vanity. *Had he even mentioned going home; what he was going to do when he got home?*

I felt sick at the realization. He really was a figment of my imagination. I had fallen in love with the perfect man because he wasn't real.

"Oh my god, I'm crazy!"

I stood staring at myself in the mirror wondering what to do now. *I'm in control of my mind, therefore I should be able to make him leave. If he isn't real, then he'll be gone when I go out there.* The me in the mirror had a stupid look of deep concentration.

How do people do it in dreams? It's gotta be like that. When I realize I'm dreaming, I become in control, right?

I paced back and forth in the bathroom. *He is gone…. NOW!* I willed it to be.

"But I don't want him to go." Tears welled up in my eyes once more.

There was a knock at the door.

"Zoey, are you up?"

I didn't answer. I stood against the vanity clutching my hairbrush. *What did it mean? Is he real? Or do I just not really want him to leave? I don't want him to leave. I want to stay here with him.*

Another Knock.

"Zoey, are you okay?"

I'm in a coma, that's what it is. I can't control my mind because it's a protective mechanism. I'm dying. I slumped down to the floor with my knees up, still clutching the brush. *That's stupid, why would I be in a coma?* The house began to shake as confusion racked my mind and I felt on the verge of losing it completely.

Jace brought him here. If he isn't real, then I can't trust Jace. I'm alone.

I dropped the brush and made fists in my hair. My makeup and hair products began to fall off the countertop, rattled to the floor. Figaro pawed at the door and meowed loudly.

The knocking on the door was getting more intense.

"Zoey, What's wrong?"

He rattled the doorknob.

"Zoey, let me in. What's going on? Are you okay? Why are you anxious? Zoey! Talk to me!"

"Go away! You're not real!"

"Crap! Zoey, not this again. I'm real."

There was a scratching sound and a thump on the door. I imagined he slid down the door and was leaning his head against it. Figaro was meowing loudly and pawing at the knob. The house continued to shake.

I don't know how long I sat there, breathing in and out; trying to stop the anxiety. Going through the steps that my therapist had encouraged me to do, I tried to go to a happy place in my mind. That was just confusing, considering… I did the breathing exercises and tried to relax my muscles. I unknotted my fists from my hair and felt my blood pulsating in my scalp. Eventually, the house stilled and my heart went back to a normal rhythm.

Gabe had said nothing, and Figaro had given up on getting out and was bathing herself on my bed.

I got up and washed my face. My eyes were puffy and red from crying, on top of a slightly black eye from the night before.

The bathroom was riddled with make-up and hair paraphernalia. I didn't care, it would be there for me to clean up later, or maybe it would clean itself up. Who knew? Who cared? For now, I needed to figure this out.

I questioned myself, wondering if it even mattered if he was just my imagination. This *place* isn't real, Why should it matter if he is real? I can deal with my sanity when I get out of here, maybe I *should* be in a mental hospital anyway.

Chapter 17 Fade Out

Gabe was sitting in the door frame when I finally opened the door. He looked up at me and I thought I saw fear in his eyes, certainly sadness, but perhaps something else.

Figaro made her break for it and promptly ran past Gabe and down the stairs.

Gabe stood and took me in his arms and held me for a long moment. He was holding me tightly, almost desperately it seemed. He pulled back and held me at arm's length, looking into my eyes. His expression was sad and worried.

"I'm okay," I whispered.

His brow furrowed and he frowned. My stomach turned.

"We need to talk," he said, taking my hand and leading me down to the living room.

From the ballroom a song, I'd only heard once, began to play. Lost Boy*[1]; a mournful melody. I could hear a beautiful voice singing the words and wondered if this song was from me, or from him. I looked up at Gabe.

He didn't seem angry, just resigned. My mind reeled. I wondered if he realized that I wasn't ready for this. I wondered if he was tired of my drama, my panic, and fear. Maybe my attempts at pushing him out were working in a different way, which meant he wasn't real... or did it??

"Run run lost boy, they said to me, far away from reality"... The words to the song flowed from the ballroom, clear and poignant.

I didn't want him to go. I'd stay there forever if it meant we could

---

[1] Lost Boy, by Ruth B.

be together. I had changed my mind. I didn't want to push him out! I didn't care if he was real.

I stopped on the stairs. "I don't care if you're real!" I yelled in desperation to get my thoughts out. He turned to look at me. He was confused, so I continued. "I'm stuck in here and I don't want to be alone, and if that makes me crazy, well… Who's gonna know? Right?"

I giggled nervously and a tear ran down my face. I pleaded with him with my eyes, begging him to understand, to give me a chance, to love me, to accept me as I was; broken.

"Please, just let me explain." he pleaded, leading me the rest of the way down the stairs.

We reached the living room and I sat down on the couch, lethargic, confused, panic-stricken. My insides were shaking and I felt sick. He was going to leave me.

I pulled my knees up to my chest and hugged them to myself. I was preparing myself for the pain that I knew was coming.

"Zoey, I'm real."

I watched him pace the room, running his hand through his hair, deep in thought.

"This would be so much easier if I weren't," he mumbled, and then looked at me. "You're gonna be okay. You're strong and smart, and you aren't alone."

"What are you doing Gabe?" I pleaded. "Don't do this."

"Zoey, I…"

"I'm sorry!" I interrupted.

He stopped to look at me, confusion etched on his face. "What? Why? You have nothing to be sorry about."

"Then what is this about? I must have done something wrong."

He sighed loudly and looked like he wanted desperately to say something, but the words wouldn't come. Then he paced the room again.

I knew the break up was coming. I'd seen it enough times, heard all the lines, I had used all the lines. It always hurt, but I didn't think it had ever hurt this bad. I realized that this time I had actually believed he loved me, and that hurt far worse than being rejected. It hurt far worse than someone growing tired of me or me growing bored of them. This hurt more than manipulation, this was rejection. He had seen me for who I really was at my core, more than anyone, and yet he was still finding reason to reject me.

I figured I'd make it easier by breaking the ice. Easier on him, easier on me. Cut it off clean and send him on his way. If he was just my imagination then I'd deal with it with my therapist. If he had been real, well, I'd never had to see him again. I stuffed my feelings down and faced it head-on.

"You've changed your mind," I said matter-of-factly and without expression.

He stared at me, sadness etched in his expression. He tried to shake his head, but I knew it wasn't genuine. He was trying to be gentle. I was getting angry, but maybe I owed him a moment to explain himself. *He'd better be quick about it.*

"I was wrong to ask you to be in my life, Zoey. I…"

I sat up and glared at him, opening my mouth to speak, but he stopped me.

"Let me explain!" he said so sternly that I paused. He took a deep breath and relaxed, mentally preparing himself to rip my heart out, apparently. I waited with my arms crossed, never dropping my death glare.

"I love you, Zoey," he said softly.

I stood up and pointed at him. "Don't you dare…" I seethed. "Get out!"

Gabe gasped, and put up his hand, as to stop me, but I flinched. He backed away, quickly. A look of shock on his face.

"Zoey, you know I'd never hurt you."

"You are hurting me!" I whined. "What's wrong with me?! Huh? Am I too much trouble, is that it?"

"No, that's not it at all. I'm telling you the truth. I am in love with you, Zoey. I…"

"Don't try that with me! You, of all people, know you can't do that to me! Get out!" I screamed.

"I'm dying!" he confessed.

I froze. Completely dumbfounded. His expression didn't change. The sadness in his eyes wasn't deception, he looked into my eyes, pleading with his. There was the punch in the gut I was waiting for, but it came in a different package. It wasn't rejection. It was loss, grief, unbelief.

"What?" was all I could say.

He closed the gap between us in a split second and tried to take me in his arms. I stopped him at arm's length and stared.

"I'm sorry I didn't tell you," he whispered.

"No." I sobbed.

"I'm in the hospital, or my body is… or was." The sadness in his eyes was intense as he explained.

"The night I got here was the night the doctor sedated me. The pain had become so bad, and they were hoping I'd be able to get through the infection in my kidney, the other one has already stopped working altogether. I have become immune to many of the antibiotics they've used." His eyes searched mine, looking for understanding. "You see, I need a new kidney. The doctors say it's stage four renal failure."

He paced away from me when he turned back around there were tears in his eyes. He was becoming pale, almost translucent. I stared, horrified; transfixed.

"I had a dream I was falling into my grave. I actually thought that I'd died. That this…" he motioned to the room, "Might be some sort of purgatory or some sort of last test or something. The pain was gone."

I was speechless; standing there with my mouth open. He continued.

"Zoey, being in this place with you has been heaven for me. I've felt well, I was able to return to my exercises; it felt so good to stretch my body again. And the food, all the glorious food." he smiled in spite of himself. "It's been so long since I could eat without feeling sick, let alone enjoying sweets!"

My legs felt weak and I sat on the edge of the couch.

"I allowed the feelings of normalcy, of wellness, to cloud my judgment." he explained, "I'm not rejecting you. The truth is, I love you. I'm *in* love with you. I love that you're clumsy and graceful, I love your voice. You're beautiful, funny and feisty." He laughed softly and a tear fell over his lashes. "It breaks my heart to think I can't spend the rest of your life with you, but I'm so happy that I got to spend the last of mine with you."

He sat down beside me and gazed into my eyes, waiting for me to say something, anything. I was lost for words. I stared at him in utter shock, trying to think of a way to make the pain stop.

"Then stay here!" I spurted, desperately. I stood and pleaded with him. "Don't leave me."

He stood and calmly shook his head. "We both know that's not possible." He looked down at his hands. It was as if he knew he had been fading away. I wondered if he could feel it.

"Can't they do that dialysis thing?" My tears were flowing freely now and I didn't even care to wipe them away. I stood and took fistfuls of his shirt in my hands and put my head on his chest, trying to hold him there. I wouldn't let him go. He wrapped me in his arms and spoke into my hair.

"I've been on dialysis for months. Paul told me you've not been to the dojo for a while. I've been gone too."

"It wasn't about your dad or your time in the hospital as a kid." I choked. "You couldn't do the hospital memory because you were afraid; afraid because you're dying."

Gabe nodded and closed his eyes, a tear rolled down his face and dripped onto my cheek.

I shook my head against his body. The guilt of not knowing, not being there for him, for missing out on what we might have had if I hadn't been so broken, settled in.

The music changed in the ballroom. Rihanna's song "Stay" played softly.

"My kidneys are dying. I have been on the donor's list for a while now, but even if I get a new one, I still have diabetes. No one wants to give a kidney to someone like me, who probably won't live anyway."

His body was trembling, just as mine was. "Don't go! I didn't mean it. I want you to stay." I pleaded.

"You'll be fine without me," He moved a stray curl from my face. " You have Jace, and he will never leave you. Remember that."

I could hear his heart racing and I opened my eyes, only to notice that I could see through him. I gasped and looked up into his eyes. He was breathing raggedly now and fear was written all over his face. But he held me in his trembling arms.

"Goodbye, Zoey," he whispered.

I stepped back, desperate to stop him. "I need you!"

He was almost invisible now, and my knees were too weak to hold me. I fell to the floor, weeping freely.

"You never needed me. I didn't once protect you. You are stronger than you know."

"You did protect me. You protected my heart!! Don't go…"

I heard his voice say, "I loved you even when you were a mess." Then he was gone.

Chapter 18 Alone

He faded away. He left me. The weight of what I had done washed over me, like waves on the shore; of sorrow and pain. I had successfully driven him out and now I was alone in this prison of mine. I had no idea how to get out and I didn't want to face the rooms alone or at all for that matter. The extent of my self-pity was pathetic. I'm glad there was no one to see me in that state.

Figaro took advantage of my seated posture and climbed into my lap, peddling her paws into my shirt. When she was satisfied that I was thoroughly kneaded, she laid down and purred.

"Hearts a Mess" by Gotye played in the ballroom, and my heart agreed.

Deep depression settled over me and I found I didn't care to get up; to even move from the floor. I leaned my head against the couch and cried until I had no more tears to cry, still, I stayed there. Eventually, I fell asleep.

When I woke up, I was laying on the rug with Figaro curled up against me. My muscles ached from sleeping on the floor. I sat up and stretched and another wave of loneliness washed over me; a small sob escaping as I breathed out. Figaro stretched and went off in the direction of her food dish.

I finally got up, moving slowly, and got a shower. I left the bedroom door open. Who was going to see me? I was alone, and couldn't handle the feeling of being anymore closed off than I already was.

Disturbed's rendition of "The Sound of Silence" played in the main hall, fueling my sadness. I was a mess.

The hot water soothed my sore muscles and I stayed in it for a long time. One cool thing about being in a fictional place is the hot water never runs out. I sat at the bottom of the shower and let the water run over me and wash away my pain, soothe me. I had cried all I could cry, now I was just going through the motions.

I dressed, brushed my hair and teeth, and stepped out onto the balcony to go to the kitchen. I figured coffee might help my mood, or at least give me some energy.

There, in the main living room, stood The Jester and his Wild Card. He smiled with those nasty teeth as the Wild Card growled his unearthly snarl. The Jester opened his mouth to say something, that I'm sure wasn't going to be great and encouraging, and I stopped him in his tracks.

"Shut it, Jester! I'm not in the mood. Get out!" I pointed to the door and waited.

The look on his face was almost comical as I'm sure, I caught him off guard. His mouth shut with an audible chomp and he looked a bit confused. Then he glared at me and opened his mouth to speak again. The tenacious jerk!

"Don't make me call Jace!" I threatened, crossing my arms in front of me.

This time he did speak and, being a lady, I refuse to repeat what he said. Let's just say it wasn't nice. But he left, pulling the whining devil dog behind him by the nape of his neck. I heard the door slam and the chandeliers made tinkly sounds as they swayed slightly.

I breathed a sigh of relief and held onto the banister to steady myself. My heart was ramming in my chest. The realization of what I had just done hit me and I started to laugh. I'd love to tell you that it was an innocent chuckle, but seriously, It was a burst of manic laughter that was just ugly.

I'd also love to tell you that I was glad that there was no one there to see that, but again, no. I turned to go to the kitchen once more, and there stood a man in a tailored suit. He was tall, immaculately dressed and groomed, and had a small, golden name tag pinned to his lapel. It read "Carl."

I screamed. "Carl, you scared the life out of me!"

His facial expression didn't change; he looked bored and incredibly snooty. "I assure you my Lady Zoey, I did not scare the life out of you."

He spoke in English accent and looked me up and down; disapprovingly.

"Your presence is being requested in the East Wing, room 502."

"What?" I asked, incredulously.

Carl sighed, closing his eyes impatiently. "Room 502, East Wing."

I stared at him in a daze. *Carl's telling me where to go now?*

"Carl, I'm not ready for another room right now, I…"

"This way my lady." He started walking towards the stairs, indifferent to my pleas.

"Seriously Carl! I'm not in the mood."

He kept walking. It occurred to me, this is my place. I didn't have to listen to Carl!

I turned around, intent on going back to my room. I took two steps back towards my room and the balcony changed directions. Carl stood in front of me again.

"This way, Ms. Zoey."

I turned around to look back and my room was behind me. I looked back at Carl. He held his hand out and beckoned me to walk that way. Then, he led the way once more. I looked back again, that was seriously messed up.

I turned around and ran back up the balcony towards my room, only to run smack dab into Carl. He was like a brick wall! I toppled over onto the floor and he just stood there like I'd never touched him.

"I grow weary of this game, Lady Zoey."

Something like that has a tendency to piss you off. It did. I stared at him thinking of all the ways I'd love to strangle that guy! "Carl!" I growled through gritted teeth, ready to give him a piece of my mind.

He didn't bother to help me up or even look at me. He simply said, "This way my Lady Zoey." and took off walking again.

I took a deep breath, picked myself up, and reluctantly followed Carl to room 502 E.

When we got there, the room stood ajar and golden light flooded out through the crack and into the dimly lit hallway. Carl stood by the door with his hands clasped in front of him.

That regal, pompous, butler, butthead!

I stood there looking at the door and then glared at Carl. He never said a word, just stood there staring into nothingness like a Royal Palace guard. I finally resigned myself to the inevitable, pushed open the door and went in, sighing audibly.

The light grew from the center of the room and began to take shape. I was standing in another movie theater lobby. This one, however, was modern and clean. A tall, lanky, pimply-faced teen stood behind the concession stand. His name tag, of course, read "Carl".

I leaned back out the door to see the butler Carl still standing in the hallway, ignoring me. I looked over to the concession stand and that Carl greeted me. His voice cracked and squeaked with all the charm of a teen boy in the throes of puberty.

"Hi, Zoey," he said shyly, with a little wave of his hand. "Uhm, can I get you a soda or some candy before your movie?" He pointed to the candy display under the glass. "It's free," he sang.

A deep feeling of dread settled over me. I politely declined and looked around for the entrance to the movie room. The lobby was big and empty. Large arcade games lined one wall and small tables sat in front of them. I spotted the door to the movie off to the left beyond the tables. The marquee read "He Loves Me Not."

Oh, this has got to be good. I thought, sarcastically.

The theater was, again, empty. I took a seat all the way at the back row of seats, with my back against the wall. I wasn't taking any chances with The Jester getting behind me this time.

Soon the lights dimmed and the movie began to play.

This movie began with a scene with my first boyfriend. His name was Danny, and he was so cute, or at least that is what the me on the screen was saying to a friend of mine, as we stood in front of our lockers at Pensacola High School. Danny walked up and began talking to the younger me. I had thought I was the luckiest sixteen-year-old girl in the world. Danny was a senior and I was a sopho-more. My friends had been so jealous.

The movie moved from scene to scene of different conversations I had had with Danny. He had been building up to his manipulation tactics, flattering me, and doing all he could to get me to give my-self to him. It was incredibly obvious to me as I sat there and watched, but I had been utterly caught up in it when I was sixteen. I had been crazy about him and he used me and then discarded me. He had been my first love and my first well, lover. I had been dev-astated at the time, but sitting in the theater it didn't really hurt to see him or this memory, I was over him.

The next short film began with another relationship. Corbin. I watched the screen and smiled at the young me and the young Corbin making eyes at each other, he had a great smile. The scenes on the screen brought up old memories, some happy and some melancholy. Then the scene changed and I watched Corbin and I argue and bicker at each other. He began to call me a tease and ac-cused me of manipulating our relationship to only my wants and needs. "What about my needs!" he was saying.

Soon another relationship played out and then another. Each of them ended when I had grown to believe I was being manipulated into an intimate relationship and I didn't feel comfortable. I began to doubt over and over that these guys ever cared about me. They only wanted to use me.

The next film was a boy named Keith who was a church kid. Keith had been different. He didn't want to have sex before marriage. I really believed he cared, until the moment came when he found out about my past. He couldn't forgive me for my past and not keeping myself "pure." "You should have saved yourself for your husband," he'd said. We ended badly.

The last film was about Aden. I watched him take me to parties and prance me around on his arm. He would buy me increasingly more sexy clothing to wear to parties and I began to feel more like his possession than his wife. If I didn't want to be intimate when he was in the mood, he would degrade me and his anger would get out of control.

The movie started over at the beginning and I sat there wondering what it was about. The movies didn't seem to correlate. I felt the emotions, but mostly I felt numb and confused.

"They never loved you, Moron!" said a deep voice off to my left.

The Jester was sitting a few seats down from me with his boots up on the chair in front of him. He looked like he had cleaned himself up and his handsome features were somehow softer, his eyes not so dark, his teeth, maybe not so sharp. There was no sign of the dog.

"You're a piece of meat!" He looked over at me with a bored expression and then back at the screen. He was simply stating facts. I didn't even feel afraid. That was new.

I stood up to walk out and he spoke again. "You're used up goods sweetheart. You got used up when you were five."

"Shut up, Jester!" I spat. "Jace already showed me the truth about that. You can't hurt me anymore. And this..." I pointed up to the screen. "This doesn't hurt either!"

"Oh no?" He put his feet down and leaned forward. "Then why didn't any of them love you? There's something wrong with ya. You're faulty."

Ouch! There it was. The pain that said he hit the nail on the mark. It must have shown on my face because he threw his head back and laughed.

"How's it feel now, Sweety?"

He was right. I didn't believe any of those men loved me. Cared maybe, but love? Not even Aden. I looked back through my mind to the first movie room and the molestation scene. That man was supposed to have cared about me, then Danny had said he loved me, then Corbin, then Keith, Timothy, then Allen, all the way to Aden. I had given myself away over and over, only to be used. They all got tired of me. Eventually, I had broken off every one of those relationships because I didn't believe they cared and they never had the courage to end it, so I did.

In each one of those relationships I had tried so hard to make them love me, and each one ended because I got tired of the fight.

I'm not lovable, there is something wrong with me.

"Ding ding ding! There she figured it out! Give the woman a prize!" the Jester yelled.

I glared at him with all the hate that fueled my anger, turned, and stomped out of the theater.

"Don't get mad at me, Cutey Pants," he yelled after me. "I'm just tryin' ta help ya." I heard him laughing all the way until I reached the lobby.

I reached the hallway and pulled the door shut behind me. Wouldn't you know it, the door wouldn't latch. I looked around for either of the Carls, but neither were anywhere to be found.

"Fantastic! Thanks for the help, Carl! So glad you're here when I need ya!!" I yelled into the distance.

I slammed the door over and over, trying to get it to latch, I couldn't lock it if it wouldn't latch. I tried lifting the knob, tried pushing down on it. Nothing, the door just swung back open each time I released it and I was left standing in the hallway with a thin line of light spilling through the crack. The hallway was otherwise dark.

The stream of profanity that came out of my mouth, as I slammed the door repeatedly, well, it would have made the burley Carl from the night club room blush.

"Carl!" I yelled. "Carl, come help me!"

Nothing.

As I stood there holding the door closed in the dark, the hall began to illuminate. Bright white light filled the space and I squinted, turning my head to look around behind me. I didn't let go of the knob.

Jace walked around to face me and placed his hand upon mine. "Only I can close this one, Zoey." His voice was comforting and kind.

I felt raw and exposed. I looked into his eyes and melted. My resolve died and the anger that fueled me and covered my pain melted away. I stared down at our hands, my heart breaking to pieces as the realization crashed down upon me, *I am not lovable, I am flawed.*

"When your innocence was taken as a child, a door was left open to your enemy," he explained. "He was then allowed to slip in a lie. That lie has been reiterated throughout your life."

"It doesn't feel like a lie, Jace. It's true." Tears streamed down my face and I finally let my hands drop from the doorknob.

"Those men all had a feeling of love for you, Zoey, but real love is to choose what is best for the person for whom you love and also for yourself," he explained, matter-of-factly. "Those men were not able to love you the way you needed to be loved. Not because there is something wrong with you, but because they themselves were wounded."

I looked up at him, and doubt filled my mind. I knew he was telling me the truth. I didn't think Jace would lie to me, but it didn't *feel* true. What felt true was that I was unlovable and wrong.

"You have been miraculously and wonderfully made. I knew you and loved you from before the foundations of the earth." He spoke with power and authority. Suddenly, I was in awe, and frankly terrified.

It wasn't a fear like the Jester brought however, it was more like I was standing before the maker of all time and space and he required my attention. I shook in complete overwhelming reverence of him.

"Remember Aden, when I revealed to you who he was in the ice rink?" he asked.

I nodded.

"I gave you a glimpse of his wounding as a teen. His father was a cruel man. He could never allow Aden to be who he wanted to be. He felt every mistake Aden made was a reflection of himself. Aden was abused, as was his father before him, and his father before him. Never allowing me to heal their wounds, the pattern continued."

I had known Aden's father. He was, in fact, a very mean man. Jace was making sense.

"You chose to give yourself away to men who did not know how to love you. You were manipulated and the lie was reiterated."

The truth settled over me like a warm blanket and I felt my heart begin to mend. "You're right. I believe you."

The door clicked shut, and I could hear what sounded like someone locking it from the inside. Jace smiled at me and the overwhelming fear abated, leaving only peace in my heart and in the room.

Sconces appeared along the walls of the hall, each glowing with yellow light.

"The truth has set you free," he said, smiling at me. Then, as before, he faded out of sight.

I was exhausted. I dragged myself to my room and went back to bed, sleeping soundly until morning. Honestly, it could have been five minutes for all I know. I'll never figure that time thing out.

The next day, I didn't even bother to get out of my pajamas. I was hungry and groggy, and frankly, worn out and lonely. I didn't want to think about Gabe, I didn't want to open any more doors. I Just wanted to get some coffee and breakfast, and do nothing.

I sat in the kitchen looking out the window and sipping my coffee. Cheese danishes were sitting on the counter when I arrived, as well as a fresh pot of coffee, and of course my vanilla creamer.

It was a beautiful day outside. The sun shone brightly and birds of all kinds sang a cacophony of tweets and whistles, that on any other day would have brought a smile to my face. Today, it was competitive noise. My nerves were shot, and I was irritable.

I finally got up, dumped the last of my coffee in the sink, and turned to set the mug on the counter.

Right behind me stood the butler, Carl, in all his haughty, pompous glory. I startled and dropped my mug on the floor. It broke into a million pieces.

Carl just looked at me and then to the mess on the floor. Unfazed and bored.

"The Master will see you now, Lady Zoey."

"The Master?"

His reply was drawn out and dripping with haughtiness. "Yes." he articulated, pausing for emphasis, pursing his thin lips together. "Please, follow me."

He waited for me to step over the glass and led me through the dining room into the living room. I wasn't even going to bother trying to argue this time.

I looked up to see that the double doors to the great hall were open and light flooded out like someone had somehow fitted the sun in there and it was burning to get out. The forbidden room, the locked door, finally accessible. Now I'd be able to see where the music had been coming from and to whom the voices belonged. I took a deep breath as nervousness settled over me.

He led me up the stairs, stepped aside the doors, and held out his hand, motioning for me to enter. I hesitated, and he gestured with his head that I should hurry up.

"We mustn't keep him waiting."

I stared at Carl for a moment and then slowly walked into the light.

Chapter 19 The Master

I stopped walking just inside the doorway to let my eyes adjust to the immense light. It engulfed me, surrounded me; living light. It was like warm water washing over me; peaceful and calming. It filled me with joy, not like I was giddy, more like I was filled with comfort. Like Christmas morning in a happy home. Like sitting in front of a fireplace on a cold day. Like falling in love; pure and beautiful. Tears ran down my face, I was completely undone in that moment.

I stood there, a fountain of tears, but I wasn't sad. It was the washing of my soul. I laughed between my sobs and wondered why I couldn't control myself. The light permeated my heart and burst through me like a new dawn over a mountain top. I had been an ugly emotional mess before, now I was a beautiful emotional mess. Like when the Grinch's heart grew five sizes that day, yeah, like that.

I looked around the room. Everyone I had ever known, anyone who ever had a role in my life was there. They mingled around the impossibly immense space. There were tables set up like a wedding venue with plates and drinks, and, of course, soft music was playing.

I saw my dad, my grandparents, Susanna, childhood friends, work associates, even Aden.

Then I saw Gabe. He was talking to someone and laughing his beautiful laugh, his eyes were happy, and my heart betrayed me, breaking a little more. No one saw me, they were just there, part of me; who I am. I knew he couldn't see me as I watched him, knew he wasn't real, only a memory. And I knew… Knew he had been real. Somehow he had been here with me, and I had sent him away.

I looked away and around the room again. My mother was there. She was young and happy. She didn't look broken and bruised. She was well. The tears came again and a sob escaped me as I watched her.

Then he called my name.

I turned and looked up. There, Jace sat atop a beautiful crystal throne at the center of the room. The light was radiating from him. He smiled at me. I think my heart burst into confetti and sparklers at that smile. And I smiled in return, sniffling and trying to compose myself.

"What is happening to me?" I asked, picking up a napkin from one of the tables and wiping my eyes.

"In my presence is fullness of joy." He wasn't bragging, he was just stating the truth.

When I didn't say anything else, he smiled and spoke again.

"Zoey, it's time to go home. You are ready."

I finished blowing my nose and felt ridiculous, barely able to control the endless stream of tears that ran down my face. My thoughts were a jumble of excitement and dread.

"But I have to, I'm not, I haven't opened all the rooms, I'm… "

"Not ready?" he asked, smiling.

I nodded, tears spilled over my lashes and ran down my face.

"You are ready Zoey. We can take care of other memories in time. I will always be with you, and you have learned to open your heart to me. I have healed you and strengthened you. You have learned the power of forgiveness, and I'm proud of you. You are ready."

"How can you be proud of me? I sobbed. "You did all the work." I laughed sardonically, feeling ashamed; unworthy.

"If my people only understood," he looked sad as he explained. "I bought your redemption at the cross. I have never asked you to get things right on your own, I never asked you to be worthy. You will be safe if you obey my commands, but I have *made* you worthy. I only ask that you trust me, that you give me permission to work in your life. The choice is yours."

He stood and slowly walked down to me. Standing in front of me, he took my hands, and his smile was so sincere and full of love. "You chose to trust me, and I am proud of you."

He turned and led me back towards the door. As we passed through the doorway to the hall, I noticed that the dome was completely open now and bright light shone down in rays of brilliant, warm yellow. The crystals on the candelabra sparkled like diamonds and scattered the light like prisms.

He led me down the stairs and through the tunnel. Carl stood holding the gate open and winked at me as I passed.

The entrance, sitting room had been repaired, cleaned, and organized. The candelabra was hung high in the dome there as well, and light danced around the room at it's bidding. The paint on the walls and door was still chipped in places, and the wallpaper was still torn and falling. There were still broken windows and the scent of lilies blew through as the curtains danced in the breeze.

He opened the front door and we stepped out. It was a beautiful spring day, just as it had been the day I arrived. Jace took my hands in his again and looked into my eyes. Oh, those ancient and magnificent eyes. They held time itself. Every moment, every breath, every thought, every life, was captured in those eyes. And that smile, I'd do anything for that smile.

He swept a piece of hair out of my face and put his hand on my shoulder. It felt like when my Pops would kneel down and talk with me as a child. I knew I was loved, I knew I was important, even if to only one person, and that was enough. He was enough.

"I will always be here, Zoey." he smiled. "I will never leave you."

He took his hand from my shoulder and I couldn't help but feel like I was losing someone. The tears came again. He wiped them away, and as he did, peace filled my heart.

"Gabe needs you now. You will be with me again someday; I will always be with you."

He turned me around to face the yard and there stood Carl, this time a tall limo driver in a smart polished suit. He bowed low to Jace and Jace smiled.

"Be kind Carl, she's been through a lot."

"Yes, Majesty," Carl replied sheepishly.

Carl put his hand on the small of my back and began to lead me away from the house. I looked back to see Jace watching us walk away. He smiled at me and walked back into the house.

Carl led me to the edge of the path that had led me to the mansion several days prior. A gunmetal gray limousine was parked there;

engine running. He opened the door and motioned for me to get in. "Help yourself to a beverage, Ms. Zoey," he said, closing the door.

Carl climbed into the driver's seat just as I was pouring a frappuccino into a glass. He rolled down the window behind the driver's seat and began a casual conversation. "Lovely day for a fall, isn't it Ms. Zoey?" he said, pulling out of the grounds of the manor and through the forest opposite the way I'd come in. He was going fast and picking up speed along the forest road.

"Do you mean it's a lovely Fall day? It's Spring!" I corrected. "Do we have to go so fast?"

The scenery was flying by in a blur and up ahead I could see we were quickly coming to a clearing. I set my drink in a cup holder and buckled my seat belt, pulling it snug, and then sat gripping the armrest tightly.

"Well, no. I suppose I could drive off the cliff slowly, but that just prolongs it, don't you think?" he explained, never taking his eyes off the dirt road.

We cleared the forest and were zooming past green pastures on either side. On both sides of the road, there were orange signs that read, "Danger, Bridge Out Ahead."

"Carl!" I yelled, losing all ability to remain calm. "What are you doing?! Where are you taking me?"

By now we were going at least eighty miles per hour and the signs were becoming more and more frequent. "Turn Around!" "Stop Now." "Danger Ravine Ahead."

"Ms. Zoey, how did you get here?" he asked, casually.

My demeanor was, shall we say, less than calm. My fingers were hurting from the death grip I had on the armrest and my heart was apparently trying to match speeds with the rushing scenery. I thought about what Carl had asked and wondered if he was really trying to have a casual conversation right now. Then I wondered if I really wanted to tell him I had fallen off a bridge running away from Aden, who was a Troll, into a void that wasn't really supposed to be there. Irritation got the best of me and I simply blurted an answer.

"You pushed me off a bridge," I yelled, and a squeal escaped me as well. I watched the ever-increasing amount of warning signs go past. We were still gaining speed. "Carl, you're making me pretty nervous. Could you please slow down?" I begged, pressing my foot on an imaginary brake pedal.

Carl laughed. "That's how you get out Ms. Zoey, the same way you got in. You fall," he explained, still laughing. Carl was having the time of his life. "Were almost there!"

"Jace said I had to open doors to get out." I was squealing, but panic made my ability to control my voice all but impossible.

"Jace meant you had to open the doors for him. You could have left at any time, but not if you wanted what you asked him for. You wanted to be healed. Now you wanna go home. This is how you get home." he explained, matter-of-factly. "Look! The cliff is right in front of us. It will all be over soon."

I looked out the window and, sure enough, the cliff loomed out in front of us like a gaping maw ready to swallow us up. We were going so fast now that I could barely read the signs as we passed. "Oh god, oh god, oh god! Carl, stop!" I screamed, and kept screaming as we went over the edge.

The world decelerated to slow motion. The car left the road; launched over the side and flew across the chasm for so long I had time to think about it. I could hear my scream in my ears like white noise, and I could see my frappuccino slowly come up out of the glass and form a blob of coffee in the air in front of me. I could also hear Carl laughing gleefully from the front of the car, like a sluggish record. He was still gripping the steering wheel like he could somehow steer us out of the fall.

Slowly the front of the car was pulled by gravity down into the ravine and I could see the ground coming up towards us, and just as we were going to be smashed to bits, I heard my scream in my ears and woke up in the forest.

Chapter 20 Back

I sat up, and the scream that woke me echoed through the forest against the mountains beyond. I was disoriented and again wondered why I had been leaning against the small side of a bridge in the middle of the forest. I put my hand on my chest, feeling my pounding heart, and realized I was still wearing the plastic necklace. The stick that had been my sword lay beside me. There was no troll, no chasm, nothing but a breeze and me, alone. The anxiety attack, caused by the Aden troll (my own imagination) actually *had* caused me to lose consciousness this time.

Maybe I hyperventilated? Huh, That was new.

I stood up, and for the first time since I had "left" my side wasn't hurting. I lifted my shirt and ran my hand over the place where the wound had been. There was nothing but smooth skin and my white shirt was free of blood. I pulled at my shirt and turned in circles trying, in vain, to see where the wound had been. I probably looked like a dog chasing his tail.

"HA! I like this shirt!" I smiled.

Suddenly, I remembered Jace's voice in my head. *"Some scars are worth the sacrifice."*

Gabe. Jace said Gabe needs me.

I took off running.

Chapter 21 Explanations

My Grams was just beginning to make dinner when I walked in. Pops was at the table talking with her as she peeled potatoes at the sink. Pops smiled, and his eyes lit up.

"Looks like a little nature did you some good. How ya feelin' Kid-do?" he asked, as Grams peeked around the wall at me, dripping water on the floor as she did.

"Uhm, Yeah, I feel great! I gotta go home!" I blurted.

There was a moment of silence while my grandparents took turns looking at me and then each other. Grams gave him that look that said *"You need to talk her down."*

Pops stood up slowly and scratched his beard. His look of concern irritated me a bit, but I was too excited to let it get to me.

"Zoey, Honey, Did you have another anxiety attack?" he asked, slowly walking towards me. "We can get through this, you don't have to rush back home. You're safe here. You know that."

I giggled. He stopped walking. Confusion replaced concern, and he looked back at Grams. I didn't mean to giggle, I was just happy. I hadn't had a purpose for a long time and I did know I was safe! I hadn't felt safe since Aden and I had gotten married. I was free.

Grams had turned off the water in the sink and was drying her hands as she joined Pops in the middle of the room to stare at me and then back at each other. They were at a loss, genuine concern written on their faces. They probably thought they'd be Baker-Acting me as they looked at me and then down at the big plastic jewel I still wore around my neck.

"I'm okay you guys," I said, motioning for them to sit.

"I did have another anxiety attack in the forest, but I'm okay; better than okay." They sat together hand in hand and listened as I told them I'd had some time alone in the forest. That I had prayed and found peace with some things I had been dealing with.

They both smiled and I could see the relief on their faces. Then I explained that I had gotten information from a friend that someone

I cared about was in the hospital. I wanted to get back to see if they were okay.

"I'm surprised you had any signal out in the forest." Grams was saying. I just kind of let her assume it had been a phone call.

They both had questions about my friend and what had happened. I didn't want to lie, but I didn't know how to tell them the truth either. I decided to keep it vague and excused myself to go pack.

I felt bad about leaving them so soon, but I had to get to Gabe. I got my ticket changed and I was on a plane home the next afternoon.

Chapter 22 Home

It wasn't hard to find the hospital Gabe was in. There are only three hospitals in town. The hard part was getting up the courage to go and see him. Maybe I was crazy, maybe I'd walk in his hospital room and he'd wonder what his student was doing visiting him at the hospital. That was kind of forward, wasn't it?

There goes that doubt again.

The decision was made for me, however, when I called and found out he was in intensive care. Family only.

Crap, what now?

I paced around my large house feeling uncomfortable and anxious. I looked around at the photos of Aden and I made the decision to pack them up and put them away. I was different now. I didn't need to hold on to him. I didn't hurt over him anymore. He was just a memory without the pain. I smiled, whispering a silent prayer of thanks.

I ran to Yum's Chinese for take out, and then picked up some packing boxes on the way home. I whiled away my evening packing away pictures and memorabilia of my life with Aden and tried to put Gabe out of my mind for a while, at least until I could figure out what to do about him. Then, I took my wedding rings from a drawer and put them in the boxes and put them all in the garage.

Cleaning and packing-up passed the time, but I had an anxiousness that would not be abated. I had to see Gabe. I had rushed home only to be stalled, and that was irritating me. I didn't know what to do. It was getting late and I decided there was nothing to do until morning, so I went to bed.

That night I had fitful rest. I had unremembered, fuzzy dreams and woke often, only to roll over and go back to more of the same. By the time early morning had come I was ready to get up, feeling awake and unrested. As I sat up in my bed, my thoughts were of Jace and Gabe. I was determined to see Gabe and called out to Jace in my mind. *"What do I do?"*

I didn't hear anything, but felt compelled to go to the hospital to see what would happen. I looked over at the red numbers on my alarm clock, and it read 6:05 am. I knew visiting hours weren't until eight o'clock.

I got up and made coffee and then sat down on the couch to check my Facebook and Instagram while I waited. I hadn't checked it in weeks. The notifications were obnoxiously full of memes and updates. Not much pertaining to me except a message from a friend in Burney whom I was supposed to have gotten ahold of whilst in Town.

Oops. I guess I'll deal with that later. Sorry Kimmy.

The house was uncomfortably quiet as my thoughts drifted, once again, to Gabe. I'd gotten used to the constant music that played in my mansion and realized that I almost always had music in the back of my thoughts. Brett Young's song "Would You Wait For Me" played through my mind and it felt right. I smiled in spite of myself.

I closed my eyes and tried to look back inside myself; to see Gabe, but it was all so blurry in my mind. My heart ached for him and I hoped beyond hope that it hadn't all been a dream. I hoped he knew me, remembered me. I hoped I wasn't crazy, but I couldn't bring myself to believe I was. I was brought out of my daydreams by the beeping of the coffee maker, and my hope grew into doubt, only to be exacerbated by the fact that I was out of creamer and had to drink my coffee black.

It was a quarter to eight when I handed my keys to the Valet at the hospital and walked through the main entrance doors. The volunteer at the information counter was a little old lady with a red crochet vest and a welcoming smile. Her name tag read "Phyllis."

"Good morning, young lady. How can I help you?" Her smile lingered as I collected my thoughts.

"Uhm, well I." I stammered. I took a deep breath and asked for Gabriel Kort, spelled with a K.

Phyllis looked down at her papers and ran her fingers down the page marked "K."

"Oh, I'm afraid he is in ICU," she said, looking up at me and blinked her wrinkled lids. "Are you family?"

Of course, I thought about lying, but I couldn't bring myself to do it. Too many unanswered questions. What if they asked for ID? What if his family was there with him? What would I say then?

I think I stood there thinking a moment too long. Phyllis repeated herself. "I say, are you family, young lady?"

"Oh, uhm, no. I'm not." I answered, feeling embarrassed and looking around me. I was the only person there. I found that comforting.

"Then, I'm afraid you will have to get permission from the family before you can go into the ICU." She said, slowly blinking again, she looked back down at the paper, running her bright red fingernail back over his name.

A handsome man wearing scrubs was walking by and stopped, looking down at Phyllis. "Oh yeah, that poor kid with the failing kidneys. Sure wish they could find him a donor." Then he shook his head in mock pity and winked at me.

I stared at him, confused until I saw his hospital badge. It said, "Carl Angelo."

My mouth flew open in shock, but before I could say anything he got on the elevator behind the information desk and was gone.

"Oh, yes. Of course." I stammered. "I uhm, forgot to mention that I am going to see if I am a donor match for Gabe, er, Mr. Kort." My heart pounded in my chest and suddenly it made sense. Gabe needed a kidney! The scar on my side. *"Some scars are worth the sacrifice."*

Phyllis' expression turned to pity. "Well, sweetheart, you are brave. You must be a close friend to be willing to be a kidney donor." She stood up and patted my arm with her own cold wrinkled hand. Then she gave me a paper for the Lab and gave me directions to get there.

It was all happening so fast I didn't have time to consider what was happening. All I could think was, *I can save Gabe!* My pace picked up and I soon found myself standing at the sign-in counter at the lab in the Nephrology/Urology Wing.

Alissa greeted me from behind the counter and held her hand out for the paper that Phyllis had given me. I handed it to her without a word. She looked at the paper and then up at me. A look of surprise on her face and then looked back down at the paper.

"Are you family?" she asked. The look of surprise quickly replaced by professionalism i.e. forced indifference.

"No, I'm a friend." I smiled nervously.

"What's your blood type?" she asked.

"Uhm, O positive."

She looked back down at the paper and then asked me to take a seat. Then she got up and left the room through a door behind her. I was left alone in a waiting room full of empty chairs and a TV playing The View. *They should call that show the chicken coop.* I thought, and took out my phone to find another way to waste time. I found I was too nervous to concentrate on anything anyway. Eventually, I ended up texting Dad to tell him I was back in town and I'd catch up with him in a few days. It wasn't long before Alissa was back with a man that looked like a doctor, with a white lab coat, name badge, and, of course, his stethoscope. She pointed at me and he smiled, nodded, and came out the door that separated the rooms.

"Good morning Ms. Jacobson," he said, holding out his hand. "I'm Doctor Barrett, Mr. Kort's doctor."

"Zoey," I said, standing to shake his hand.

"Nice to meet you, Zoey." he smiled. "I'm going to get right to the point, Zoey." He gestured to the chair for me to sit, and we sat together. "Mr. Kort is in a bad way. Of course, if you are here then you already know this."

I didn't know what to say, so I just nodded.

"Well, no one in his family is a match and although he is on the donor's list, these things take time." He looked at me to see if I was getting what he was saying.

I nodded again.

"What I am trying to say, Zoey, or rather ask, is, are you really willing to do this? This is a big decision and should you be a match, we would need you to be ready within a week. There are dietary restrictions, tests, and of course the risks of a surgery like this are there, just like any other surgery. Then there is the recovery time…"

"I… I'm ready." I blurted it out and then blushed at my abrupt answer. " I mean, yeah, I can do that. I'm willing. I just…"

"Yes?"

"I can't pay for it."

Doctor Barrett smiled and patted my hand. "That will be covered by a donor foundation."

"Oh, Good," I said, relieved. I was getting in way over my head way too fast.

He smiled and stood up. "Okay. Well we'll give you additional information and you'll have more time to think about it, but we can start the testing now." He put out a hand to help me up. By this time there was a nurse standing at the door, smiling at me.

"We usually just start with a blood test and then call you when the results are in." Doctor Barrett explained. "But you are a universal donor, so we'd like to go ahead and get blood and tissue samples today, if that is okay with you? But Zoey, don't get your hopes up."

I nodded again. My heart was racing and it all seemed to be happening so fast. How would I explain it to his family? Would they know who had donated? I had so many questions, but a nod was all I could seem to accomplish in this conversation.

I guess exams are gonna have to wait. I thought.

The doctor nodded at the nurse and she smiled and led me down a long hall and began taking blood samples. I don't think I have ever filled out so much paperwork.

Chapter 23 Dad

The days that followed the blood tests dragged by. I reread the pamphlets they'd sent home with me cover to cover multiple times and triple-checked the contract and accompanying paperwork to make sure I'd signed everything. How long could it possibly take to figure out if we were a match?

I contacted the donor association and filled out all of their paperwork as well. I was afraid I'd have carpal tunnel before it was all over.

My time was filled with blood and tissue tests, x-rays, ultrasounds, and diet changes. I was drinking more water than ever. I think I knew the location of every public bathroom in Pensacola.

I was trying to take good care of myself. I had a sense of purpose I'd never felt before, and I still hadn't told anyone what I was planning. I didn't want anyone to try to talk me out of it, but I thought I'd better tell Dad. I called him and asked him to have lunch with me. I wanted him to see how well I was doing too. It felt like weeks since we'd talked. For him, it had only been a week.

We met up at his favorite dive restaurant and sat in a booth in the back. My dad has a genuine way of making me feel loved just by the way his eyes light up when he sees me. When he saw me this time he laughed, hugged me, and looked me over like something might be broken.

"Boy Kiddo, California did you some good, didn't it?" he smiled. Apparently, he could tell I was better just by looking at me. "It was Gram's cookin' wasn't it?" he said, patting me on the shoulder.

"She misses you Dad. You really should take some time to go visit."

"Well, maybe I should." he agreed, turning to the hostess to ask for a table.

We ordered our food and it hit me, I had no idea what to tell him. I couldn't tell him what had actually happened. I wasn't even sure how much was in my mind and how much was real. I knew my healing was real, I knew Jace was real, and logically I surmised that if Gabe was really in the hospital then he'd been real as well. I hadn't known he was in the hospital when I left Florida. I sat picking at the straw paper, deep in thought.

Nothing here is real, except the things that are real. I smiled in spite of myself. When I looked up Dad was watching me with a curious expression.

"Is my little girl in love?" he asked.

"Little girl?" I raised an eyebrow.

"Don't change the subject," he snickered. "Out with it."

I wanted to tell him all about Gabe, but I didn't know how. I decided to word it as if we had been talking online since I went to California. I didn't say it exactly like that but, worded it in such a way that it would seem that way. I didn't want to lie, but how could I tell him the truth? I'd been such a mess before, the last thing he needed to think was that I'd lost my mind. "Don't worry, you'll like him, Dad."

"Well, that's great Kiddo. When can I meet him?"

Crap.

"We're taking it slow, Dad," was all I could think to say. Thankfully our server brought our food and his attention was turned to eating. I did an inner sigh of relief.

"Well Pops said you decided to come home early," he said, with his mouth full. "So, you must be more serious than you're lettin' on, hmm?"

I had to think fast. "Well, he ended up in the hospital. So, I came home, uhm, to see him." The truth was good, right?

He put his drink down with a look of worry on his face. "Oh yeah? What happened? Car accident?"

"No, he, uh… has some health issues."

Dad put his fork down and put his elbows on the table, crossing his hands in front of himself. "Zoey Lynn! What's with all the secrecy? Is this guy a drug dealer, or another slimy lawyer?"

I laughed nervously. "No, Dad. He's a great guy. He's a preacher's kid." I smiled sheepishly.

Dad rolled his eyes. "What are you not telling me?"

Why does he always have to know me so well? I put my fork down and looked him in the eye. "Nothing, Dad. He is a diabetic. He needs a kidney."

I picked up my fork and quickly shoved another big bite in my mouth. I couldn't answer with a mouth full, right?

Dad groaned and rubbed his eyes. "Zoey, you're not thinking what I think you're thinking?"

I smiled sheepishly with my mouth full.

"A kidney?"

I nodded.

Dad pushed his plate away from himself and sighed deeply, poking a finger into his right temple to soothe a headache.

I wiped my face and braced for the onslaught.

"You can't just give an organ to a guy you're sparking with, Kiddo." His face was turning red. "Buy him a freaking puppy!" he snapped.

The restaurant went quiet and people were looking in our direction. Dad seemed oblivious as he stared at me. He took a deep calming breath and started again.

"Zoey, He's not your husband. Not that I'd have wanted you to give that man anything! The fact is that he isn't even a family friend. There are donor lists for this kind of thing. Let the doctors take care of him."

"I don't even know if I'm a match yet, Dad."

"You're risking your life for someone you hardly know! You could die!"

"I know him, I've known him for a while! I'll be okay, Dad."

"You don't know that!" He was raising his voice again, and he poked at his temple, rubbing in little circles.

I looked around and then shushed him. "Keep it down, Dad."

He collected himself, taking another breath, this time closing his eyes. He looked angry and when he opened his eyes I saw fear there.

"I forbid you to do this, Zoey!" His last-ditch effort.

"I'm not a little girl anymore, Dad."

"You're acting like one!" he snapped.

He got up from the table and dug through his wallet. He threw down money for the meal and shoved the wallet back into his pocket.

"You're all I've got, Zoey. You need to think long and hard about this. You're gonna end up leaving your ol' Dad sad and alone!" He turned and stormed out.

Guilt tactics. How did I not see that coming?

I looked around and smiled apologetically at the other diners in the restaurant. Soon everyone lost interest and the attention was off me once more.

I had lost my appetite. I sat there for several minutes before the server brought the bill. He smiled a sad smile and asked if I was okay. I nodded and gave him the money for the bill. "Keep the change."

He nodded and smiled again. I just wanted out of there, wishing we'd have sat closer to the door. It felt like all eyes were on me as I walked towards the door and back out onto the sidewalk.

I decided to walk down the road to the park with the fountain. I sat on a bench and watched as the water splashed over the bowl. My thoughts were heavy, and I was feeling alone. My heart longed for Gabe's company. I just wanted him with me, wanted him okay.

Maybe I was making a mistake. I had made some pretty bad choices over the years. Dad had reason not to trust my judgment. I just couldn't bring myself to believe I was wrong this time. I may have a chance to save Gabe, I had to try.

"Sometimes the understanding of others is a luxury you can't afford."

It was a still, small voice in my mind, and I smiled, knowing Jace was still with me.

Chapter 24 Tests of Another Kind

No one at the hospital was really allowed to tell me anything about Gabe, I think most of them just assumed I already knew how he was doing though. I just acted like I knew when the nurses discussed him in casual conversation. I would smile and nod mostly and let them think I was just a quiet person.

After six days of waiting and wondering I found out that I was, in fact, a match, but they would have to wait until Gabe was strong enough to have the operation.

By Friday I was finally able to see him. They assumed I was welcomed by the family and I wasn't going to argue when they gave me the visitors pass.

I had never been so nervous in all my life. I had been less nervous on my wedding day. My hands shook and I felt nauseous as I walked down the sterile hallway towards the ICU ward.

I recognized Gabe's sister and mother as they passed me and I smiled. They smiled back as they passed, just a friendly smile from a stranger, but my heart soared!

Anna was pretty, with chestnut hair and blue eyes. She was thin and bright looking, with a confident air about her. Her mother had blond hair, with delicate features. I had never seen them before! Only in the picture that Gabe had placed in his room back when we were together in the mansion.

That meant he had to be real, didn't it? I picked up my pace.

When I got to his room I knocked on the wall next to the curtain that gave only a feeling of privacy to his room, and waited for an answer. The nurse behind me instructed me to go ahead and go in, as he would be too weak to speak loudly enough to tell me to come in. I smiled and simply said, "Oh, of course, thank you," and pushed the curtain open, quietly walking in.

The room was dimly lit and quiet, save for the beeping from a machine at his bedside. He looked terrible and seemed to gasp for breath. I stopped to stare for a moment. He was ashen and unshaven, and his face was puffy and swollen. His hair was longer than I remembered it ever being at the dojo.

His eyes flickered open and then closed again. I walked closer.

"Hello, Gabe," I whispered.

His eyes remained closed, but he smiled and mumbled something I couldn't hear. I placed my hands on the railing of his bed and leaning over him slightly.

"What?" I asked. "I can't hear you."

I moved closer and he whispered. "I love this dream."

"I'm sorry, I didn't mean to wake you," I said, wondering if I should leave.

His eyes flickered open and closed again and he reached up to put his hand on mine. His was swollen and cold.

"You didn't wake me, this is my favorite dream." He smiled with his eyes closed and then, it seemed, he fell back to sleep. I didn't know what to do, so I just stood there with his hand on mine.

After a few moments, his breath deepened and I knew he was asleep. I stood there for a bit longer, not knowing what to do. What had I expected? I didn't know. *Maybe it's best if I just leave.* I thought.

I slipped my hand from his and laid his hand softly beside him. I was about to turn around when he spoke, a little louder this time.

"Zoey?"

"Hi Gabe, er, Mr. Kort." *There goes that doubt, rearing its ugly head.* I fiddled with my fingers and moved my hair out of my face.

Gabe laughed, a soft airy laugh, and then grimaced in pain. "Don't start that again," he whispered. He closed his eyes, reaching again for my hand. I put my hand in his and he sighed.

"I thought I was dreaming again." He opened his eyes. "You are really here though, aren't you?"

I nodded, tears welling up in my eyes. He looked so pale and weak. I thought I must be too late.

"How are you?" I asked softly.

He took a ragged breath, "Better now." he answered, and squeezed my hand weakly.

"Gabe."

He opened his eyes and looked at me. I could see that it took effort to keep them open.

"Are you okay? I mean, really?"

He nodded. They gave me a new pancreas three or four days ago and I've had no signs of rejection so far," he whispered, and closed his eyes again. "They found a donor to give me a kidney too. Isn't that great?" He grimaced again and then relaxed.

One of the machines beside him made a clicking noise and then a hum. It was his pain medicine. He sighed again.

"I'm really tired," he said, taking a labored, deep breath. His eyes opened to meet mine once more. "Will you be here when I wake up?"

I tried to answer him, but he had already drifted off to sleep again. This time I didn't wake him when I laid his arm down next to him and covered it with his blanket.

I stood there watching him for several minutes. He remembered me. It was all real. My heart was so happy, but I was worried too. He looked so frail. I knew I was doing the right thing, I just hoped it would be on time. I chose to believe Jace's words when he told me Gabe needed me..

I turned to leave and saw Gabe's mother and sister standing in the doorway, staring. I had no idea how long they had been there.

"Who are you?" Anna asked. Looking at me and then over to Gabe, like I had been trying to smother him or something.

Gabe's mother only stared with wide eyes and then glanced back at the nurse's station.

What was I supposed to tell them? So many things went through my head, but all that came out was, "Hi, I'm Zoey." I waved an awkward gesture and smiled meekly.

They looked at each other and back at me. It was the longest moment of my life.

"You're Zoey?" his mother asked, and I realized I didn't know her name.

I nodded slowly. "You know me?"

Gabe's mother crossed the room and embraced me before I had time to react. I instinctively hugged her back and waited for her to release me; wondering how she could possibly know who I was.

When she let me go she had tears in her eyes. "Gabe has been saying your name in his sleep since last Friday. We didn't know who you were. You must be someone very special to him." She smiled and asked me to sit down.

I sat, completely panicking inside. What was I supposed to tell her? My mind raced to find an explanation. I decided to ask her first, maybe get a leg up on the conversation.

"Gabe never mentioned me before?" I asked.

Gabe's mom looked at Anna and she shrugged, then nodded.

"Well, he did a while back." She looked a little embarrassed. "He used to talk about a woman named Zoey in his class that he would have liked to ask out, but she didn't give him the 'time of day.' Or so he said. I guess you finally came around?"

I couldn't help but laugh. Gabe stirred and all of our attention went to him until he settled and was quiet again.

"Gabe said you were married." Said Anna.

"I'm a widow," I answered.

They looked at each other and then back to me.

"I'm sorry it took me so long to get here, I uhm, I've been out of town."

"Well, then you probably don't know."

I looked at Anna and she smiled. "Know what?" I asked, looking to both of them for an answer.

They both beamed. "Gabe got a pancreatic transplant from a deceased donor three days ago and now they have found a matching donor for his kidney, a living donor! Can you believe that?"

I blushed, in spite of myself and looked at my feet. I don't know why it made me feel so self-conscious. Perhaps because I hadn't told anyone except Dad, what I had planned to do. Maybe because I was afraid. Maybe because it was my secret, and the only way I could show how much I loved Gabe.

"Zoey?" she asked. "What's wrong?"

But before I could answer, Anna answered for me.

"She's the donor, Mom!"

Her mom looked shocked. Looking to Anna and then to me. "Is this true, Zoey?"

I nodded, still looking at my feet like I was ashamed. I wasn't ashamed, I just wanted this to be mine. I wanted it to be between Gabe and me. It struck me that I didn't have him all to myself anymore, and it felt, well, sad. I didn't want to share him. But, I had lost him once and I wasn't going to lose him again, even if it meant risking my life to save him. Maybe that's a little melodramatic, but that's how it felt.

She threw her arms around me again and sobbed. I wrapped my arms around her and patted her, in my awkward way of trying to soothe. I felt ridiculous. Anna smiled at me as I looked over her mom's shoulder.

In that awkward moment, I realized I had a song behind my thoughts. Burn the Ships, by For King and Country, and I smiled on the inside. *No turning back now*, I thought.

"We're all very grateful for your... Gift," Anna said, walking over to put her hand on my back. Her mother sobbed louder and nodded. I chuckled, and patted her all the more.

Gabe's mother, Darlene, (I was eventually introduced) Anna, and I spoke in hushed tones for some time while Gabe rested. I answered their questions as if the time that Gabe and I had spent together was there in Pensacola, and not in an indescribable place in my subconscious. How on earth we would ever tell them that was beyond me. But that was a bridge to cross way down the road. I eventually went home with permission to visit any time.

I was checked into the hospital four days later to run tests and more tests to make sure I was healthy enough for the procedure. Surgery was the next morning.

Gabe was strong enough to risk another surgery and the doctors were going to go ahead as planned. I still hadn't told anyone and made Darlene and Anna promise they wouldn't tell Gabe until after the surgery was done.

I didn't visit Gabe in the time in between seeing him and surgery.I had spoken with Darlene on the phone, but I was too afraid he might tell them something I couldn't explain in some sort of drugged stupor if he saw me again. Besides, he slept most of the time and Darlene said that he thought my visit had been a dream.

They rolled me into the operating room and put that mask thing on my face, instructing me to count down from ten. I think I made it to seven.

I woke with three small laparoscopic scars on my abdomen. It was nothing like the wound I had had in the mansion. The pain was pretty intense though, and I was grateful for the pain meds. They had me in ICU for the rest of that day and then moved me to a regular room soon after. Anna and Darlene came to visit me as often as they could get away from Gabe. They had kept my secret, and promised to let me be the one to tell him.

I called my Dad as soon as I was feeling better and he came to sit with me at the hospital. At first, he was worried, and truthfully, I think he was mad at me.

I was discharged after four more days in the hospital, and would begin rehab in a day or two depending on my recovery. Dad drove me home and went back to work that day.

Anna showed up later and made sure I had everything I needed and filled me in on Gabe's condition. He was doing as well as could be expected, time would tell if his body accepted the donor kidney. I asked why Gabe wasn't given the kidney from the person who gave him the pancreas. She explained that the young man had died in a motorcycle crash. His kidneys had been damaged in the accident.

Dad was there when I woke up. He was sitting in a chair by my bed with his head in his hands.

"Hi, Dad!" I said groggily.

"You doing okay, Kiddo?" The anger was gone and now he just seemed worried.

I nodded.

He stood up and scratched his head. "Zoey, Honey, you loan a friend fifty bucks, you don't give them an organ!"

"I love him, Dad, and you will too. You'll see." I explained, trying to sit up and realizing that was way too painful.

He rushed to my side and propped me up gently with a pillow. "Are you alright honey," he asked, looking around, like he might find something to make me better, like my stuffed bunny from when I was little.

"I'm gonna be fine Dad, I just need rest."

He nodded. "We are going to talk about this later young lady!"

I nodded, "I know, Dad"

He nodded and sat back down. "Now go back to sleep. I'll be here awhile if you need anything."

"Thanks, Dad."

When I woke again later, I could hear talking in the other room and Dad was laughing. Then I heard Darlene's voice too. I wanted to get up and see what was going on, but sitting up still proved too painful.

I listened, straining my ears to hear as much as I could. *What is Dad talking to Darlene about?* Unfortunately, I couldn't hear much. It wasn't long until Anna came in and sat down by my bed.

"Our parents are hitting it off nicely," Anna said, smirking. I could see a glimpse of her brother in those mischievous eyes. Adopted or not, they had the same expressions.

"Well, by all means, go stop them!" I replied. The thought of my Dad flirting with my boyfriend's mom was too much.

Anna laughed.

Chapter 25 While You Were Sleeping

It had been a week since the surgery and I was going to my rehab appointment. It was my second appointment, the doctors were keeping close tabs on me and Anna had volunteered to drive when Dad had to work. We were becoming friends, and although she was a little younger than me, I really began to cherish her.

She reminded me so much of her brother, but she had a great sense of style and loved everything fashion, often hinting that she could help me with my wardrobe. I had a feeling her ideas would make me very uncomfortable. She thought I should break out of my comfortable way of dressing. I reminded her that sundresses and jumpsuits weren't that comfortable after surgery. We could talk about fashion when I was feeling better.

All in all, things were going well. The closer I got to the hospital, however, the more nervous I got. After my rehab, I was going to see Gabe.

"He's going to be happy to see you, ya know." she encouraged."You're his girlfriend for Pete's sake!"

I just nodded, faking a smile. I couldn't get much past her, she was observant and watched me inquisitively. Finally, she asked, "You are his girlfriend, aren't you? This isn't one of those 'While You Were Sleeping' scenarios is it?

My heart raced, and I giggled a strange nervous noise of a giggle. "No." *Not exactly.*

She just raised an eyebrow at me and then parked the car.

Darlene was working, and Anna went to the cafeteria to let me go see Gabe alone. I don't know if she was just being thoughtful or if my mood tipped her off that maybe I needed a moment alone with him. Either way, I was grateful.

He was in a regular room now, room 213. I knocked and heard him say "come in." I didn't know if he was expecting me or not. I walked in slowly, shyly, trying not to wring my hands.

There was a nurse taking blood standing between us as I approached. She was just finishing up. She turned, smiled, and walked out, closing the door behind her. Suddenly, I felt naked, exposed. His eyes found mine and the look he gave me was not welcoming, more curious.

"Hi Zoey." he said, looking at me and then down to pick at something on his blanket. He looked better. The swelling in his body had gone down and except for the weight loss, he looked himself, if not a bit gaunt.

"Hi." I replied, "Uhm, did I come at a bad time? I can...."

"No!" he blurted, looking back up at me. "Uh, how are you? I uh, haven't seen you at the Dojo for a while." He looked sheepish. "I haven't actually been at the Dojo for a while. I've been pretty sick, but you know that, don't you?"

I nodded. I was confused. He acted like he didn't know me, but he had remembered me in the ICU, I didn't get it.

"Well, it's nice to see you. Have a seat." he offered, gesturing to a chair.

I didn't know what else to do, so I sat down (with a little effort); I was still very tender. Gabe's eyes got big with concern and he tried to sit up straighter. Only to groan and settle back against the pillows.

We both asked at the same time, "Are you okay?"

He answered first. "Yeah, I'm okay, but why are you not okay?"

"I'm okay," I replied.

He scrutinized me. "You know what I mean!" he said. There's the Gabe I knew.

"What's wrong, Zoey?"

"Do you remember, Gabe!?" I blurted out.

His eyes got big, but he quickly regained his composure. "Do I remember what?"

Panic, anxiety, freak out... Pick one. All at once, I thought that maybe it was true, he had been a figment of my imagination. I had just given a kidney to my self-defense instructor and told his family I was his girlfriend. I really had snapped. I stared at him wide-eyed, shaking.

"I gotta go!" I stood up gingerly and turned to walk out.

"Zoey, wait!"

I stopped but, I didn't turn around. I knew if I did I would burst into tears.

"Was it real?" he asked.

I took a deep breath to settle myself, clenching my fists. It was my turn to play coy. "Was what real?"

He sighed. It was a moment before he spoke. "The mansion, was it real?"

The tears came then, and I couldn't hold them back. Sobs hurt a lot after giving a kidney, and my knees almost buckled. I wrapped my arms around myself protectively and bent over slightly from the pain.

"Zoey!" I heard the sheets rustle and I turned. He was trying to get up.

"Are you crazy?!" I snapped, wiping my face. It was an ugly cry and my voice was high pitched and winey. I moved as quickly as I could and pressed him back down against the bed

"You'll hurt yourself."

I pulled the blankets back over him and gently tucked him in, never making eye contact. I could feel his eyes on me.

He reached up and cupped his hand under my chin. My eyes met his and another tear escaped my lid.

"It was real. Wasn't it."

"I nodded."

"Why are you in pain?" he asked.

I scowled at him. "Because, well, I thought I had been mistaken. You acted like you didn't know me."

He ran his hand through his hair like he always did, and I ached to hold him. "I'm sorry, Zo. I thought I might have dreamt it all."

"Come here." He gestured for me to sit on the bedside, but the motion was too painful and I gasped.

"What is it? What's wrong?" he asked, looking at my midsection and then back at me. "Was the gash on your side real too?"

I nodded. "Sort of."

"Let me see," he demanded. Trying to reach for the back of my shirt and bumping my side in the process. I gasped again and stepped away.

He stared at me, completely dumbfounded. He reached out for me. "Zoey, I…" the tortured look in his eyes was painful to see.

I'm not sure why I was so reluctant to tell him the truth. I guess I knew he wasn't going to like it. He'd be grateful, of course, but yeah, he wasn't gonna be happy.

"The wound in the mansion wasn't real."

Gabe looked confused. "Then what did you do?" He looked at me and then back to my side.

"The wound I had in the mansion was just to let me know what I needed to do."

"What you needed…?"

I took a deep breath and lifted my shirt high enough for him to see the bandages in three places.

He looked at me and his hand went to his side. Tears welled up in his eyes. "You?" he asked, as tears flowed down his cheeks.

I nodded, as tears ran down mine. "I couldn't let you die."

"I thought you didn't want me. I thought you wanted me out of your life. You pushed me out!"

"I was afraid." I stood up as erect as I could. "I'm not afraid anymore."

He looked around his bed as if he'd lost something and, finding it, picked up his remote control. He pushed the down button as low as the bed would go and then motioned for me to come over.

I sat gingerly on his bed and he wrapped his arms around me as best he could. We were a pathetic duo. I couldn't even get low enough to kiss him and he couldn't get close enough to kiss me. I would just have to settle on his arms around me for the time being.

I touched his face and he closed his eyes against my hand.

"Thank you, Zoey," he whispered.

He lay quietly for a few minutes, thinking and watching me.

"Remember when I told you that Jace and I had talked about some things?" he asked quietly.

"Yeah."

"He said if I'd help you, you'd help me. I thought it was a dream."

I chuckled.

"Thank you doesn't seem to be enough. You saved my life."

I smiled and looked into his eyes. "You saved mine first."

Chapter 26 Moving Forward

The next few months were full of doctor appointments for Gabe and me. His transplants were well received by his body, but he had to take it easy for a long time. He's had to avoid crowds, and limit his time in the sun. He will be on medication for the rest of his life, and he'll always have to monitor his eating, although he can splurge once in a while, which is better than it was before. No more shots and no more finger pricks.

It took a little while for me to start feeling normal again, as my body had to adjust to one kidney. The doctors had told me it would. My scars are healed and the tenderness is gone. I feel good and I have never been happier. I've never been more free.

I ran into Madison from my old job at the insurance agency yesterday. She's going through a nasty divorce and custody battle with her ex-husband over their three children. It was strange, I never knew what she was going through back when I was working there, but I see now that the way she treated me had nothing to do with me, and everything to do with her insecurities. She cried in the produce aisle at Publix grocery store and apologized for being mean to me way back then. I think I surprised her when I hugged her and told her that things would work out. We made plans to grab a coffee together when things settle down.

I was given some extensions on my college exams due to the operation. My professors were surprisingly supportive once they found out what I had done. My English Professor even cried when I told her. As it turns out, she had a relative that had died of kidney failure. She hugged me and gave me all the notes that I had missed over the weeks I was out.

The support we received from our families and friends was amazing. My dad and Gabe's mom became friends instantly (which worried us both a little). And Anna and I became fast friends as well.

A friend of Gabe's has been watching over the dojo for a while. Remember Paul? I am learning to appreciate Paul. He comes across as a bit of a meathead at first, but he's not a bad guy. Gabe helps when he feels up to it. Which has been more and more lately. I see him getting stronger, and it makes me happy.

Gabe and I have officially been dating. It's funny how quickly you can get used to everything being at your disposal, but honestly, it's been nice to have to cook for one another and to go shopping together. I don't particularly enjoy making coffee, but I love it when Gabe comes over to enjoy some with me. We do things for each other, and I love it. He does things Aden would never have done. He's kind and thoughtful.

Last week Gabe took me out for a picnic, just him and me. He laid out a blanket and had sandwiches and chips and lots of things that aren't necessarily good for you laid out for us to nibble on. I'm learning balance and he is also learning to take one day at a time with his nutritional needs. It was a beautiful gesture. We took a long walk afterward and he led me to a beautiful bridge that crossed a stream lined with Perennials. It reminded me of the little bridge in California, although much larger. I stayed away from the edge. It was there that he got down on one knee and proposed to me.

The ring is beautiful, a family heirloom that belonged to his late grandmother. Obviously, I said yes. He had already talked to my dad, those sneaky boogers!

We have decided on a Spring wedding, with Susanna as my Maid of Honor and Paul to be the best man. Of course, I asked Anna to be a bridesmaid too.

My dress will be white, who cares about tradition? I'm so free! Besides, this is Gabe's first wedding and I want him to have it just the way he wants it. He wants me in white. He says that's the way he sees me. I love that man and I owe it all to Jace, or as many call him, Jesus.

All of my memories are the same as they have always been. They are not changed, except that they don't hurt anymore. Jace didn't change my memories, he just gave me a different perspective. You see, our memories aren't what hurt us. The lies that we believe in those memories are what cause us pain. When we are shown the truth about a situation or about ourselves, the pain leaves. Truth sets us free.

I have memories that still hurt, that I didn't look at while I was inside myself. I know how to deal with those now. When the time is right I will open the door to those memories and look at them and invite Jace in. I have time to get to those and Jace is patient. He will prepare me to open those doors, and if he'll do it for me, he'll do it for you.

Made in the USA
Columbia, SC
04 September 2022

66458103R00136